THE
DRIVER

MARK
DAWSON

THE
DRIVER

WELBECK

First Published in 2022 by Welbeck Fiction Limited, part of Welbeck Publishing Group
This paperback edition published in 2023 by Welbeck Publishing Group
Offices in: London – 20 Mortimer Street, London W1T 3JW &
Sydney – 205 Commonwealth Street, Surry Hills 2010
www.welbeckpublishing.com

A CIP catalogue record for this book is available from the British Library

Paperback ISBN: 978-1-78739-705-7

Printed and bound by CPI Group (UK) Ltd., Croydon, CR0 4YY

10 9 8 7 6 5 4 3 2 1

PART I

TABBY WILSON

Tabby Wilson updated her Craigslist profile on the night she was murdered. She tweaked her personal information a little and added a new selfie that she had taken that same afternoon. It was a good likeness of her: she was wearing wispy lingerie, her skin was smooth and blemish-free, and she had on a crazy blonde wig that made her look a little like Lana Del Rey. She looked fine, she thought. Her expression was sultry and provocative, almost daring men to contact her. She was slender and had big eyes, androgynous with that alien look that was so popular on the blogs that she bookmarked and the magazines she thumbed through in Walmart or when she was waiting at the laundromat.

It was important that she looked her best. The Craigslist ad was her shop window, and as she touched up the blemishes in Photoshop, she was pleased with the results. She had perfect skin, a short bob of dark hair and those big eyes were green and expressive. She was twenty-one and had left school when she was seventeen to have a baby. She had two kids now, each with a different father, although she never saw either man. Her mom helped to bring up the kids. Until recently, she had worked in Walmart. She lived in a one-bedroom apartment in Vallejo funded by the alimony that her son's father had been ordered to pay. Apart from the fact that stacking shelves wasn't what she had in mind for her career, the alimony and her wages didn't cover all of her expenses. Things got worse when she was fired because she was always late. She got a couple of other dead-end jobs, but they didn't cut it either and she'd walked out just as soon as they had started.

Tabby liked to think that she was a positive person, so she concentrated on her ambitions. She had always wanted to be a model. There was money in that, lots of money, and she was sure that she was pretty enough and had a good enough figure to make a go of it. She created Pinterest and Instagram pages that she filled with photographs: selfies with the camera held as far away from her face as possible, others showing her in the full-length bedroom mirror, and a selection that she had culled from the shoot that a photographer friend had conducted in exchange for a night with her.

She knew that she needed to do something to get her career moving in the right direction. She spent a lot of time working on her page, and it wasn't long before she noticed the ads for modelling. She'd clicked on a site that offered free hosting for the portfolios that girls sent in. She'd set up an account and uploaded the best photos from the shoot. She'd started to see enquiries right away. She was hoping for legitimate offers and the agencies who'd replied said that they could book her for those kinds of jobs. When she'd clicked on their sites, it was obvious that what they were really looking for were hookers and escorts.

She'd started to take the offers more seriously when she saw how much money she could earn. Sex sold; she'd always known it, and now here was the proof. She couldn't really see a downside, except

4

that she couldn't see the point of giving someone else half of the money she made.

She could do it all herself.

That was when she had started advertising on Craigslist.

* * *

That night's job had been booked on the phone. The john had emailed her to say that he was interested, and she had done what she always did: gave him the number of her work phone so that she could talk with him and lay out the prices and what he could expect to get in return. Insisting on a call also gave her the chance to screen the guys who had never booked her before. There were always weirdos, and she'd been knocked around by a couple. Talking to someone was better than reading an email to get an idea of what they were like. She had refused bookings with several men who had just sounded wrong on the phone. Tabby liked to say that she was a good judge of character. She was careful, too.

This guy, though? He sounded all right. A Southern accent, a bit of a hillbilly twang going on, but he'd been polite and well spoken. He'd explained to her that he was a police officer, in town for a law enforcement conference, and said that he wanted a little bit of fun. He had no problem with her charges, so she had arranged to meet him.

She was on the corner of Franklin and Turk at eight, just as they had arranged, smoking a cigarette and watching the traffic go by. She was thinking about her kids and about how she had made enough money already this week to pay the rent, pay for the groceries and maybe even take them to Six Flags for a treat. There was one at Vallejo. She was thinking about that as the Cadillac slowed to a stop beside her. Her old man had been a mechanic, and she had been big into cars when she was younger so that she could impress him; she recognised it as an Eldorado, probably twenty years old. It wasn't in the best condition. The front-right wing was dinged, the licence plate was barely attached to the chassis, and the engine backfired as the driver reached over and opened the passenger-side door for her.

He called out her name in the same redneck accent that she remembered from the phone call.

She picked up her bag and stepped into the car.

She was never seen again.

1

The grey mist had rolled in off the bay two days earlier, and it hadn't lifted yet. It softened the edges of objects within easy sight, but out beyond ten or fifteen feet, it fell across everything like a damp, cold veil. June was often the time when it was at its worst – they called it June Gloom for a reason – but the fog was always there, seeping down over the city at any time, without warning, and often staying for hours. The twin foghorns – one at either end of the Golden Gate Bridge – sounded out their long, mournful, muffled ululations. John Milton had been in town for four months, and he still found it haunting.

It was nine in the evening, the street lamps glowing with fuzzy coronas in the damp mist. Milton was in the Mission District, a once-blighted area that was being given new life by the artists and students who swarmed in now that crime had been halted and rents were still low. It was self-consciously hip now, the harlequinade of youth much in evidence: long-haired young men in vintage suits and fur-trimmed Afghans, and girls in short dresses. The streets looked run-down and shabby. The girl Milton had come to pick up was sitting on a bench on the corner. He saw her through the fog, difficult to distinguish until he was a little closer. He indicated right, filtered out of the late-evening traffic and pulled up against the kerb.

He rolled the passenger-side window down. The damp air drifted into the car.

'Madison?' he called, using the name that he had been given.

The girl, who was young and pretty, took a piece of gum out of her mouth and stuck it to the back of the bench upon which she was sitting. She reached down for a rucksack, slung it over her shoulder, picked up a garment bag and crossed the pavement to the Explorer. Milton unlocked the door for her, and she got in.

'Hi,' she said in a lazy drawl.

'Hi.'

'Thanks for being so quick. You're a lifesaver.'

'Where do you want to go?'

'You know the McDonald's in Balboa Park?'

He thought for a moment. Four months driving around San Francisco had given him a decent grasp of local geography. 'I know it.'

'That's where we're headed.'

'Okay then.'

Milton changed into first and pulled back out into the sparse traffic. The rush hour had dissipated. He settled back into his seat and nudged the car up to a steady forty-five. He looked in the mirror at his passenger; Madison had opened her rucksack and taken out a book. It looked thick and substantial; a textbook, he thought. When the dispatcher had relayed the booking, she had told him to look for a blonde, although her skin was a very dark brown, almost black. Her hair was light and straightened, and Milton wondered whether it might be a wig. Curvaceous and small, she was dressed in jeans and a chunky sweater. Definitely very pretty. She read her book in silence. Milton flicked his eyes away again and concentrated on the road.

They passed through Mission Bay and Potrero Hill and continued on into Balboa Park. The McDonald's, a large drive-thru, was in the grid of streets south of Ocean Avenue. There were advertisements for three-for-two on steak burritos and cups of premium roast coffee for a dollar.

'Here you go,' he said.

'Thanks. Is it okay if we wait?'

'What for?'

'A call. We're just stopping here.'

'Fine – but I'll have to keep the clock running.'

'That's okay. I got to wait until the call comes, and then we'll be going someplace else. Is that okay with you?'

'As long as you can pay, we can stay here all night.'

'I can pay,' she said with a broad smile. 'How much do I owe you?'

Milton looked down at the meter. 'Twenty so far.'

'Twenty's no problem.' She took a purse out of her bag, opened it and took out a note. She reached forward and handed it to him. It was a hundred.

He started to feel a little uncomfortable.

'That should cover it for a couple of hours, right?'

Milton folded it and wedged it beneath the meter. 'I'll leave it here,' he said. 'I'll give you change.'

'Whatever.' She nodded at the restaurant, bright light spilling out of the window onto the line of cars parked tight up against it. 'I'd *kill* for a Big Mac,' she said. 'You want anything?'

'I'm fine, thanks.'

'You sure?'

'I ate earlier.'

'All right.'

She got out. He clenched and unclenched his fists. He rolled the window down.

'Actually,' he said, 'could you get me a coffee? Here.' He reached in his pocket for a dollar bill.

She waved him off. 'Forget it. My treat.'

Milton watched as she crossed the car park and went into the restaurant. There was a queue, and as she slotted into it to await her turn, Milton undid his seat belt and turned around so that he could reach into the back. She had left her bag on the seat. He checked that she was facing away and quickly unzipped it, going through the contents: there was a clutch bag, two books, a mobile phone, a bottle of vodka, a box of Trojans and a change of clothes. He zipped the bag and put it back. He leant back against the headrest and scrubbed his forehead with the palm of his hand.

He had been very, *very* stupid.

The girl returned with a bagged-up Happy Meal, a tall soda and a large coffee. She passed the Styrofoam cup through the open window, slid into the back seat, took the bottle of Stolichnaya from her bag, flipped the plastic lid from the soda and poured in a large measure.

'Want a drop in your coffee?'

'No, thanks,' he said. 'I don't drink.'

'Not at all?'

'Never.'

'Is that, like, a lifestyle choice?'

He wasn't about to get into that with her. 'Something like that,' he said vaguely.

'Suit yourself.'

She put the straw to her mouth and drew down a long draught.

'Madison,' Milton said, 'I need you to be honest with me.'

She looked up at him warily. 'Yeah?'

'There's no delicate way to put this.'

She stiffened, anticipating what was coming next. 'Spit it out.'

'Are you a prostitute?'

'You're a real charmer,' she said.

'Please, Madison – no attitude. Just answer the question.'

'I prefer "escort".'

'Are you an escort?'

'Yes. You got a problem with it?'

'Of course I do. If we get pulled over, I could be charged with promoting prostitution. That's a felony.'

'If that happens – which it won't – then you just tell them that I'm your friend. How they gonna say otherwise?'

'You make it sound like it's happened to you before.'

'Hardly ever, and whenever it has, it's never been a big deal.'

'No,' Milton said. 'I'm sorry. It's a big deal for me.'

'Seriously?'

'I don't need a criminal record. You're going to have to get out. You can call another taxi from here.'

'Please, John,' she said. He wondered for a moment how she knew his name, and then he remembered that his picture and details were displayed on the laminated card that he had fixed to the back of his seat. 'I can't afford this right now.'

'And I can't take the risk.'

'Please,' she said again. He looked up into the mirror. She was staring straight at him. 'Come on, man. If you leave me here, I'll never get a ride before they call me. I'll miss the party, and these guys, man, this agency I work for – they've got a zero-tolerance policy when the girls no-show. They'll fire me for sure, and I can't afford that right now.'

'I'm sorry. That's not my problem.'

'Look, man, I'm begging you. I've got a little kid. Eliza. She's just two years old – you've got no idea how cute she is. If I get fired tonight, then there's no way I'm going to be able to pay the rent. Social services will try to take her away from me again, and that just can't happen.'

Milton stared out at the queued traffic on Ocean Avenue, the glow of a hundred brake lights blooming on and off in the soupy fog as they waited for the junction to go to green. He drummed his fingers on the wheel as he turned the prospect over in his mind, aware that the girl was looking at him in the mirror with big, soulful, hopeful eyes.

He knew he was going to regret this.

'On one condition: no drugs.'

'Sure thing. No drugs.'

'You're not carrying anything?'

'No, man. Nothing, I swear.'

'No cocaine. No pills. No weed.'

'I swear it, on my daughter's life. I haven't got a thing. I'm already on probation. I got to pee in a cup twice a week, man. If I get caught with anything in my system, they'll take her away from me just like that. People say a lot of things about me, John, but one thing they don't say is that I'm stupid. It's not worth the risk.'

He watched her answer very carefully. She was emphatic and convincing, and he was as satisfied as he could be that she was telling the truth.

'This is against my better judgement,' he said, 'but, all right.'

'Thanks, John. You don't know how much I appreciate this.'

He was about to answer when her mobile buzzed. She fumbled for it in her bag and put it to her ear. Her tone became deferential and compliant. He didn't catch any names, but it was obviously about where they were headed next. The conversation was short. She put the phone back into her bag.

'You know Belvedere?'

'Don't go up there very often.'

'Full of rich folks.'

'I know that. That's where we're headed?'

'Please.'

'You got an address?'

She gave it to him, and he entered it into the satnav slotted into a holder that was suction-cupped to the windscreen. The little unit calculated and displayed the best route.

'The 101 up to the bridge,' he said, reading off the screen. 'It's going to take forty minutes. That all right?'

'Perfect.'

'You going to tell me what's out there?'

'Like I say, rich folks throwing a mad party. That's where it's at.'

2

Madison was talkative as they drove north through Sunset, Richmond and Presidio, hanging a left at Crissy Field and joining the 101 as it became the Golden Gate Bridge. She explained how her business worked as they drove. She met her driver at a prearranged spot every night. She said he was called Aaron and that he was twitchy but, generally, a stand-up kind of guy. He had let her down badly tonight. They were supposed to have met at eight at Nob Hill, but he hadn't showed, and when she finally got through to him on his mobile, he said that he was unwell and that he wouldn't be able to come out. There was a number for a taxi firm on the back of the bench she had been sitting on. She called it. It was one of the firms that sent jobs Milton's way. The dispatcher had called him with her details, and he had taken the job.

She wasn't shy about her work. She explained how she got jobs through an agency, with the rest coming from online ads she posted on Craigslist. The agency gigs were the easiest; they made the booking, and all she had to do was just show up, do whatever it was that needed to be done, collect the cash and then go. The money was split three ways: the driver got

15

twenty per cent and the rest was split equally between the agency and the girl. Milton asked how much she made, and she was a little evasive, saying that she did okay but skimping on the detail. There was a moment's silence as he thought of the flippant way that she had given him the hundred. He concluded that she was probably earning rather a lot and then he chastised himself for his credulity. The story about the struggle to find the rent suddenly seemed a little less likely. He wondered whether there even was a little girl. Probably not. He chuckled a little as he realised that he had been well and truly suckered.

The bridge was lit up rusty gold as they passed across it, the tops of the tall struts lost in the darkness and the fog.

He heard the sound of a zip being unfastened. He looked into the mirror and saw her taking a black dress from the garment bag.

'I need to get changed,' she said. 'No peeking, John, all right?'

'Of course.'

'Don't be a pervert.'

He concentrated on the gentle curve as the bridge stretched out across the bay, but he couldn't resist a quick glance up at the mirror. She had removed her jumper and now she was struggling to slip out of her jeans. She looked up into the mirror, and Milton immediately cast his eyes back down onto the road ahead; she said nothing, but when he flicked his eyes back up again, there was a playful smile on her lips.

They crossed over into Sausalito and then Marin City.

'Done,' she said. 'You can look now.'

He did. Milton knew very little about women's clothes, but the simple black cocktail dress she was wearing had obviously been purchased in an expensive boutique. It was sleeveless, with a plain design and a deep collar that exposed her décolletage.

'You look very pretty,' he said, a little uncomfortably.

'Thank you, John.'

* * *

It was coming up to ten when Milton took the ramp off the interstate at Strawberry and negotiated the traffic circle around the tall brick spire that marked the turning onto Tiburon Boulevard. It was a long, narrow stretch of road that cut north to south right along the coast. White picket fences marked the boundaries of vast paddocks where million-dollar horses grazed. The lights from big houses that commanded impressive estates glowed from the crowns of the darkened headland to the left. They reached Belvedere proper and turned up into the hills.

The fog was dense here, and as they drove on, the vegetation closed in on both sides, the beams of the headlights playing off the trunks and briefly lighting the deep darkness within. Milton could only see fifty feet ahead of them. The flora grew a little wilder and less tended. To the left and right were thickets of bayberry and heather, a thick jumble of branches that tumbled right up to the margins of the road.

There was poison ivy, as tall as two men and thick as the branches of a tree. There was shining sumac and Virginia creeper and salt hay and bramble. Light reflected sharp and quick in the eyes of deer and rabbits. The road was separate from the houses that sat at the end of their driveways, and that night, the darkness and the fog enveloping the car like a bubble, Milton knew that they were alone.

'You know where we're going?' he asked.

'Turn onto West Shore Road. There's a private road at the end.'

He looked in the mirror. Madison had switched on the courtesy light and was applying fresh lipstick with the aid of a small mirror. She certainly was pretty, with nice skin and delicate bones and eyes that glittered when she smiled, which was often. She was young; Milton would have guessed that she was in her early twenties. She was small, too, couldn't have been more than five-three and a hundred pounds soaking wet. She looked vulnerable.

The whole thing didn't sit right with him.

'So,' he said, 'you've been here before?'

'A few times.'

'What's it like?'

'All right.'

'What kind of people?'

'I told you – rich ones.'

'Anyone else you know going to be there?'

'Couple of the guys,' she said. Was she a little wistful when she said it?

'Who are they?'

She looked into the mirror, into his eyes. 'No one you'd know,' she said, and then he knew that she was lying.

He thought she looked a little anxious. They drove on in silence for another half a mile. He had been in the area a couple of times before. It was a beautiful location, remote and untroubled by too many visitors, full of wildlife and invigorating air. He had hiked all the way down from Paradise Beach to Tiburon Uplands and then turned and walked back again. Five miles, all told, a bright summer afternoon spent tracking fresh prints into the long grass and then following them back again in the opposite direction. He hadn't seen another soul.

He looked in the mirror again. 'Do you mind me asking – how long have you been doing this?'

'A year,' she said, suddenly a little defensive. 'Why?'

'No reason. Just making conversation.'

Her temper flickered up. 'As long as you don't try to tell me I should find something else to do, okay? If you're gonna start up with that, then I'd rather you just kept quiet and drove.'

'What you do is up to you. I'm not in any place to tell you anything.'

'Fucking A.'

'I'm just thinking practically.'

'Like?'

'Like, how are you getting back?'

'I'll call another cab.'

'Back to the city?'

'Sure.'

'That's if you can find someone who'll come out this late at night. With fog as bad as this and supposed to be getting worse? I know I wouldn't.'

'Lucky I'm not calling *you*, then.'

He spoke carefully. He didn't want to come over like some concerned father figure. He guessed that would put her even more on the defensive. 'You got no one to look out for you while you're here?'

She hesitated, looking out into the gloom. 'My guy usually waits and then drives me back again. Keeps an eye on things, too, makes sure I'm all right.'

'I can't do that for you.'

'I wasn't asking.'

'I've got a day job. I need to get back to sleep.'

'I told you – I wasn't asking. *Jesus, man!* This isn't the first time I've done this. I'll be all right. The men are okay. Respectable types. Bankers and shit. A frat party – maybe I'm a little concerned to be out on my own. But here? With guys like this? Nothing to worry about. I'll be fine.'

The GPS said the turn was up ahead. Milton dabbed the brakes and slowed to twenty, searching for the turn-off in the mist. He found it; it was unlit, narrow and lonely, and the sign read PINE SHORE. He indicated even though there was no one on the road ahead or behind him and then slowed a little more.

He looked at the clock in the dash; the glowing digits said that it was half-ten.

The road ran parallel to West Shore Road for half a mile or so, and then Milton saw lights glowing through the trees. It turned sharply to the left and then was interrupted by an eight-foot brick wall and, in the midst of that, a majestic wrought-iron gate that looked like it belonged on a Southern plantation. A white gatehouse was immediately ahead. Beyond the gate, on the right-hand side of the road, a blue wooden sign had been driven into the verge. The sign said PINE SHORE ASSOCIATION in golden letters that sloped from right to left. There was a model lighthouse atop the gate. Milton considered it: a private community, prime real estate, close enough to the city, and with Silicon Valley not too far away. It all smelt of money.

Lots and lots of money.

'Through there,' she said.

'How many houses in here?'

'Don't know for sure. I've only ever been to this one. Twenty? Thirty?'

'How do we get in?'

'They texted me the code.' The glow of her mobile lit up her face as she searched for the information she needed. '2-0-1-1.'

He nudged the car forwards and lowered his window. The low rumble of the tyres on the rough road surface blended with the muffled chirping of the cicadas outside. He reached out to the keypad and punched in the code. The gate opened, and they followed a long driveway enclosed on both sides by mature oaks. Large and perfectly tended gardens reached

down to the road. There were tree allées, expansive lawns, fol-
lies, knot gardens and boxwood parterres.

They reached the first house. It was a large, modern building set out mostly on one level with a two-storey addition
at one end. It spread out across a wide parcel of land. There
were two separate wings, each with floor-to-ceiling windows that cast oblongs of golden light that blended away
into the grey shroud that had fallen all around. A series of
antique lamps threw abbreviated, fuzzy triangles of illumi-
nation out across the immaculate front lawn. There was a
forecourt verged by fruit trees. Milton reverse-parked in a
space; there was a Ferrari on one side and a Tesla Roadster
convertible on the other. Two hundred thousand dollars of
peerless design and engineering. His Explorer was old and
battered and inadequate in comparison.

Milton switched off the engine. 'You weren't kidding.'

'About what?'

'There's money here.'

'Told you.' She unclipped her seat belt and put her hand
on the door handle, but then she paused for a moment, as if
unwilling to open the door.

'Are you all right?'

'Sure. It's just—'

'You're nervous? I can take you back if you want.'

She shook her head. 'I'm not nervous.'

'Then what?'

'I'm here to meet someone, except I haven't seen him for a
while, and he doesn't know I'm coming. The last time I saw

him, it— well, let's say it didn't go so well, didn't end well for either of us. There's probably a very good chance he tells me to get the fuck out as soon as he sees me.'

'I'm going back into the city. It's not a problem.'

'No. I don't have any choice. I want to see him.'

'It'd be no trouble. No charge.'

'I'm fine. Really. It's completely cool. I'm just being stupid.'

She opened the door and got out, reaching back inside for her coat and bag.

She shut the door.

She paused.

She turned back to him.

'Thanks for driving me,' she said into the open window. She smiled shyly and suddenly looked very young indeed. The chic dress and stratospheric heels looked out of place, like a schoolgirl playing dress-up. She turned towards the house. The door opened, and Milton noticed a male face watching them through the gloom.

Milton wondered, again, how old she was. Nineteen? Twenty?

Too young for this.

Her footsteps crunched through the gravel.

Dammit, Milton thought.

'Madison,' he called through the window. 'Hang on.'

She paused and turned back to him. 'What?'

'I'll wait.'

She took a step closer to the car. 'You don't have to do that.'

'No, I do. You shouldn't be out here on your own.'

She liked to keep her face impassive, he could see that, but she couldn't stop the sudden flicker of relief that broke over it. 'Are you sure you're okay with that? I could be a couple hours – maybe longer, if it goes well.'

'I've got some music and a book. If you need me, I'll be right here.'

'I'll pay extra.'

'We'll sort that out later. You can leave your bag if you want.'

She came back to the car and took the smaller clutch bag from the rucksack. She put the condoms inside and took a final swig from the bottle of vodka. 'Thanks. It's kind of you.'

'Just— well, you know, just be careful, all right?'

'I'm always careful.'

3

Milton got out of the car and stretched his legs. It was quiet but for the occasional calls of seals and pelicans, the low whoosh of a jet high above and, rolling softly over everything, the quiet susurration of the sea. A foghorn boomed out from across the water, and seconds later, its twin returned the call. Lights hidden in the vegetation cast an electric blue glow over the timber frame of the building, the lights behind the huge expanses of glass blazing out into the darkness. Milton knew that the house was high enough on the cliffs to offer a spectacular view across the bay to Alcatraz, the bridge and the city, but all he could see tonight was the shifting grey curtain. There was a certain beauty in the feeling of solitude.

Milton enjoyed it for ten minutes, and then, as the temperature chilled and began to drop further, he returned to the Explorer, switched on the heater, took out his phone and plugged it into the dash. He scrolled through his music until he found the folder that he was looking for. He had been listening to a lot of old guitar music and he picked *Dog Man Star*, the album by Suede that he had on before he picked Madison up. There had been a lot of Britpop on the barrack's stereo while he had slogged through Selection for the SAS and it brought back memories of happier times. Times when his memories didn't burden him like they did now. He liked the swirling layers of shoegazing and dance-pop fusions from the Madchester era and the sharp, clean three-minute singles that had evolved out of it. Suede and Sleeper and Blur.

He turned the volume down a little and closed his eyes as the wistful introduction of 'Stay Together' started. His memories triggered: the Brecon Beacons, the Fan Dance, hours and hours of hauling a sixty-pound pack up and down the mountains, the lads he had gone through the process with, most of whom had been binned, the pints of stout that had followed each exercise in inviting pubs with roaring log fires and horse brasses on the walls.

The credentials fixed to the back of the driver's seat said JOHN SMITH. That was also the name on his driver's licence and passport, and it was the name he had given when he had rented his nine-hundred-dollar-a-month single-room-occupancy apartment with no kitchen and shared bathroom in the Mission District. No one in San Francisco knew him as John Milton or had any idea that he was not the anonymous, quiet man that he appeared to be.

He worked freelance, accepting his jobs from the agencies who had his details. He drove the night shift, starting at eight and driving until three or four. Then he would go home and sleep for seven hours before working his second job from twelve until six, delivering boxes of ice to restaurants in the city for Mr Freeze, the pseudonym of a cantankerous Ukrainian immigrant Milton had met after answering the 'positions vacant' ad on an internet bulletin board. Between the two jobs, Milton could usually make a hundred dollars a day. It wasn't much in an expensive city like San Francisco, but it was enough to pay his rent and his bills and his food, and that was all he needed, really. He didn't drink. He didn't have any expensive habits. He didn't have the time or the inclination to go out. He might catch a film now and again, but most of his free time was spent sleeping or reading. It had suited him very well for the four months he had been in town.

It was the longest he had been in one place since he had been on the run, and he was starting to feel comfortable. If he continued to be careful, there was no reason why he couldn't stay here for even longer. Maybe put down some roots? He'd always assumed that that would be impossible and had discouraged himself from thinking about it, but now?

Maybe it would be possible after all.

* * *

He gazed out of the window. He could see the glow from other houses further down the road. The nearest was another big building with lights blurring through the murk. As he watched, a sleek black town car turned into the driveway and parked three cars over from him. The doors opened, and two men stepped out. It was too dark and foggy to make out

27

anything other than their silhouettes, but he watched as they made their way to the door and went into the house.

The dull thump and drone of bass was suddenly audible from the house. The party was getting started. Milton turned up the stereo a little to muffle it. He changed to The Smiths. Morrissey's melancholia seemed appropriate in the cloying fog.

Time passed. He had listened to the whole of *Meat is Murder* and was halfway through *The Queen is Dead* when he heard a scream through the crack in the window.

His eyes flashed open.

He turned down the stereo.

Had he imagined it?

The bass throbbed.

Somewhere, footsteps crunched through the gravel.

A snatch of angry conversation.

He heard it again, clearer this time, a scream of pure terror.

Milton got out of the car and crossed the forecourt to the front door. He concentrated a little more carefully on his surroundings. The exterior was taken up by those walls of glass, the full-length windows shining with the light from inside. Some of the windows were open, and noise was spilling out: the steady bass over the sound of drunken voices, conversation, laughter.

The scream came again.

A man was standing with his legs apart on the front porch.

'You hear that?' Milton said.

'Didn't hear nothing.'

'There was a scream.'

'I didn't hear anything, buddy. Who are you?'

'A driver.'

'So back to your car, please.'

The scream sounded for a fourth time.

It was hard to be sure, but Milton thought it was Madison.

'Let me in.'

'You ain't going in, buddy. Back to the car. *Now.*'

Milton sized him up quickly. He was big, and he regarded Milton with a look that combined distaste and surliness. 'Who are you?'

'I'm the man who tells you to fuck off. Like already, okay?' The man pulled back his jacket to reveal a shoulder holster. He had a big handgun.

Milton punched hard into the man's gut, aiming all his power for a point several inches behind him. The man's eyes bulged as the pain fired up into his brain, and he folded down, his arms dropping to protect his groin. Milton looped an arm around his neck and yanked him off the porch, dragging him backwards so that his toes scraped tracks through the gravel, and then drove his knee into the man's face. He heard the bones crack. He turned him over, pinning him down with a knee into his gut, reached inside his jacket and took out the gun. It was a Smith & Wesson, the SW1911 Pro Series. 9mm, ten rounds plus one in the chamber. A very good, very expensive handgun. Fifteen hundred dollars new. Whoever this guy was, if he bought his own ironwork, he must have been getting some decent pay.

Milton flipped the S&W so that he was holding it barrel first and brought the butt down across the crown of the man's head. He spasmed and then was still.

Another scream.

Milton shoved the gun into the waistband of his jeans and pushed the door all the way open. A central corridor ran the length of the building with doors and windows set all along it and skylights overhead. The walls were painted white, and the floor was Italian marble. The corridor ended at a set of French doors. Vases of orchids were spaced at regular intervals across the marble.

He hurried through into the bright space beyond. It was a living room. He took it all in: oak parquetry floor inlaid with ebony, a gilded fireplace that belonged in a palazzo as the focal point of the wall, rich mahogany bookshelves and fine fabric lining one wall and the rest set with windows that would have provided awesome views on a clear day. The ceiling was oak and downlights in the beams lit the room. The furnishings were equally opulent, with three circular sofas that would each have been big enough to accommodate ten or eleven people. The big windows were ajar and gleaming white against the darkness outside. A night breeze blew through the room, sucking the long curtains in and out of the windows, blowing them up towards the ceiling and then rippling them out over a rust-coloured rug.

Milton took in everything, remembering as much as he could.

Details:

The DJ in a baseball cap mixing from two laptops set up next to the bar.

The pole with two girls writhing around it, both of them dressed as nuns.

The girl dancing on the well-stocked bar, wearing a mask of President Obama.

The music was loud, and the atmosphere was frantic. Many of the guests were drunk, and no attempt had been made to hide the large silver salvers of cocaine that had been placed around the room. Milton watched a man leading a half-naked woman up the wide wooden staircase to the first floor. Another man stuffed a banknote into the garter belt of the girl who was dancing for him.

The scream.

Milton tracked it.

He made his way farther inside. The windows at the rear of the room looked out onto wide outdoor porches and manicured grounds. He could just see through the fog to the large illuminated pool, the spa and the fire flickering in an outdoor firepit. He passed into a library. Silk fabric walls blended with painted wainscoting. There was a private cloakroom and a large wood-burning fireplace. A handful of guests stood there, all male.

Madison was cowering against the wall, slowly rocking backwards and forwards.

There was a man next to her. He put his hand on her shoulder and spoke to her, but she pulled away. She looked vulnerable and frightened.

Milton quickly crossed the room. 'Are you all right?'

She looked right through him.

'Madison – are you all right?'

She couldn't focus on him.

'It's John Smith.'

Her eyes were glassy.

'I drove you here, remember? I said I'd wait for you.'

The man who had been speaking to her faded back and walked quickly away. Milton watched him, caught between his concern for her and the desire to question him.

'They want to kill me,' she said.

'What?'

'They want me dead.'

Another man appeared in the door and came across to them both. Another guard.

Milton turned his head to look at him. 'What's going on?'

'Nothing.'

'Look at her. What's happened?'

He snorted out a derisive laugh. 'She's tripping out, man. They said she went into the bathroom, and when she came out, she was like that. But you don't need to worry. We'll look after her. We're going to drive her back to the city.'

'She says someone wants to kill her.'

'You want me to repeat it? Look at the state of her. She's off her head.'

Milton didn't buy that for a moment. Something was wrong, he was sure of it, and there was no way he was going to leave her here.

'Who are you?' the man asked him.

'I drove her out here. You don't need to worry about another car. I'll take her back.'

'No, you won't. We're taking care of it, and you're getting out of here. Right now.'

'Not without her.'

Milton moved towards him so that they were face to face. The man was about the same height as him but perhaps a little heavier. He had low, clenched brows and a thick, flattened nose. He had nothing in common with the well-dressed, affluent guests next door. Hired muscle in case any of the guests got out of hand. Probably armed, too, like his pal with the broken nose and the headache outside. Milton took another deep breath. He stared forward with his face burning and his hands clenching and unclenching.

'What?' the man said, squaring up to him.

'I'd be careful,' Milton advised, 'before I lose my temper.'

'That supposed to be a threat, pal? What you gonna do?'

Milton's attention was distracted for just a moment, and he didn't notice Madison sprint for the door. He shouldered the man out of the way and gave chase, but she was quick and agile and already halfway across the library and then into the living room beyond. Milton bumped into a drunken guest, knocking him so that he toppled over the back of the sofa and onto the floor, barely managing to keep his own balance. 'Madison!' He stumbled after her, scrambling through the room and into the foyer and then the cool of the night beyond. The visibility was bad. He called out to her, 'Madison! Wait!'

She crossed the driveway and kept going, disappearing into the bushes at the side of the gardens.

She vanished into the fog.

The man outside was on his knees, still dazed, struggling to get to his feet.

Milton started in pursuit but came to a helpless stop. He clenched his teeth in frustration. He couldn't start crashing across the neighbouring properties. Their occupants would call the police, and then he would be arrested, and they would take his details. He had probably stayed too long as it was. Perhaps they had already been called. Bringing attention to himself was something that a man in his position really couldn't afford.

He ran for the Explorer, started the engine and rolled the car up the road. He turned right, further into Pine Shore, and as the headlights raked through the murky gloom, he saw Madison again, at the front door of the next house, knocking furiously. He watched as the door opened and an old man with scraps of white hair and an expression that flicked from annoyance to concern came out and spoke with her. She shrieked at him, repeating one word – 'help' – before she pushed her way into the house.

Milton stepped out of the car and then paused, impotent, as the sounds of an argument were audible from inside. Madison stumbled outside again, tripping down the porch steps. She scrambled to her feet as Milton took a step towards her, the old man coming outside after her, a phone in his hand, calling out in a weak and uncertain voice that he had phoned 911 and that she needed to get off his property. He saw Milton, glared at him and repeated that he had called the cops.

Milton paused again. Madison sprinted to the old man's fence and clambered over it, ploughing through a flower bed and a stand of shrubs, knocking on the front door of the next big house, not waiting to have her knock answered before continuing on down the road.

Milton heard the growl of several motorcycle engines. Four sets of lights blasted around the corner, powerful headlamps that sliced through the fog. He turned and looked into the glare of the high beams. The shape of the bikes suggested big Harleys. The riders slotted the hogs in along the side of the road. The engines were killed, one by one, but the headlights were left burning.

A car rolled up alongside them. It was difficult to make it out for sure, but it looked like an old Cadillac.

Milton got back into the Explorer and drove slowly up the road after Madison. It was dimly lit and he couldn't see where she had gone. He dialled the number she had used to book him earlier. There was no answer.

Another set of headlights flicked on behind him, flashing across the rear-view mirror. The town car from before had pulled out of the driveway to the party house. Milton redialled the number as he watched its red tail lights disappear into the fog, swerving away behind the shoulder of dark trees at the side of the road.

He turned the car around and went through the gate in case Madison had doubled back and tried to make her way back up towards West Shore Road. The vegetation was dark and thick to either side, no light and no sign of anyone or anything. No sign of her anywhere. He parked.

After five minutes, he heard the engines of the four motorbikes and watched as they looped around in a tight turn and roared away, heading back out towards the road, passing him one after the other and then accelerating sharply. The Cadillac followed. Five minutes after that he heard the siren of a cop car. Milton slid down in the seat, his head beneath the line of the window. The police car turned through the gate and rolled towards the house. He waited for change to it to come to a stop, and then, with his lights off, he drove away. He had already taken more risks than was prudent. The cops would be able to help Madison more than he could, and he didn't want to be noticed out here.

That didn't mean that he didn't feel bad.

He flicked the lights on and accelerated gently away.

4

Milton stirred at twelve the next day. His first waking thought was of the girl. He had called her mobile several times on the way back to the city, but he had been transferred straight to voicemail. After that, he had driven home in silence. He didn't know her at all, yet he was still terribly worried. He made his bed, pulling the sheets tight and folding them so that it was as neat as he could make it, a hang-up from a decade spent in the army. When he was done, he stared out of the window of his room into the seemingly never-ending shroud of fog in the street beyond. He feared that something dreadful had happened.

His apartment had a shared bathroom, and he waited until it was unoccupied and then showered in the lukewarm water. He ran his right hand down the left-hand side of his body, feeling for the broken ribs that he had suffered after *Santa Muerte* had stomped him in the dust and dirt outside Juárez. There had been no time to visit a doctor to fix them, but they had healed well enough. It was just another fracture that hadn't been dealt with properly, and he had lost count of the number of times that that had happened.

Milton took his razor and shaved, looking at his reflection in the steamy mirror. He had short dark hair flecked with a little grey. There was a scar on his face, running horizontally from his earlobe, across his cheek and terminating just below his right nostril. He was even-featured, although there was something 'hard' about his looks. He looked almost swarthy in certain lights, and now that he had shaved away the untidy beard that he had sported while he had travelled north through South America, his clean, square, sharply defined jawline was exposed.

His day work was physically demanding, and hefting the weighty boxes from the depot into the back of the truck had been good for his physique. His old muscle tone was back, and he felt better than he had for months. The tan he had acquired while he was in South America had faded, and the tattoo of an angel's wings across his shoulders and neck stood out more clearly now that his skin was paler. He dried himself and dressed in jeans and a work shirt, locked the door and left the building.

*   *   *

Top Notch Burger was a one-room restaurant at the corner of Hyde and O'Farrell. Milton had found it during his exploration of the city after he had taken his room at the El Capitan. It was a small place squeezed between a hair salon and a shoe shop, with frosted windows and identified only by the single word BURGER written across dusty signage.

Inside, the furniture was mismatched and often broken, the misspelt menu was chalked up on a blackboard, and hygiene looked as if it was an afterthought.

The chef was a large African-American man called Julius and, as Milton had discovered, he was a bona fide genius when it came to burgers. Milton came in every day for his lunch, sometimes taking the paper bag with his burger and fries and eating it in his car on the way to Mr Freeze, and on other occasions, if he had the time, he would eat it in the restaurant. There was rarely anyone else in the place at the same time, and Milton liked that; he listened to the gospel music that Julius played through the cheap Sony stereo on a shelf above his griddle, sometimes read his book and sometimes just watched the way the man expertly prepared the food.

'Afternoon, John,' Julius said as he shut the door behind him.

'How's it going?'

'Going good,' he said. 'What can I get for you? The usual?'

'Please.'

Milton almost always had the same thing: bacon and cheddar on an aged beef patty in a sourdough bun, bone marrow, cucumber pickles, caramelised onions, horseradish aioli, a bag of double-cooked fries and a bottle of ginger beer.

He was getting ready to leave when his phone rang.

He stopped, staring as the phone vibrated on the table.

No one ever called him at this time of day.

'Hello?'

'My name's Trip Macklemore.'

'Do I know you?'

'Who are you?'

Milton paused, his natural caution imposing itself. 'My name's John,' he said carefully. 'John Smith. What can I do for you?'

'You're a taxi driver?'

'That's right.'

'Did you drive Madison Clarke last night?'

'I drove *a* Madison. She didn't tell me her second name. How do you know that?'

'She texted me your number. Her usual driver wasn't there, right?'

'So she said. How do you know her?'

'I'm her boyfriend.'

Milton swapped the phone to his other ear. 'She hasn't come home?'

'No. That's why I'm calling.'

'And that's unusual for her?'

'Very. Did anything happen last night?'

Milton paused uncomfortably. 'How much do you know—'

'About what she does?' he interrupted impatiently. 'I know everything, so you don't need to worry about hurting my feelings. Look – I've been worried sick about her. Could we meet?'

Milton drummed his fingers against the table.

'Mr Smith?'

'Yes, I'm here.'

'Can we meet? Please. I'd like to talk to you.'

'Of course.'

'This afternoon?'

'I'm working.'

'After that? When you're through?'

'Sure.'

'Do you know Mulligan's? Green and Webster.'

'I can find it.'

'What time?'

Milton said he would see him at six. He ended the call, gave Julius ten dollars and stepped into the foggy street outside.

* * *

The business had its depot in Bayview. It was located in an area of warehouses, a series of concrete boxes with electricity and telephone wires strung overhead and cars and trucks parked haphazardly outside. Milton parked the Explorer in the first space he could find and walked the short distance to Wallace Avenue. Mr Freeze's building was on the corner, a two-storey box with two lines of windows and a double-height roller door through which the trucks rolled to be loaded with the ice they would deliver all around the Bay Area.

Milton went in through the side door, to the locker room and changed into the blue overalls with the corporate logo – a block of motion-blurred ice – embroidered on the left lapel. He changed his Timberlands for a pair of steel-capped work boots and went to collect his truck from the line that was arranged in front of the warehouse.

He swung out into the road and then backed into the loading bay. He saw Vassily, the boss, as he went around to the big industrial freezer. His docket was fixed to the door: bags of ice to be delivered to half a dozen restaurants in Fisherman's Wharf and an ice sculpture to a hotel in Presidio.

He yanked down the big handle and muscled the heavy freezer door open. The cold hit him at once, just like always, a numbing throb that would sink into the bones and remain there all day if you stayed inside too long.

Milton picked up the first big bag of ice and carried it to the truck. It, too, was refrigerated, and he slung it into the back to be arranged for transport when he had loaded them all. There were another twenty bags, and by the time he had finished carrying them into the truck, his biceps, the inside of his forearms and his chest were cold from where he had hugged the ice. He stacked the bags in three neat rows and went back into the freezer. He just had the ice sculpture left to move. It was of a dolphin, curled as if it was leaping through the air. It was five feet high and set on a heavy plinth. Vassily paid a guy fifty dollars for each sculpture and sold them for three hundred. It was, as he said, 'a big-ticket item'.

Milton couldn't keep his mind off what had happened last night. He kept replaying it all: the house, the party, the girl's blind panic, the town car that had only just arrived before it had pulled away, the motorcycles, the Cadillac. Was there anything else he could have done? He was embarrassed that he had let Madison get away from him so easily when it was so obvious that she needed help. She wasn't his responsibility.

He knew that she was an adult, but he also knew he would blame himself if anything had happened to her.

He pressed his fingers beneath the plinth, and bending his knees and straining his arms and thighs, he hefted the sculpture into the air, balancing it against his shoulder. It was heavy, surely two hundred pounds, and it was all he could manage to get it off the floor. He turned around and started forwards, his fingers straining and the muscles in his arms and shoulders burning from the effort.

He thought about the call from her boyfriend and the meeting that he and Macklemore had scheduled. He would tell him exactly what had happened. Maybe he would know something. Maybe Milton could help him find her.

He made his way to the door of the freezer. The unit had a raised lip, and Milton was distracted; he forgot that it was there and stubbed the toe of his right foot against it. The sudden surprise unbalanced him, and he caught his left boot on the lip too as he stumbled over it. The sculpture tipped away from his body, and even as Milton tried to follow after it, attempting to bring his right arm up to corral it, he knew there was nothing he could do. The sculpture tipped forwards faster and faster, and then he dropped it completely. It fell to the concrete floor of the depot, shattering into a million tiny pieces.

Even in the noisy depot, the crash was loud and shocking. There was a moment of silence before some of the others started to clap, others whooping sardonically. Milton stood with the glistening fragments spread around him, helpless. He felt the colour rising in his cheeks.

Vassily came out of the office. 'What the *fuck*, John?'

'Sorry.'

'What happened?'

'I tripped. Dropped it.'

'I can see that.'

'I'm sorry.'

'You already said that. It's not going to put it back together again, is it?'

'I was distracted.'

'I don't pay you to be distracted.'

'No, you don't. I'm sorry, Vassily. It won't happen again.'

'It's coming out of your wages. Three hundred bucks.'

'Come on, Vassily. It doesn't cost you that.'

'No, but that's money I'm going to have to pay back. Three hundred. If you don't like it, you know where to find the door.'

Milton felt the old, familiar flare of anger. Five years ago, he would not have been able to hold it all in. His fists clenched and unclenched, but he remembered what he had learnt in the Rooms – that there were some things that you just couldn't control, and that there was no point in worrying about them – and with that in mind, the flames flickered and died. It was better that way. Better for Vassily. Better for him.

'Fine,' he said. 'That's fine. You're right.'

'Clean it up,' Vassily snapped, stabbing an angry finger at the mess on the floor, 'and then get that ice delivered. You're going to be late.'

5

Milton drove the Explorer back across town and arrived ten minutes early for his appointment at six with Trip Macklemore. Mulligan's was at 330 Townsend Street. There was a small park opposite the entrance, and he found a bench that offered an uninterrupted view. He put the girl's rucksack on the ground next to his feet, picked up a discarded copy of the *Chronicle* and watched the comings and goings. The fog had lifted a little during the afternoon, but it looked as if it was going to thicken again for the evening. He didn't know what Trip looked like, but he guessed the anxious-looking young man who arrived three minutes before they were due to meet was as good a candidate as any.

Milton waited for another five minutes, watching the street. There was no sign that Trip had been followed or that any surveillance had been set up. The people looking for him were good, but that had been Milton's job for many years, too, and he was confident that they would not be able to hide from him. Satisfied, he got up, dropped the newspaper into the rubbish bin next to the seat, collected the rucksack, crossed the road and went inside.

The young man he had seen coming inside was waiting at a table. Milton scanned the bar; it was a reflex action drilled into him by long experience and reinforced by several occasions where advance planning had saved his life. He noted the exits and the other customers. It was early, and the place was quiet. Milton liked that. Nothing was out of the ordinary.

He allowed himself to relax a little and approached. 'Mr Macklemore?'

'Mr Smith?'

'That's right. But you can call me John.'

'Can I get you a beer?'

'That's all right. I don't drink.'

'Something else?'

'It's okay – I'm fine.'

'You don't mind if I do?'

'No. Of course not.'

The boy went to the bar, and Milton checked him out. He guessed he was in his early twenties. He had a fresh complexion that made him look even younger and a leonine aspect, with a high clear brow and plenty of soft black curls eddying over his ears and along his collar. He had a compact, powerful build. A good-looking boy with a healthy colour to his skin, Milton guessed that he worked outside, in a trade that involved plenty of physical labour. He was nervous, fingering the edge of his wallet as he tried to get the bartender's attention.

'Thanks for coming,' he said when he came back with his beer.

'No problem.'

'You mind me asking – that accent?'

'I'm English.'

'That's what I thought. What are you doing in San Francisco?'

Milton had no wish to get into a discussion about that. 'Working,' he said, closing it off.

Trip put his thumb and forefinger around the neck of the bottle and drank.

'So,' Milton said, 'shall we talk about Madison?'

'Yes.'

'She hasn't come back?'

'No. And I'm starting to get worried about her. Like – *seriously* worried. I was going to give it until ten and then call the police.'

'She's never done this before?'

'Been out of touch as long as this?' The boy shook his head. 'No. Never.'

'When did you see her last?'

'Last night. We went to see an early movie. It finished at eightish, she said she was going out to work, so I kissed her goodnight and went home.'

'She seemed all right to you?'

'Same as ever. Normal.'

'And you've tried to call her?'

'Course I have, man. Dozens of times. I got voicemail first of all, but now I don't even get that. The phone's been shut off. That's when I really started to worry. She's never done that before. She gave me your number last night—'

'Why did she do that?'

'She's careful when she's working. She didn't know you.'

Milton was as sure as he could be that Trip was telling the truth.

The boy drank off half of his beer and placed the bottle on the table. 'Where did you take her?'

'Up to Belvedere. Do you know it?'

'Not really.'

'There's a gated community up there. She said she'd been up there before.'

'She's never mentioned it.'

'There's a couple of dozen houses. Big places. Plenty of money. There was a party there. A big house just inside the gate. She didn't tell you about it?'

He shook his head. 'She never told me anything. Can't say it's something I really want to know about, so I never ask. I don't like her doing it, but she's making money, thousand bucks a night, sometimes – what am I gonna do about that? She makes more in a night than I make in two weeks.'

'Doing what?'

'I work for the electric company – fix power lines, maintenance, that kind of thing.'

'What does she do with the money?'

'She saves it.'

'She have a kid?'

'No,' he said.

Milton nodded to himself: *suckered.*

'She's saving as much as she can so she can write. That's her dream. I suppose I could ask her to stop, but I don't think she'd pay much attention. She's strong-willed, Mr Smith. You probably saw that.'

'I did.'

'And anyway, it's only going to be a temporary thing – just until she's got the money she needs.' He took another swig from the bottle. Milton noticed his hands were shaking. 'What happened?'

'I dropped her off, and then I waited for her to finish.'

'And?'

'And then I heard a scream.'

'Her?'

'Yes. I went inside to get her.'

He paused, wondering how much he should tell the boy. He didn't want to frighten him more than he already was, but he figured Trip needed to know everything.

'She was in a state,' he continued. 'She looked terrified. She was out of it, too. Wouldn't speak to me. I don't even know if she saw me.'

'Out of it? What does that mean?'

'She ever do drugs?'

'No way,' Trip said. 'Never.'

'That's what she told me, too.' Milton frowned. 'I went in to see her, and look, if I had to say one way or another, then I'd say she was on something. She said everyone was trying to kill her. Very paranoid. Her eyes wouldn't focus, and she wasn't making any sense.'

'Maybe her drink was spiked?'

'Maybe,' Milton said. But maybe not. He thought it was more likely that she was doing drugs. A job like that? Milton had helped a girl in the Balkans once during the troubles over there, and she had worked up a ferocious heroin habit. The way she had explained it, she'd needed something to deaden herself to the things she had to do to stay alive, and that had been as good as anything else. And Madison had kept the finer details of her hooking away from Trip, so wasn't it likely that she'd keep this from him, too? Didn't it stand to reason? No sense in pushing that now, though.

'What happened after that?'

'She ran. I went after her, but she was too quick for me, and to be honest, I'm not sure what I would've done if I'd caught her, anyway. I got in the car and drove up and down, but there wasn't any sign of her. I called her mobile but didn't get anywhere. In the end, I waited as long as I could, and then I came back. I was hoping she might have found her way home.'

Trip blanched with worry. 'Fuck.'

'Don't panic,' Milton said calmly. 'There might be a reason for it.'

'I don't think so. Something's wrong.'

Milton said nothing. He pushed Madison's rucksack along the floor with his foot. 'Here,' he said. 'She left this in the car. You better take it.'

Trip picked up the bag, put it on his lap, opened it and idly took out the things inside: her books, the bottle of vodka, her purse. 'What do I do now?'

'That's up to you. If it was me, I wouldn't wait to call the police. I'd do it now—'

'But you said not to panic.'

'I know, and the chances are that there's a perfectly good explanation for what's happened. She'll come home, and you'll just have to explain to them that it was a false alarm. They won't mind – happens all the time. But if something is wrong, if she is in trouble, the sooner you get the police onto it, the better it's likely to be.'

'How do I do that? Just call them?'

'Better to go in.'

'Yes,' Trip said, nodding vigorously. 'I'll go in.'

'You want some backup?'

'What – you'll come too?'

'If you like.'

'You don't have to do that,' he said, although his relief was palpable.

It was the right thing to do. The way Milton saw it, they would want to speak to him, and it would save time if he was already there. It would show willing, too; Milton was a little anxious that there might be questions about him driving a prostitute to a job, and he thought it would be better to be upfront right from the start. He would deny that he had known what was going on — which was true, at least up to a point – and hope for the best. And, he thought, the boy was becoming increasingly anxious. He suspected he might appreciate a little moral support.

'Come on,' he said. 'You drive here?'

'I don't have a car. I got the bus.'

'I'll give you a ride.'

6

They were met in the reception area by a uniformed cop who introduced himself as Officer Francis. He was an older man with the look of a long-standing veteran. His hair was shot through with streaks of grey, his face was creased with lines, and he sat down with a sigh of contentment that said that he was glad to be off his feet. He wasn't the most vigorous officer that Milton had ever seen, but he wasn't surprised by that: with something like this, why waste the time of a more effective man? No, they would send out one of the older guys, a time-server close to his pension, someone who would listen politely and give them the impression that they had been given the attention that they thought their problem deserved, and then he would send them on their way.

'You're Mr Macklemore?'

'That's right.'

'You're the boyfriend.'

'Yes.'

'And you, sir?'

'John Smith.'

'How are you involved in this?'

'I'm a taxi driver. I dropped Madison off last night.'

'You know Mr Macklemore?'

'We just met.'

'So you're here why?'

'I'd like to help. I was one of the last people to see Madison.'

'I see.' He nodded. 'All right, then, Mr Macklemore, why don't you tell me what's happened and then we can work out what to do next.'

Trip told the story again, and Officer Francis listened quietly, occasionally noting down a detail in a notebook that he took from his breast pocket. When Trip was finished, Francis asked Milton a few questions: how had Madison seemed to him? Did he have any idea why she had run off the way she did? Milton answered them all honestly.

'You know she was hooking?'

'I didn't,' Milton said.

'Really?'

'No. I didn't. Not until we got there. It was just another job for me. I know the law, officer.'

'And you've come here without being asked,' he said, pursing his lips.

'Of course. I'd like to be helpful.'

'Fair enough. I'm happy with that. What do you think happened?'

'I don't know. Whatever it was, she was frightened.'

'Whose party was it?'

'I'm afraid I don't know that.'

'A lot of rich folks up there,' Francis mused. 'I can remember when you could buy a place with a nice view of the bay for a hundred grand. You wouldn't get an outhouse up there for that these days. Plenty of the tech guys have moved in. Driven up the prices like you wouldn't believe.'

Francis closed the notebook and slipped it back into his breast pocket.

'Well?' Trip said.

'I gotta tell you, Mr Macklemore, this isn't what we'd call a classic missing persons case. Not yet, anyway. She's only been gone a day.'

'But it's totally out of character. She's never done anything like this before.'

'That may be, sir, but that don't necessarily mean she's missing. She's young. From what you've said, it sounds like she's a little flighty, too. She's got no history of mental illness, no psychiatric prescriptions, and you say she wasn't on drugs. Just because you can't find her, that don't necessarily mean that she's missing, you know what I mean?'

'No,' Trip said. 'I don't agree.'

'Not much I can do about that, sir,' Francis said, spreading his hands.

Milton shook his head. 'I agree with Mr Macklemore, detective. I'm not sure I'm as relaxed about it as you are.'

The policeman glanced up at Milton with a look of mild annoyance. 'What do you mean?'

'You didn't see the state she was in last night.'

'That may be— I'm sorry, what was your name again?'

'Smith.'

'That may be, Mr Smith, but she wouldn't be the first working girl I've seen freak out, then check out for a bit.'

'Not good enough,' Trip complained angrily. 'It's because she's a hooker you're not going to assign someone to this, right? That's the reason?'

'No. That's not what I said.'

'But it's what you meant.'

Francis stood and held out his hands, palm first. 'Take it easy, son. If she's still not back tomorrow, you give us another call, and we'll see where we are then. For now, I'd go back home, make sure your phone's switched on and try to relax. I've seen plenty of cases like this. *Plenty*. Seriously. I'm telling you, ninety-nine times out of a hundred, they come back, a little embarrassed about the whole thing, and everything gets explained.'

'And the other time?'

'Not going to happen here, Mr Macklemore. Really – go home. She'll turn up. You'll see.'

* * *

They made their way outside and onto the street.

'What the fuck was *that*?'

'Take it easy,' Milton said.

'You think he was listening to a word we said?'

'Probably not. But I'm guessing that's standard operating procedure. And he's right about one thing – it's been less than a day.'

'You agree with him?'

'I didn't say that. And no, I don't. Not with everything.'

Milton had expected a reluctance to get involved, and part of him could accept the logic in what the officer had said; it *was* still early, after all. But the more he thought about what had happened last night, the more he had a bad feeling about it.

The way she had looked.

The way she had run.

The car speeding away.

The bikers. What were they doing at a high-end party like that?

Milton had made a living out of relying on his hunches. Experience told him that it was unwise to ignore them. And they were telling him that this didn't look good.

Trip took out a packet of Luckies. He put one into his mouth and lit it. Milton noticed that his fingers were trembling again. 'That was a total waste of time. Total waste. We could have been out looking for her.' He offered the packet to Milton.

'It wasn't,' he said, taking a cigarette and accepting Trip's offer of a light. 'At the very least, he'll file a report that says that you came in tonight and said she was missing. Now they'll have something to work with. And the clock will have started. I wouldn't be surprised if they treat it more seriously then.'

'So what do I do now? How long do we have to wait before they'll do something? Two days? Three days? When's the right time before they accept that something is wrong?'

'If she's not back in the morning, I'd call again. I'd make a real nuisance of myself. You know what they say about the squeaky hinge?'

'No.'

'It gets the oil. You keep calling. Do that until ten or eleven. If it doesn't work, and if she's still not back by then, go back to the precinct and demand to see a detective. Don't leave until you've seen one. Authority's the same the world over: you give them enough of a headache, eventually they'll listen to you – even if it's just to shut you up.'

'And until then? It's not like I'm gonna be able to sleep.'

'There are some things you can do. Do you know anything about the agency she was working for?'

'No. She never said.'

'Never mind. Google all the emergency rooms in a twenty-mile radius. There's one in Marin City, another in Sausalito, go as far north as San Rafael. That's the first place to look. If something's happened to her, if last night was some sort of episode or if she's hurt herself somehow, then that's probably where she'll be. And when you've tried those, try all the nearby police stations – Belvedere, Tiburon, the Sheriff's Department at Marin. You never know. Someone might've said something.'

'Okay.'

'Does she have a laptop?'

'Sure.'

'There might be emails. Can you get into it?'

'I don't know. There'll be a password. I might be able to guess it.'

'Try. Whoever booked her is someone we'll want to talk to. The police will get to it eventually, assuming they need to, but there's nothing to stop us having a look first.'

Trip looked at him, confused. '*Us?*'

'Of course.'

'What – you're going to help me?' He was almost pitifully grateful.

'Of course I'm going to help.'

'But you don't even know us. Why would you do that?'

'Let's just say I like helping people and leave it at that, all right?'

His time in A.A. had taught Milton plenty of things. One of them was that it was important to make amends; recovering alcoholics considered that almost as important as staying away from the first drink. It wasn't as easy for him to do that as it was for others. Most of the people that he would have had to make amends to were already dead, often because he had killed them. Milton had to make do with this. It wasn't perfect, but it was still the best salve he had yet discovered for soothing his uneasy conscience.

7

Governor Joseph Jack Robinson II was a born talker. It was just what he did. Everyone had a talent: some men had a facility for numbers, some for making things, some for language; hell, others could swing a bat and send a ball screaming away to the fences. Governor Robinson was a speaker, and Arlen Crawford had known it within five seconds of hearing him for the first time. That was why he had given up what could have been a very profitable career in law and turned down the offer of a partnership and the millions of dollars he would have been able to make. He had postponed the chance to take an early retirement and the house on the coast he and his wife had always hankered after. The governor's gift was why he had given all that up and thrown in his lot with him. That was back then, two years ago, when Robinson was governor, just starting out on this phase of his political career, but Arlen Crawford had never regretted his decision, not even for a second. It could have gone wrong, a spectacular flameout that took everyone and everything around him down too. But it hadn't, and now J.J.'s star was in the ascendant, climbing into the heavens, streaking across the sky.

Arlen Crawford had seen nothing to make him think that he had misjudged him.

He took his usual place at the back of the room and waited for the governor to do his thing. There had been plenty of similar rooms over the course of the last few months, all the way across the country from the Midwest to the coast of the Pacific: school gymnasia, town halls, factory dining rooms, warehouses, anywhere where you could put a few hundred seats and fill them with enthusiastic voters who were prepared to come and listen to what the candidate had to say.

It was like that today; they were in the gymnasium where the Woodside Cougars shot hoops, with its polished floor that squeaked when he turned his shoe on it, a banked row of seats where moms and pops and alumni and backers of the school would gather to cheer on the kids, and a scoreboard at one end that said COUGARS and AWAY, the neon numerals set to zero. A lectern had been placed against the wall that faced the bleachers with enough space for six rows of folded chairs to be arranged between the two. A poster that they had fixed to the lectern said AMERICA FIRST. A larger banner that they had pinned to the wall behind it read ROBINSON FOR PRESIDENT.

The room was full. Crawford guessed there were five hundred people inside. There were a few curious students, not Robinson's normal constituency, but Crawford had insisted. It made him look more 'hip' and helped in his campaign to broaden his appeal to a younger audience. Crawford knew, too, that the governor was occasionally prone to phoning it in if the room was too friendly; it did him no harm at all to think that there was the possibility of awkward questions in the Q&A that would follow his speech. The rest of the audience were naturally right-leaning voters from the area, all of them given a little vim and vigour by the dozen or so backers that the campaign brought with them on the bus. They were doing their thing now, hooting and hollering as they watched a video of the governor's achievements as it played on the large screen that had been fixed to the wall.

The video ended, and Robinson walked through a storm of applause to the lectern.

'Thank you, Woodside. Thank you.'

Crawford looked around the room: five hundred avid faces hanging on every word.

'So what brought us here today? Why aren't we catching a game, the 49ers or the Raiders? I know, both teams stink, but it's better than coming here and listening to me for an hour, right?' He waited for the laughs to die down. 'What brought us together is a love of our country, isn't it? Because we can see that America is in trouble. She needs our help.'

Robinson stopped. He waited. One of the women in the audience called out, '*We're listening!*'

Robinson grinned and then gave the same speech that he'd given yesterday, and the day before that. He spoke of how many working-age men were out of work, how mortgages were being called in at a rate that hadn't been seen since the Great Depression, how divorce was through the roof. He raged against the current president and his policies, drew attention to the size of the national debt and the speed with which it was growing.

He went on in the same vein for another ten minutes. It was a bravura display, yet again. In his two years as Robinson's chief of staff, Crawford had probably heard him speak a thousand times, and that, right there, was another in a long line of brilliant speeches. He had the knack of making his audience feel as if he was one of them; the kind of fellow you could imagine having a beer with, shooting the breeze and setting the world to rights. It wasn't a conscious thing, a talent that he could calibrate and deploy with care and consideration; it was totally natural, so much so that he didn't even seem to realise what he was doing.

He stepped away from the lectern and made his way along the front row of the folding chairs, pumping offered hands, sometimes taking them in both of his and beaming that brilliant megawatt smile.

Crawford watched and smiled and shook his head in admiration.

No doubt about it: Joseph Jack Robinson was a natural.

He stayed with them for half an hour, listening to their stories, answering their questions and signing autographs, then they all followed him back downstairs and out to the campaign bus. Crawford and Catherine Williamson, the press manager, trailed the crowd.

Catherine looked at Crawford and raised her manicured eyebrow, an inverted tick of amusement that the governor had done it again. Crawford looked back at her and winked. J.J. did that, now and again; he surprised even the staffers who had been with him the longest. It seemed to be happening more often these days. As the speeches got more important, as the television crews that tailed them everywhere grew in number, as his polling numbers solidified and accrued, Robinson pulled the rabbit out of the hat again and again and again.

It was why they were all so excited.

This felt real.

It felt like they were backing a winner.

Crawford followed the governor up the steps and onto the bus.

'Great speech,' he told Robinson as he opened his brief-case and took out the papers he needed for the trip.

'You think?'

'Are you kidding? You had them eating out of your hand.'

Robinson shrugged and smiled. Crawford found that habit of his a little annoying, the *aw-shucks* modesty that was as false as the gleaming white veneers on his teeth. The governor knew he was good. Everything was done for a reason: every grin, every knowing wink, every handshake and backslap and beam of that radiant smile. Some of the rivals he had crushed on the way had been good, too, but not as good as him. They had a nagging sense of the ersatz that stuck with their audiences and curdled over time, seeds of doubt that grew into reasons why the voters chose Robinson instead of them when they finally got to the polling booths. The governor didn't suffer from that. He was a good man, completely trustworthy, honest to a fault, or, more relevantly, that was what they thought. The greatest expression of his genius was to make the whole performance look so effortlessly natural.

'Those questions on immigration . . .' Robinson began.

'Go vague on the numbers. We don't want to get caught out.'

'Not the numbers. The message. It's still holding up?'

'People seem to agree with you.'

'Damn straight they do. If I can't say it like it is, what's the point?'

'I know – and I agree.'

'These fucking *wetbacks*,' Robinson said with a dismissive flick of his wrist, 'taking jobs that belong to Americans; damn straight we should be sending them back.'

Crawford looked around, making sure they weren't overheard. 'Easy,' he advised.

'I know, I know. *Moderation*. I'm not an idiot, Arlen.' He dropped down into the seat opposite and unbuttoned the top button of his shirt. 'Where next?'

'Radio interview,' Catherine said. 'And we're an hour late already.'

Robinson was suddenly on the verge of anger. 'They know that?' he demanded.

'Know what?'

'That we're gonna be late.'

'Don't worry. I told them. They're cool.'

They were all used to his temper. He switched unpredictably, with even the smallest provocation, and then switched back again with equal speed. It was unnerving and disorientating for the newest members of the entourage, who had not had the opportunity to acclimate themselves to the vagaries of his character, but once you realised it was usually a case of bark over bite, it was just another vector to be weighed in the calculus of working for the man.

Catherine disappeared further up the bus.

'No need to snap at her,' Crawford said.

'You know I hate being late. My old man used to drill it into me—'

'You'd rather be thirty minutes early than a minute late. I know. You've told me about a million times. How's the head?'

'Still pretty sore. You should've told me it was time to go.'

'I did.'

'Not early enough. We should have left about an hour before we did. You didn't insist.'

'Next time, I will.'

'We probably shouldn't even have been there.'

'No,' he said, 'we should.'

The party had been a little more raucous than Crawford would have preferred, but it was full of donors and potential donors, and it would've been unseemly to have given it the bum's rush or to have left too early. The hour that they had been there had given the governor plenty of time to drink more than he should have, and Crawford had spent the evening at his side, a little anxious, trying to keep him on message and making sure he didn't do anything that would look bad if it was taken out of context. It had been a long night for him, too, and Crawford knew he would have to find the energy from somewhere to make it through to the end of the day.

'You get the Secret Service if you have to. Tell them to drag me out.' He paused theatrically. 'Do I have a detail yet?'

'Not yet,' Crawford said, playing along.

'You know what I'm looking forward to most? The code name. You know what they called Kennedy?'

'No, sir.'

'LANCER. And Reagan?'

'No, sir.'

'RAWHIDE. What do you reckon they'll call me?'

'You want me to answer that? Really?'

'No.' He grinned. 'Better not.'

8

Crawford settled back in his seat as the bus pulled out of the school car park, closed his eyes and allowed himself to reminisce. They had come a long way. He remembered the first time he had met J.J. God, he thought, it must have been at Georgetown almost twenty years ago. He had been involved in politics ever since he'd arrived on campus, standing for various posts and even getting elected to a couple of them. J.J. had been the same. They had both been in the same fraternities – Phi Beta Kappa and Kappa Kappa Psi – and they had served on the same committees.

Eventually, they stood against each other for president of the Students' Association. After a convivial two-week campaign, Robinson had defeated him. But *defeated* was too polite a word; it had been an *annihilation*. A good old-fashioned straight-up-and-down slobberknocker. Crawford knew the reason. J.J. had always been a handsome boy, something of a surfer dude back in those days, and the aura of charisma that clung to him seemed so dense as to be able to deflect all of Crawford's clever thrusts. It was like a suit of armour.

The campaign was civil enough so as to require them to temper their attacks, but the list of deficiencies in his opponent that Crawford had hoped to exploit – his vanity, his privileged background, the suspicion that he was doing this for his résumé rather than from a spirit of public service – were all neutralised the moment he switched on his smile and dazzled his audience with a serving of his West Coast charm. They had debated each other twice, and both times, even the most biased of observers would have had to admit that Crawford had destroyed J.J. on the issues at hand. It didn't seem to make the slightest scrap of difference; J.J.'s election victory was the largest landslide in college history.

It was a good lesson learnt: style trumped substance every single time. It was ever thus.

Crawford retired from student politics with good grace. He was better as the man in the background, the overseer with the long view to better plot strategy and tactics, and he was happy to cede the spotlight to characters like J.J. They had both become friendly during their jousting, despite the occasional low blow, and Crawford had agreed to work with on the Students' Association to make his term of office productive and useful. By and large, it was. They stayed in loose touch as they went their separate ways on graduation.

Crawford was always going to go into law. His father was an attorney, and he had known that he would follow in his footsteps since he was young. Crawford made a career for himself in property and taxation, esoteric subjects that were complicated enough to be remunerative for the few who could master them. His firm served the nascent technology industry in Silicon Valley, and his roster of clients included Microsoft and Apple. He did well. There was the big house in Palo Alto, the BMW in the driveway and a boat. The trophy wife who wouldn't have looked twice at him if they had met at college. Two healthy and happy kids. And it still wasn't enough. Law was never what he would have described as fun or even satisfying, even though he was good at it. Eventually, each month became a long and depressing slog that was made bearable only by the massive pay cheque at the end of it.

Stuck in a rut, Crawford stayed at the firm more than long enough for it to lose its lustre. Law had been the easy decision out of school, cashing in his degree for the easy money despite the nagging suspicion that he would have been better satisfied doing something else: academia, perhaps, or something where he could write. And then he turned forty, and he realised, with a blinding flash of self-awareness that was frightening in its certainty, that he was wasting his life. He quit the next day, called an old friend at Georgetown and asked him for a job.

The man had obliged. Crawford had been teaching the legislative process to keen young up-and-comers for three years when two very different offers came at the exact same time: the first was the offer of millions as a partner at a lobbying firm in Washington, and the second was J.J. Robinson inviting him out to dinner.

He had watched his old opponent's career with a strange mixture of jealousy and relief that it wasn't him. Robinson had run for the House of Representatives as a twenty-eight-year-old

Republican but had been handily defeated by the incumbent. Instead, he had switched his target to the Attorney General-ship, and after defeating a host of minor opponents, he had been elected at the age of thirty. Two years later, Robinson defeated the Democratic governor of Florida and finally took the high office that he had always craved. He had managed to hold onto his youthful appearance, a fact that gave his opponents some-thing to latch onto when they laid into him; he was routinely derided as the 'Boy Governor' and not to be taken seriously. He lost popularity over misjudged taxation and immigration poli-cies and was ousted by his Democratic challenger after just one term of office. He licked his wounds in a lobbying practice for a short while before winning the governorship again, this time serving for ten years.

Crawford had taken up his offer of dinner. He remembered the conversation. There had been some small talk, nothing consequential, until Robinson explained the reason for get-ting back in touch. He was forty-six now, a political veteran, and he was looking for a new challenge.

He was running for president.

And he wanted Crawford to be his chief of staff.

* * *

The bus pulled up outside the campaign office, and the entou-rage duly decamped. The office was the same as the others all across the country. It was entirely generic. It didn't seem to matter where they were, everything looked the same. There was some comfort to be had in that, Crawford thought. There was the usual clutch of pollsters working the phones, entering data into laptops, pecking at the platter of sandwiches from the deli around the corner, the cellophane wrapper still halfway across. Empty soda cans were stacked on desks. Some wore headphones, nodding their heads to the music that seeped out. Crawford knew some of them from the convention last year, but most were new recruits, drawn into the candidate's orbit by the tractor beam of his charisma, offering their time for free.

He saw Sidney Packard standing to one side, a half-eaten sandwich in one hand and his phone in the other. It was pressed to his ear, and he had an expression of deep concentration on his face. Packard was older, bald-headed and wrinkled, and when he moved, his limbs flowed with a lazy confidence. He had been in the police before, and before that, there was talk of the army. He was head of the security detail, and he had been working with the governor for the last ten years. It was an interesting job.

Crawford watched him speaking, and eventually, the other man noticed that he was looking at him and gave him a single, curt nod. Crawford interpreted that as good news, went to the nearest platter of sandwiches and loaded up a plate.

The radio crew had already set up their gear in the conference room, so Crawford went looking for the governor. He opened the door to the bathroom, and there he was; he was buttoning his shirt and fastening his belt. He recognised the young staffer, too. She was adjusting her clothes in the stall behind the governor.

'I'm sorry,' Crawford said.

The woman seemed confused. Robinson drew her out and put his arm around her. 'This is Karly Hammil,' he said. 'She's working for us now.'

'Yes,' Crawford replied. 'I know. I hired her. Hello, Karly.'

She seemed to brace herself against the washbasin and just about managed a shy smile, an attempt to maintain the appearance of propriety that was redundant in the circumstances. Robinson, on the other hand, did not appear to have the capability of being embarrassed. It was as if he had just come out of the stall after using the toilet. Nothing unusual. Nothing out of order. It was an act he had, no doubt, perfected over many years. My God, Crawford thought, there had been plenty of practice. He had seen that shit-eating grin many times since he had started working for him.

'Well, then,' Robinson said. 'We ready?'

'We are,' Crawford said.

Robinson winked at Crawford as he stepped outside and moved over towards the food.

Crawford followed behind him.

'You can't keep doing this,' he said, and the note of resignation he heard in his voice made him feel even more pathetic.

'Relax.'

'How many times do I have to tell you?'

'No lectures today, Arlen.'

'If just one of them tells their story, you do know what'll happen, right? You do understand?'

'Arlen—'

'I'm just checking, because I don't think you've thought about it.'

'No one's saying anything, are they?'

Crawford bit his lip. 'If they did, that'd be the end of it for you. End of the road. That kind of thing— J.J. I'm telling you, you need to listen to me. This isn't the 60s. You're not JFK.'

'Not yet.'

Crawford clenched his teeth; the man was infuriating. 'It's toxic,' he protested.

Robinson took Crawford's right hand in his and squeezed it tight. Depending on his mood and what was required, the governor had several ways of shaking hands. He might place his left hand by the elbow or up around the shoulder or take your hand in both of his. That meant that he was especially interested, underscoring a greeting and making the recipient feel as if they were the most important person in the room. Other times, he would squeeze the shoulder, or for those he really wanted to bring within the dazzling aura of his personality, he might loop the arm across the shoulders and pull them in for a hug. He did this now, releasing Crawford's hand, draping his arm around his shoulders and squeezing him tight.

'I'm keeping a lid on it,' he said. 'You need to stop worrying. You'll get an ulcer.'

Crawford felt like sighing at the sheer boring predictability of it and the frustration that, despite it all – despite increasingly doom-laden warnings of what would happen to the campaign if any of his indiscretions were to be aired in public – the governor just would not listen to him.

9

Milton drove back to Belvedere. It was a little after eight as he navigated the Explorer out of the city, heading north out of the Mission District until he picked up the 101 and then passed through Presidio. He paid more attention this time, orientating himself properly and memorising as much of the landscape as he could. Newly formed whitish fog filtered through the harp strings of the bridge and then puffed out its chest as though pleased with its dramatic entrance; its only applause was the regular blare of the two foghorns, the lapping of the waves as they disappeared under the silent mass and the constant hum of the traffic. He passed turn-offs for Kirby Cove Campground and the Presidio Yacht Club, continued on after Southview Park and Martin Luther King Jr Park, the big cemetery at Fernwood and then, as he turned east and then back south, Richardson Bay Wildlife Sanctuary and McKegney Field with the placid waters of Richardson Bay off to the west. The darkness and the fog – deep and thick – reduced visibility to a handful of yards. Milton drove carefully.

He turned off the coast road and continued to the gate.

The radio was on and tuned in to a talk radio channel; the presenter was speaking to one of the Republican candidates ahead of the presidential election. He sat for a moment, half-listening to the conversation: immigration, how big government was wrong, taxation. The man had a deep, mellifluous voice accented with a lazy drawl. Milton had heard of him before: the governor of Florida, seen as a front-runner in the race. Milton had little time for politicians, but this one was convincing enough.

He turned the dial to switch the radio off, lowered the window and entered the code that Madison had given him last night.

2-0-1-1.

The final digit elicited a buzz, and the gate remained closed.

The code had been changed.

Milton looked at the gate and the community beyond. Why had the code been changed? He tried the combination a second time, and as the keypad buzzed at him again, he noticed the dark black eye of a CCTV camera pointed at him from the gatehouse. He hadn't noticed that being there last night.

He put the car into reverse, and the camera jerked up and swivelled as it tracked him. He turned around and drove slowly back down the drive until he was around the corner and out of sight. He killed the lights and then the engine and reached into the back for the black denim jacket he had stuffed into the footwell. He had a pair of leather gloves in the glove compartment, and he put them into the pockets of the jacket along with a pair of paperclips he removed from old invoices. He took the S&W 9mm that he had confiscated from the guard outside the house and slipped it into the waistband of his jeans. He put the jacket on, opened the door and, keeping within the margin of the vegetation at the side of the road, made his way back towards the gate again.

About fifteen yards from the gate, a wooden pole carried the high-tension power cabling from the substation into the estate. Three large cylindrical transformers were rigged to the pole, twenty feet in the air, and the wire crossed over to a corresponding pole on the other side of the wall. From there, individual wires delivered the current to the houses.

Milton took out the S&W and racked a bullet into the chamber. There were better ways to disable a power supply – Mylar balloons filled with helium would have shorted it out very nicely – but he was working on short notice, and this would have to do. He took aim at the ceramic insulators that held the wire onto the pole. It was a difficult shot; the insulators were small targets at a reasonable distance, it was dark and the fog was dense. He fired once, but the shot missed. He resighted the target, braced his right wrist with his left hand and fired again. The insulator shattered, and the wire, sparks scattering into the gloom, swept down to earth in a graceful arc.

The light above the gate went out.

Milton cut into a dense copse of young firs that crowded close to the left of the road and, using it as cover, moved carefully to the wall. It was made of brick and topped with iron spikes. He reached up and dabbed a finger against the top, feeling for broken glass or anti-climb paint. All he could feel was the rough surface of the brick. Satisfied, he wrapped each gloved hand around a spike and, using them for leverage, hauled himself up, his feet scrabbling for purchase. He got his right foot onto the lip of the wall and boosted himself up until he was balancing atop it. The vantage point offered an excellent view of the community beyond. He could see half a dozen big houses in the immediate vicinity and, as the road turned away to the east, the glow of others. There was no one in sight. He stepped carefully over the spikes and lowered himself onto the ground.

The big house where the party had been held was quiet. All the windows were dark. Milton moved stealthily into the cover of a tree and, pressing himself against it, scoped out the road. It was empty in both directions. There was no one visible anywhere. He ran quickly across, vaulting the low fence and making his way through the large garden to the back of the house. He remembered the layout from the quick glimpse through the window last night: the T-shaped swimming pool with the underwater lamps; the series of terraces on different levels; trees and bushes planted with architectural precision; the firepit; the dark, fogged waters of the bay.

A redwood platform abutted the house here, a sheer drop down the cliff to the rocks below on the right-hand side. The surf boomed below, crashing against the cliff, and the air was damp with salty moisture.

Milton followed the platform.

He pressed himself against the back wall and risked a glance through the windows. The living room beyond was very different now from how it had been the previous night. It was empty. The furniture had been returned to more usual positions around the room. The DJ equipment was gone. The bar, which had been strewn with bottles and glasses, was pristine. The salvers of cocaine that had been so ostentatiously left on the tables had been removed. The room was cool and dark and quiet. The windows were still open a little at the tops, and the curtains shivered in and out on each breath of wind – the only movement that Milton could see.

It was as if the party had never even happened.

Milton flitted quickly across the window to a door that was set into a long extension that had been built across one side of the house. He tried the door. It was locked. Taking off his gloves, he took the paperclips from his pocket and bent them into shape. He slid one into the lower portion of the keyhole, used it to determine which way the cylinder turned, applied light tension and then slid the other clip into the upper part of the keyhole and felt for the pins. He pressed up and felt the individual pins with the tip of the clip, finding the stiffest one and pushing it up and out of the cylinder. He repeated the trick for the remaining four pins, adjusting the torque for each. He turned the cylinder all the way around, and the door unlocked.

Milton scrubbed the lock with the sleeve of his shirt, put the gloves back onto his hands and went inside. It was a utility room. He closed the door behind him, leaving it unlocked, and then paused for a moment, listening carefully. He could hear nothing. He was confident that the house was empty. He walked quickly into a huge kitchen with wide windows, then a hallway, then into the living room. It was gloomy, but there was just enough suffused moonlight from outside for him to see his way.

He checked the downstairs quickly and efficiently. There was another formal living room with a large, carved stone mantel. A secret doorway in the bookshelves led to a speakeasy-style wet bar. The dining room looked like it was being used as a conference room, with a speakerphone in the middle of the table and videoconferencing equipment at the other end. A spiral staircase led down to a wine cellar that had been built around crouching monk corbels that had been turned into light fittings; there were hundreds of bottles, thousands of dollars' worth of wine, but nothing of any obvious interest.

Milton found the stairs and climbed to the first floor. There were four bedrooms, all with en-suite bathrooms. He climbed again to the second floor: three more bedrooms, all enormous. He searched them all quickly and expertly. There were no clothes in the closets and no products in the bathrooms. No signs of habitation at all.

It looked as if the house was vacant.

Distantly, down the stairwell, two storeys below, Milton heard the sound of the front door opening.

He froze.

Footsteps clicked across the wooden floor.

'Power's out,' the voice said.

'The fuck?'

'Whole road, from the look of things.'

'Place like this, millions of dollars, and they lose the power?'

'Shit happens.'

'If you say so.'

'I do.'

'You got a flashlight?'

'Here.'

There was a quiet click.

'You know this is a waste of time.'

'It's gotta get done.'

'What we gotta do?'

'Just make sure everything looks the way it should.'

'Why wouldn't it? What we looking for?'

'Anything that looks like there was a crazy-ass party here.'

'Looks clean to me.'

'Had professionals in – everything you can do, they did.'

'So what are we doing here?'

'We're making sure, okay? Double-checking.'

Milton stepped further back, to another door. He moved stealthily. He could hear footsteps down below. He opened the door; it led to another bedroom. The footsteps downstairs were hard to make out. Was that somebody walking up the stairs to the floor below, the first floor? Or somebody walking through the foyer on the ground floor? He couldn't tell, but either way, he was stuck. If he crossed the landing there, he would have to go past the stairwell, and then he might be visible from below for a certain amount of time.

'You ever seen a place like this? Look at all this shit. This is where the real money's at.'

'Concentrate on what you're doing.'

They were definitely up on the first floor now.

'Go up there. Check it out.'

'Just gonna be more bedrooms.'

'And crazy-ass parties end up in the bedroom, so go up and check them all out.'

'What about you?'

'I'm calling the boss.'

Milton could hear scuffed footsteps coming up the stairs; it was the unenthusiastic, resentful one of the pair. That was probably fortunate.

He dropped to the floor and slid beneath the bed.

'It's me,' the other man was saying, his voice now muffled by the closed door. 'We're at the house. Yeah – looks good. Clean as a whistle. Power's out, though. Alarm was off. Whole neighbourhood. I don't think that's anything to bother us. One of those things.'

Milton held his breath as the door to the bedroom opened and heavy footsteps sounded against the boards. A torch swept the room. The bed was low down, the boards and the mattress snug against his back, and he couldn't see his feet; he thought they were beneath the valance, but he couldn't be completely sure. He felt horribly vulnerable and suddenly cursed himself for picking the bed over the walk-in cupboard he could have sheltered in. He could have pulled the gun in there, too. If the man saw him under here, there would be nothing he could do. It was a rookie mistake.

He was trapped.

He turned his head to the right and looked through a gap between the fabric and the floor. He saw the soles of a pair of boots: heavy treads, worn and scuffed leather uppers, lots of buckles.

The boots made their way from one end of the room to the other.

A door opened, creaking on rusty hinges, and then closed again.

The man downstairs was still on the phone. 'Up to you, obviously, but I say we check the garden, then get out of here. All right? All right. Sweet. We'll see you there.'

The torch swept across the floor, the light glowing through the thin cotton valance.

The boots came closer, shoes on polished wood. Milton saw them again, closer this time. He could have reached out and touched them.

The boots moved out of sight, away to the door; steps sounded, going away again.

'Nothing up here,' the man said.

'You sure? They want us to be absolutely sure.'

'Check yourself if you don't believe me.'

'If you say it's okay, it's okay. Take it easy.'

Milton slid carefully out from under the bed and stayed low, crouching, listening. He heard steps, a pause, more steps, a door opening downstairs, then closing, then another door, a heavier door and finally, silence.

He moved quickly but quietly out onto the landing, gently pulled the door closed and then descended, treading on the sides of the steps as he made his way down to minimise the risk of putting weight on a creaking board. He did the same on the next set of stairs. He was halfway down the final flight, facing the big front door and about to make the turn to head back along the long hall to the kitchen and the rear door, when he heard the sound of a key in the front door's lock.

He froze: too late to go back up, too late to keep going down.

The door didn't open.

He realised what it was: they had forgotten to lock it.

The fresh, cool evening air hit Milton's face as he opened the rear door and stepped out into the garden. He breathed it in deeply. He heard the sound of two powerful motorcycle engines grumbling and growling into life, the sound fading as they accelerated away.

He shut the door behind him and walked carefully and quickly to the road.

10

Milton made his way towards the house that Madison had run to last night, the one with the old man who had threatened to call the police. It was another big place, a sprawling building set within well-tended gardens and fronted by a stone wall topped with ornamental iron fencing. Milton buzzed the intercom set into the stone pillar to the right of the gates and waited. There was no answer. He tried again with the same result. He was about to leave when he saw the old man. He came out of a side door, moving slowly and with the exaggerated caution of advanced age. Behind him was a wide lawn sloping down to the shore. A collie trotted around the garden with aimless, happy abandon, shoving its muzzle into the flower beds in search of an interesting scent.

'Can I help you?'

'I hope so,' Milton said. 'Could I have a word?'

Milton assessed him as he approached. He was old; late eighties, he guessed. He was tall, but his frame had withered away with age so that his long arms and legs were spindly, sharply bony shoulders pointing through the fabric of the polo shirt that he was wearing.

'What can I do for you?'

'I was here last night.'

The man thought for a moment, the papery skin of his forehead crinkling. He remembered, and a scowl descended. 'This morning, you mean?'

'That's right.'

'She woke me up, all that racket – my wife, too. You with her?'

'No, sir. But I drove her out here.'

'So what are you? A cab driver?'

'That's right.'

'What's your name, son?'

'John Smith. And you?'

'Victor Leonard.'

'Sorry about all the noise, Mr Leonard. The disturbance.'

'What the hell was she so exercised about?'

'I was hoping you might be able to tell me – did she say anything?'

Milton watched through the bars of the gate as Leonard pursed his withered lips. 'Didn't make a whole heap of sense. She was in a terrible panic. Just asking for help. I've no idea what she wanted help for. She had her cell phone out and kept trying to make a call, but it didn't look like she was getting through. I could see she needed help, so I told her she could come in. Didn't help – she got a whole lot worse. Couldn't make any sense out of her. My wife called 911, told her the police were coming, but that seemed to panic her. She bolted.'

'And?'

'And nothing much. Police came around half an hour later. It was a single officer; he had a look around the place. Said he looked around the whole neighbourhood, but he couldn't find her anywhere. They asked me the same questions I guess they ask everyone: what did she look like, what was she wearing, what did she say, all that. I told them what I could remember.' He paused.

'Which was . . . ?'

'She was high. Big eyes – pupils practically as big as saucers. And she wasn't making any sense. If that's not someone under the influence of something or other, I don't know what is. You ask me, whatever she thought her problems were, they were in her mind – hallucinations or whatever you want to call them.'

'Did you see where she went?'

'Over the fence. Straight into Pete Waterfield's garden. She pounded on his door, but he's off on vacation with his grandkids, and when she didn't get an answer, she kept on going.'

'Where?'

'Over there,' he said, pointing.

'That leads down to the cliffs?'

'Sure does. You see the boat he's got parked down there? Behind the car?' Milton said that he did. 'She stopped there for a moment. I saw her try to make a call on her phone again, but I guess it didn't get anywhere, like the others, because she upped and made a run for it. And that's the last time I saw her.'

'Yes,' Milton said. 'Me too. The cliffs are fenced off there?'

'Around the house, sure they are. But not further down.'

'You think she might have gone over the edge?'

'I hope not. That's a fifty-foot drop right onto the rocks.' He paused. 'What's it got to do with you, anyway? She's just a customer, right?'

'I'm worried.'

'Ain't like no taxi drivers I know, get worried about the people they drive.'

'I think something bad has happened to her.'

'Nothing bad happens around here, Mr Smith.'

'I don't know about that.' Milton took a business card for his taxi business from his pocket. 'I appreciate you talking to me. Maybe I am worrying too much, but maybe I'm not. The police won't even treat this as a missing person enquiry until she's been gone a couple more days, and even then, it's not going to be very high up their list of priorities. I wonder, if you think of anything else, or if you hear anything, or if anyone says anything to you, could you give me a call?'

'Sure I can.'

Milton passed the card through the bars of the gate.

'One more thing,' he said. 'The house over there' – he pointed to the house he had just been inside – 'do you know who owns it?'

'The company place?'

'What do you mean?'

'It's owned by a company, one of the tech firms down in Palo Alto. Was on the market last year. Ten million dollars. What do you think of that?'

Milton made a show of being impressed.

'Good for the rest of us, too. They send executives – guys they've just hired – to stay there before they can find a place of their own. None of them ever make much of an effort round here with the rest of us. Not unreasonable, I suppose. Why would they? They're only stopping on the way to something else.'

'Know who's in there now?'

'Afraid not. It's empty, I think.'

'Apart from last night.'

'You can say that again.'

Milton thanked him, and the old man went back to his front door. Milton turned back to the big house again. The place was quiet, peaceful, but there was something in that stillness that he found disturbing. It was as if the place was haunted, harbouring a dark secret that could only mean bad things for Madison.

11

Milton pressed the buzzer on the intercom and then stepped back, waiting for it to be answered. It was early, just before nine, and the sun was struggling through thinning fog. The brownstone was in Nob Hill, a handsome building that had been divided into apartments over the course of its life. Rows of beech had been planted along both sides of the street twenty or thirty years ago, and the naked trees went some way to lending a little bucolic charm to what would otherwise have been a busy suburban street. The cars parked beneath the overhanging branches were middle-of-the-road saloons and SUVs. The houses looked well kept. Both were good indications that the area was populated by owner-occupiers with decent family incomes. Milton thought of Madison and her reticence to talk about the money she was making. It must have been pretty good to be able to live here.

'Hello?'

'It's John Smith.'

The lock buzzed. Milton opened the door and climbed the stairs to the second floor.

Trip was waiting for him inside the opened door.

'Morning, Mr Smith.'

'Anything?'

Trip shook his head.

Milton winced. 'Two days.'

'I know. I'm worried now.'

He led the way into the sitting room.

'You've spoken to the police?'

'About ten times.'

'What did they say?'

'Same – they won't declare her missing until this time tomorrow. Three days, apparently; that's how long it has to be. It's because of what she does, isn't it?'

'Probably.'

'If this was a secretary from Sacramento, they would've been out looking for her as soon as someone says she's not where she's supposed to be.'

Milton gestured to indicate the apartment. 'Do you mind if I have a look around? There might be something you've missed. The benefit of fresh eyes?'

'Yeah, that's fine. I get it.'

'Could you do me a favour?'

'Sure.'

'Get me a coffee? I'm dying for a drink.'

'Sure.'

That was better. Milton wanted him out of the way while he looked around the apartment. He would have preferred him to have left the place altogether, but if he worked quickly, he thought he would be able to do what needed to be done.

The place was comfortably sized: two bedrooms, one much smaller than the other, a bathroom, a kitchen-diner. It was nicely furnished. The furniture was from IKEA, but it was at the top end of their range; Milton knew that because he had visited the store to buy the things he needed for his own place. There was a sofa upholstered in electric blue, a large bookcase that was crammed with books, a coffee table with copies of *Vogue* and *Harper's Bazaar* and a crimson rug with a luxurious deep pile. A plasma screen stood on a small unit with a PlayStation plugged in beneath it and a selection of games and DVDs alongside. There was a healthy-looking spider plant standing in a pewter vase.

Milton went straight to the bedroom. It was a nice room, decorated in a feminine style, with lots of pastel colours and a pretty floral quilt cover. He opened the wardrobe and ran his fingers along the top shelf. He opened the chest of drawers and removed her underwear, placing it on the bed. The drawer was empty. He replaced the clothes and closed the drawer again. Finally, he took the books and magazines from the bed-side table. He opened the magazines and riffled their pages. Nothing. Once again, beyond the detritus of a busy life, there was nothing that provided him with any explanation of what might have happened to her in Pine Shore.

He went back into the sitting room. A MacBook sat open on the coffee table.

'Is this hers?'

'Yes.'

'Did you have any luck?'

'No. Couldn't get into it.'

Milton tapped a key to kill the screen saver, and the log-in screen appeared. He thought of the specialists back in London. Breaking the security would have been child's play for them, but his computer skills were rudimentary; he wouldn't even know where to start.

'The police will be able to do it if they have to.'

'You think that'll be necessary?'

'Maybe.'

Trip had left a cup of coffee next to the laptop. Milton thanked him and took a sip.

'So,' he said, 'I went back to Pine Shore last night.'

'And?'

'It was quiet. Peaceful. I had a look in the house—'

'You went in?'

'Just looked through the window,' he lied. 'It was clean and tidy, as if nothing had ever happened.'

'Who lives there?'

'One of the neighbours told me it belongs to a company.'

'Which one?'

'I don't know. It was sold last year. I looked it up online. It was bought by a trust. The ownership is hidden, but the deal was for ten million, so whichever company it was has plenty of cash.'

'A tech firm.'

Milton nodded. 'I think so.'

'You get anything else?'

'Another neighbour said she ran into his house. He said she was out of it, didn't make much sense. He called the police, and that was when she ran off again. He's not going to be able to help much beyond that.'

The boy slumped back. 'Where is she?'

Milton took a mouthful of coffee and placed the cup back on the table again. 'I don't know,' he said. 'But we'll find her.'

'Yeah,' he replied, but it was unconvincing.

'You know what – you should tell me about you both. Could be something that would be helpful.'

'What do you want to know?'

'Everything you can think of. Maybe there's something you've overlooked.'

Trip sparked up a cigarette and started with himself. He was born and raised in New York and had had a rough start. He was bad at school and there had been some petty crime, including a robbery for which he had been caught and given three years in a juvenile facility. He was twenty when he finally came out. He had relatives in San Francisco, moved west to get out of the way of temptation and enrolled at community college to try to round out a few qualifications so that he could fix himself up with a job. He found out that he had an aptitude for electronics and he took a course in electrical engineering. He parlayed that into an apprenticeship, and now he was employed fixing up the power lines.

He met Madison while he was out celebrating his first pay packet. She had been at the bar on her own, reading a book in the corner and nursing a vodka and Coke. He introduced himself and asked if he could buy her a drink. She said he could, and they had started to get to know each other. She was a big talker, always jawing, and he said how it was sometimes impossible to get a word in edgeways. (Milton said he had noticed that, too.) She was living out of town at the time, taking a bus to get into work. She said she was a secretary. Trip figured out the truth by the time they had been on their third date, and he had been surprised to find that it didn't bother him. If he didn't think about it, it was bearable. And, of course, the money was great, and it was only ever going to be temporary. He always tried to remember that. She had big plans, and she was just escorting until she had saved enough to do what she wanted to do.

'She wants to write,' Trip said. 'A journalist, most likely, but something to do with words. She's always been into reading. You wouldn't believe how much. All these' – he pointed at the books on the bookcase – 'all of them, they're all hers. I've never been into reading so much myself, but you won't find her without a book. She always took one when she went out nights.'

Milton looked at the bookcase, vaguely surprised to see so many books, always a clue to a personality. They were an odd mixture: books on astrology and make-up, novels by Suzanne Collins and Stephenie Meyer. Some books on fashion. The collected poems of Ralph Waldo Emerson. Milton pulled it out to look at the cover. Several pages had their corners turned down. Not what he would have expected to find. He slipped it back into its slot on the shelf.

'That's one of the things I love about her. She gets so passionate about books. She writes, too. Short stories. I've seen a couple of them, the ones she doesn't mind showing me. And I know I'm no expert and all that and I don't know what I'm talking about, but the way I see it, I reckon some of her stuff's pretty good.'

'What's she like as a person?'

'What do you mean?'

Milton searched for the right word. 'Is she stable?'

'She gets bad mood swings. She can be happy one minute and then the whole world is against her the next.'

'You know why?'

Trip screwed the cigarette in the ashtray and lit another. 'Family.'

He explained. Madison had two sisters and a brother; she was the oldest of the four. Her father had left the family when she was five or six. Her mother, Clare – a brassy woman full of attitude – told the children it was because he was a drunk, but Madison had always suspected that there was something else involved. She had no memories of her father at all, and whenever she thought of him, she would plunge into one of her darker moods. Clare moved a series of increasingly inappropriate men into the house, and it was after one of them started to smack her around that the police were called. The authorities got involved and the kids were moved into foster care. Clare got Madison's sisters and brother back after a year, once she was able to demonstrate that she could provide a stable environment for them, but she had left Madison with the family who had taken her in. She would run away to try to get back home and then be taken back into the foster system.

There was a series of different places, several well-meaning families, but she never settled with any of them.

'Have you spoken to her mother?'

'Last night. She hasn't seen her. Same goes for her sisters and brother.'

'Does she get on with them?'

'So-so. Depends when you ask, really.'

'Why didn't her mother take her back?'

'She never said. I think Madison was a little wild when she was younger, though. She was a tough kid to live with. She can still be a handful now.'

'How?'

'She has a temper on her. If she feels like she's being ignored or rejected, it all comes back again, and then, you know' – he made a popping noise – 'look out.'

'Could that be a reason for what's happened? Something's upset her?'

'No,' he said. 'She's been really good with her mom for the last couple of months. They've been speaking a lot. Now she's got money, she's been buying things for them – for her mom, her sisters, for her nieces and nephews, too. I've tried to tell her she shouldn't need to do that, but she likes it. They never had much money growing up, and now she has some, she likes to spread it around, I guess.'

'All right,' Milton said. 'Go on.'

He did. Around the time of seventh grade, Madison moved to live with her aunt in San Diego. The woman was young, and Madison felt that they had something in common. It was a better town, too, with better schools, and she was encouraged to work hard. That was where her love of reading and writing found expression, and she started to do well. For the first time in her life, he said, she felt wanted and useful, and she started to thrive.

'Have you spoken to her? The aunt?'

'No. I don't have her number.'

Milton's phone vibrated in his pocket. He scooped it up and looked at the display. He didn't recognise the number.

'John Smith,' he said.

'Mr Smith, it's Victor Leonard from Pine Shore. We spoke last night.'

'Mr Leonard – how are you?'

'I'm good, sir,' the old man said. 'There's something I think you should know – about the girl.'

'Yes, of course – what is it?'

'Look, I don't want to be a gossip, telling tales on people and nonsense like that, but there's a fellow who's been saying some weird things about what happened up here the other night. You want to know about it?'

Trip raised his eyebrows: who is it?

'Please,' Milton said.

12

Milton was getting used to the forty-minute drive to Pine Shore. Trip was in the passenger seat next to him, fidgeting anxiously. Milton would have preferred to go alone, but the boy had insisted that he come, too. He had been quiet during the drive, but the mood had been oppressive and foreboding; Milton had tried to lighten it with some music. He had thumbed through his phone for some Smiths but then, after a couple of melancholic minutes, realised that that hadn't been the best choice. He replaced it with the lo-fi, baggy funk of the Happy Mondays. Trip seemed bemused by his choice.

Milton drove to the address that Victor Leonard had given him and parked. It was eleven in the morning. Milton climbed up a set of steps that rose up beyond the level of the pavement and rapped the ornate iron knocker three times. There was a vertical panel set into the side of the door, and Milton gazed inside. He made out the shape of a telephone table, a flight of stairs leading up to the first floor, a jumble of shoes against the wall, coats draped off the banister. It looked messy.

A man turned out of a doorway to the left of the lobby and came towards the door; Milton stepped away from the window.

The door opened.

'Dr Brady?'

'Yes? Who are you?' Andrew Brady was very tall, with a plump face, greasy skin and a pendulous chin. His hair was chestnut streaked with grey, and his small eyes had retreated deep into their sockets. He was unshaven, and despite his height, he was overweight and bore his extra pounds in a well-rounded pot belly. He was wearing a fuchsia-coloured windbreaker, a mesh cap and a pair of wading boots that were slicked with dried mud up to just below his knees.

'My name is John Smith. This is Trip Macklemore.'

'I'm sorry, fellas,' he said. 'I was just going out. Fishing.' He indicated the waders and a fishing rod that was propped against the wall behind him.

'Could we speak to you? It would just take a moment.'

Brady glared out from the doorway at them with what Milton thought looked like an arrogant sneer. 'Depends on what about.'

'The commotion around here the other night.'

'What commotion?'

'There was a girl. You didn't hear?'

'The girl – oh, yes.'

'I understand you spoke to her?'

Brady's eyes narrowed suspiciously. 'Who told you that?'

Milton turned and angled his face towards the house diagonally opposite. 'Mr Leonard. I spoke to him earlier. Is it true?'

'No,' Brady said. 'It isn't.'

'Do you think we could have ten minutes of your time? It's important.'

'What do you both have to do with her?'

'I'm her boyfriend,' Trip explained.

'And you, Mr Smith?'

'I'm a taxi driver. I drove her up here the night she went missing. I'd like to see that she gets home safely again.'

'How honourable,' Brady said with a half-smile that could have been derisory or amused – it was difficult to tell. 'A knight of the road.' The bluster was dismissed abruptly, and Brady's face broke out into a welcoming smile. 'Of course, of course – come inside.'

Milton got the impression that this was a man who, if not exactly keen to help, liked people to think that he was. Perhaps it was a doctor's self-regard. He bent down to tug off his boots and left them against the wall amidst the pile of shoes. Milton guessed he was in his early fifties, but he might have been older; the greasy skin made it difficult to make an accurate guess.

Brady led them both into the living room. There was a kitchen in the far corner and a breakfast bar with bar stools arranged around it. There was a large television tuned to CNN, a shelf of medical textbooks and, on the wall, a picture of a younger Brady – perhaps ten years younger – posing in army uniform with a group of soldiers. The photograph was taken in a desert; it looked like Iraq. He cleared the sofa of the discarded remnants of a newspaper so that they could sit down.

'Could I get you something to drink?'

'No, thanks,' Trip said, struggling with his impatience.

Milton smiled encouragingly at the boy. 'No,' he repeated. 'That's all right. We're fine.'

Brady lowered himself to the sofa. 'So what did Victor have to say about me?'

'Just what he said that you've been saying.'

'Which was—'

'That she – the girl, Madison – was here. That she knocked on the door and you took her in. He says you used to special-ise in getting kids off drugs and that you run a retreat here. Kids with problems come up here, and you help them get clean. That true?'

'Yes, that's true.'

'And Madison?'

'No, that isn't true. And I don't know why he'd say that.'

'It didn't happen?'

'I heard the clamour – my God, the noise she was making, it'd be impossible not to hear her. She must've clambered over the wall at the bottom of the garden and went straight across, screaming for help at the top of her lungs. I was up working.'

'At that hour?'

'I was an army doctor, Mr Smith. Served my country in the Gulf, both times.'

Milton tried to make a connection with him. 'I served, too,' he said.

'Iraq?'

'Yes.'

'Doing what?'

'Just a squaddie the first time I went out. Then Special Forces.'

'SAS?'

'That's right.'

'You boys are tough as hell. Came across a few of your colleagues.'

'You know what,' Milton said, smiling at him. 'I will have that coffee.'

Brady smiled. 'Not a problem. Young man?'

'No,' Trip said. 'I'm fine.'

Brady got up and went to the kitchen. There was a coffee machine on the countertop, and Brady made two cups of black coffee. 'You been to Afghanistan, too?' he asked.

'Several times,' Milton replied.

'What's it like?'

'It wouldn't be on my bucket list, put it like that.'

'Never been out there myself, but that's what I heard from the guys I know who have. Ragheads – you ask me, we leave them to get on with whatever it is they want to do to each other. One thing you can say about them, they know how to fight – right?'

Milton ignored his distaste for the man. 'They do.'

'Gave the Russians a bloody nose when they tried to bring them in line, didn't they?

Brady rambled on for a moment, his remarks scattered with casual racism. Milton nodded and made encouraging responses, but he was hardly listening; he took the opportunity to scan the room more carefully: the stack of unpaid bills on the countertop; the newspaper, yellow highlighter all over a story about the Republican primary for the presidential elections; a precarious stack of vinyl albums on the floor; the textbooks shoved haphazardly onto the shelves; framed photographs of two children and a woman Milton guessed must have been Brady's wife. Nothing stood out. Nothing out of the ordinary. Certainly nothing that was a reason for suspicion.

'Milk and sugar?'

'No, thanks. Black's fine.'

Brady passed him a mug of coffee and went back around to sit. 'So – the girl.'

Trip leant forwards. 'Madison.'

'Must be.'

'Did you speak to her?'

'Not really. I went to the door and called out, but she didn't even pause. Kept going straight on.'

'She didn't come in?'

'No, she didn't. Like I said, she ran off.'

'Why would Mr – Leonard tell me that you said she did come in?' Milton asked, sipping the hot coffee.

'You'll have to ask him that. Between us, Victor's an old man. His faculties . . . well, let's be charitable about it and say that they're not what they once were.'

'He's lying?'

'I'm not saying that. Perhaps he's just mistaken. It wouldn't be the first time.'

'Right.'

Brady spoke easily and credibly. If he was lying, he was good at it.

The doctor sipped his coffee and rested the mug on the arm of the chair. 'You've reported her missing?'

'Of course,' Trip said tersely.

'And?'

'They were useless.'

'She's not a kid, though, is she? Most likely reason must be that she's gone off somewhere on her own. I'm sure she'll come back when she feels like it.'

'She's *missing*,' Trip said, his temper up a little.

Milton felt the atmosphere in the room change; the boy was angry, and the doctor's air of self-importance would only inflame things. They had got all they were going to get from this visit. It was time to go.

He stood. 'Thanks for the coffee. I'm sorry we had to bother you.'

Brady stood, too. 'I'll tell you what,' he said, reaching into his pocket and fishing out a business card. 'This is my number. I'll be happy to help out if you need anything. I'm on the board of the community association here. If you want to speak to anyone else or if you want to put flyers out, that sort of thing, please do just give me a call. Anything I can do, just ask.'

Milton took the card. 'Thank you,' he said as they made their way back down the corridor. They shook hands at the door. Brady's hands were bigger than his, but they were soft, and his grip was flaccid and damp, unimpressive.

Milton thanked him again, and impelling Trip onwards with a hand on his shoulder, they made their way down the steps to the pavement. Milton turned back to the house and saw Brady watching them from a side window; the man waved at him as soon as he realised that he had been seen. Milton turned back to the car, went around and got inside.

'*Bullshit*,' Trip said. 'One of them is lying, right?'

'Yes,' Milton said. 'But I don't know who.'

13

Milton met Trip in Top Notch Burger at noon the next day. Julius bagged up Milton's cheeseburger and the 'original' with jalapeños that the boy had ordered, and they ate them on the way back to Pine Shore. Trip had printed a missing person poster overnight, and they had stopped at a Kinko's to run off two hundred copies. The poster was a simple affair, with a picture of Madison smiling into the camera with a paper birthday hat perched on her head. 'MISSING' was printed above the photograph in bold capitals, her name was below the photograph and then at the foot of the flyer were Trip's mobile number and his email address.

Milton parked outside Andrew Brady's house, and they split up and set to work. He had purchased a stapler and staples from the copy-shop, and he used them to fix flyers to telegraph poles and fences. He went door to door, knocking politely and then, if the residents were home, explaining what had happened and what he was doing. Reactions varied: indifference, concern, a couple of the residents showing mild hostility. He pressed a copy of the flyer into the hands of each and put one through the letterboxes of those who were not home. It took Milton an hour to cover the ground that he had volunteered to take.

He waited for Trip in the car and stared up at the plain wooden door to Andrew Brady's house. The doctor had been the subject of several conversations with the other residents as he made his way around the neighbourhood. Milton had visited the library that morning, and his research, together with the information he was able to glean, enabled him to build up a more comprehensive picture. Brady was an interesting character, that much was obvious, and the more Milton learnt about him, the more questions he had.

Brady had moved into Pine Shore in the mid-90s. There was the doctor himself; his French wife, Collette; and their two young children, Claude and Annabel. Brady was the son of an army general who had served with distinction in Korea. He had followed his father into the military and had apparently enjoyed a decent, if not spectacular, career. He had been pulled back from the frontline for unspecified reasons and moved into an administrative role. It had evidently been a disappointment after his previous experience. He gave an interview to the local press upon his appointment as chief of surgery at St Francis Memorial Hospital explaining that while he would always love the army and that his military career had made him the man he was, he was a man of action and not suited to 'riding a desk'. He wanted to do something tangible and 'make a difference in the community'.

The family appeared to be affluent. Their house was one of the more expensive in the neighbourhood, and there was a

Lexus and an Audi in the driveway. Milton had asked around. Some of the residents spoke with a guarded warmness about them. Andrew and Collette were gregarious to a fault, becoming friends with their immediate neighbours. Andrew had been elected to the board of the residents' association, and it appeared that most of the other members were on good terms with him. There was Kevin Heyman, the owner of a large printing business. There was Charles Murdoch, who ran a real estate brokerage with another neighbour, Curtis McMahon. Those families were close, and there was talk of barbeques on the Fourth of July and shared festivities in the winter.

The closeness wasn't shared with all, and for all those who described Brady as friendly and approachable, there were others who described him as the head of a closed and overbearing clique. While some spoke of his kindness, often visiting the sick to offer the benefit of his experience, others saw him as a loud-mouthed blowhard, looking down on his neighbours and pretending to be something that he was not.

Milton heard stories that called his honesty into question. The most troubling concerned his professional reputation. During his time at the hospital, there had been a serious road incident on the interstate outside of San Mateo. A truck loaded with diesel had jackknifed across the 101, slicking the tarmac with fuel so that a series of cars had ploughed into it. The resulting fireball had been hot enough to melt the metal guard rails that ran down the median. Brady had been forced to resign in the aftermath of the crash after local reporters suggested that he had talked up his role in the recovery effort. He had claimed that he had driven himself to the scene of the disaster and, badging his way past the first responders, he had made his way into the heart of the inferno and administered first aid to survivors as they were pulled from the wreckage of their vehicles. The fire service later denied that he had been present at all and stated that he would never have been allowed to get as close to the flames as he had claimed.

In another incident, Brady recounted the story of being on his boat in Richardson Bay when a yacht had capsized and started to sink. He boasted that he had swum to the stricken boat and pulled a man and his son to safety. It was subsequently found that there was no record of a boat getting into difficulty that day and no father and son ever came forward to corroborate the story. An anonymous source even suggested that Brady had not even been on the water.

He had not taken another job since his resignation, and the suggestion had been made that there had been a large pay-off to get rid of him. He had retreated to Pine Shore and made himself busy. He took it upon himself to act as the resident physician, attending neighbours and offering help that was sometimes not welcome. He had assisted locals with minor ailments and worked hard to help the kids with addiction issues, seemingly intent on gaining the trust and respect of the community. Despite that, he continually told tales that were simple enough to debunk, and when they were, they damaged the good that he had done. He suggested that he had worked with the police. He boasted that he was a qualified pilot. He spoke of having obtained a degree in law through distance learning while he was in the army.

It seemed to Milton that Brady was intent upon making himself the centre of the community. His role as the chair of the residents' association seemed particularly important to him, and there was grudging acceptance from many that he did good and important work to make Pine Shore a better place to live. But not everyone felt the same way. More than one person confided to Milton that there was bad blood when it came to the committee. The chairmanship was an elected post, and it had been contested when the previous incumbent had stood aside.

The other candidate in an election that was described as 'pointlessly vicious' was Victor Leonard.

Trip opened the passenger door and slid inside.

'How did it go?' Milton asked him.

'Got rid of all of them.'

'Learn anything?'

'That this place is full of crap. You?'

'The same.'

Milton told him what he had learnt about Brady.

'He told others that he worked in Washington after coming out of the army. Homeland Security. He's full of shit, Mr Smith. How can we trust anything he's told us?'

'I'm not sure we can,' Milton admitted.

'So where does that leave us? You ask me, Madison was in there.' He stabbed his finger angrily against the window three times, indicating Brady's house.

'I don't know. But we need to find out.'

14

One of the campaign boosters was a big wine grower, exporting his bottles all over the world for millions of dollars a year, and one of the benefits of that largesse was an executive box at Candlestick Park. Arlen Crawford could take it or leave it when it came to sports, but his boss was an avid fan. The 49ers were his team, too, so the prospect of taking in the game against Dallas was something that had kept him fired up. It wasn't all pleasure, Crawford reminded him as they walked through the busy stadium to the level that held the luxury suites. Plenty of potential donors had been invited, too, not all of them on board with the campaign yet. They needed to be impressed. Robinson needed to deploy that beguiling grin, and his charisma needed to be at its most magnetic.

They reached the door, and Robinson opened it and stepped through into the box beyond. There was a long table laden with cold cuts, beers and snacks and, beyond that, an outside seating area. The governor's smile was immediate and infectious; he set to work on the other guests, working his way through the room, reaching out to take hands, sometimes pressing them between both of his, rewarding those who were already on the team with jovial backslaps or, for the lucky few, a powerful hug. It took him fifteen minutes to reach the front of the box and the open French doors that allowed access to the outside seats.

Crawford stepped down to the front of the enclosure and allowed himself a moment to breathe.

The field was brilliant green, perfectly lush, the gridiron markings standing out in vivid white paint. The stadium PA picked up the intensity as the teams made their way out through an inflatable tunnel in the corner of the stadium. Fireworks shot into the air, flamethrowers breathed tendrils of fire that reached up to the upper decks, music thumped, cheerleaders shimmied in formation. The 49ers' offence was introduced by the hyperbolic announcer, each armoured player sprinting through a gauntlet fashioned by the defence, chest-bumping those that had made the procession before him.

Crawford turned away from the noise and the pageantry to watch the governor deep in conversation with the multimillionaire who owned cattle ranches all the way across the south. Two good old boys, Crawford thought to himself. Winning him over would be a slam dunk for Robinson. They would be drinking buddies by the end of the afternoon, and a cheque with a lot of zeroes would be on its way to them first thing in the morning.

Suddenly tired, Crawford slid down into a seat and closed his eyes. He thought about the sacrifices he had made to get them as far as this. Robinson was the main draw, the focus, but without Crawford and the work that he did for him, he would be just another talker, high on star power but low on substance and destined for the level he was at right now. If Robinson was the circus, Crawford was the ringmaster. You couldn't have one without the other. It just wouldn't work.

He opened his eyes as the home team kicked off, the kicker putting his foot through the ball and sending it high into the air, spinning it on its axis all the way to the back of the end zone. The return man fielded it and dropped to one knee. Touchback.

The others settled into their seats. Robinson saw Crawford, grinned and gave him a wink.

He hoped that all this effort was going to be worth it.

15

Tuesday night's A.A. meeting was Milton's favourite. He stopped at a 7-Eleven and bought two jars of instant coffee and three different types of cookies. Yet more mist had risen from the ocean and was beginning its slow drift across the town. It was a cloudy night, the moon hidden. The signage of a bar on the opposite side of the street from the church was buzzing, flicking on and off. Milton parked and left the engine idling for a moment, the golden beams of the head-lights glowing and fading against the banked fog. He killed the engine, got out and locked the door and crossed the street. He took the key from his pocket, unlocked the door and descended into the basement of the church.

It was a tired room, with peeling beige paint and cracked half-windows that were set far up towards the ceiling, revealing the shoes and ankles of the pedestrians passing by. Milton filled the urn with water and set it to boil. He took the coffee from the cupboard and then arranged the biscuits that he had brought on a plate, a series of neat concentric circles. The mugs hadn't been washed from the last meeting that had used the room, so he filled the basin and attended to them, drying them with a dishcloth and stacking them on the table next to the urn.

Milton had been coming to meetings for more than three years. London, all the way through South America, then here. He still found the thought of it counter-intuitive, but then the complete honesty that the programme demanded would always be a difficult concept for a man who had worked in the shadows for most of his adult life. He did his best.

It had been more difficult at the start, in that church hall in West London. There was the Official Secrets Act, for a start, and what would happen to him if it came out that he had a problem. He had hidden at the back, near the door, and it had taken him a month to sit all the way through a meeting without turning tail and fleeing. He had gradually asked a regular with plenty of years of sobriety and a quiet attitude if he would be his first sponsor. He was called Dave Goulding, a musician in his late forties, a man who had been successful when he was younger and then drank his money and his talent away. Despite a life of bitter disappointment, he had managed to get his head screwed on straight, and with his guidance, Milton had started to make progress.

The first thing Dave insisted upon was that Milton attend ninety meetings in ninety days. He had given him a spiral-bound notebook and a pen and told him that if he wanted him to remain as his sponsor, he had to record every meeting he attended in that notebook. Milton did that. After that, a little trust between them developed, and they worked on his participation in the meetings. He wasn't ready to speak at that point – that wouldn't come for more than a year – but he had been persuaded to at least give the impression that he was engaged in what was going on. Dave called the back row at meetings the Denial Aisle and had drummed into him that sick people who wanted to get well sat in the front. Milton wasn't quite ready for that, either, but he had gradually moved forwards. Each month he moved forward again until he was in the middle of the action, stoic and thoughtful amidst the thicket of raised arms as the other alcoholics jostled to speak.

He had found this meeting on his first night in 'Frisco. It was a lucky find; there was something about it that made it special. The room, the regulars, the atmosphere; there was a little magic about it. Milton had volunteered to serve the drinks on the second night when the grizzled ex-army vet who had held the post before him had fallen off the wagon and been spotted unconscious in the parking lot of the 7-Eleven near Fisherman's Wharf. Milton always remembered Dave explaining that service was the keystone of A.A., and since taking care of the refreshments was something he could do without opening himself up to the others, it was an excellent way to make himself known while avoiding the conversations that he still found awkward.

He opened the storage cupboard, dragged out the stacked chairs and arranged them in four rows of five. The format of the meeting was the same as all of the others that Milton had attended. A table was arranged at the front of the room, and Milton covered it with a cloth with the A.A. logo embroidered on it in coloured thread. There were posters on the wall and books and pamphlets that could be purchased. Milton went back to the cupboard, took out a long cardboard tube and shook out the poster stored inside. It was made to look like a scroll; he hung it from its hook. The poster listed the Twelve Steps.

Milton was finishing up when the first man came down the stairs. His name was Smulders, he worked on the docks, he had been sober for a year, and he was the chairman of this meeting. Milton said hello, poured him a coffee and offered him a biscuit.

'Thanks,' Smulders said. 'How've you been?'

'I've had better days.'

'Want to talk about it?'

'Maybe later,' he said – the same thing he always said.

'You know what I'm going to say, right?'

'That I shouldn't brood.'

'Exactly. Get it off your chest.'

'In my own time.'

'Sure. Mmm-hmm. Good cookies – gimme another.'

Milton had already begun to feel a little better.

* * *

It was a normal meeting. The chair arranged for a speaker to share his or her story for the first half an hour and then they all shared back with their own experiences. Smulders had asked one of the regulars, a thirty-something docker that Milton knew called Richie Grimes, to tell his story. They sat down, worked through the preliminaries and then Smulders asked Richie to begin.

'My name is Richie,' he said, 'and I'm an alcoholic.'

Milton was dozing a little, but that woke him up. Richie was a nice guy.

'Hi, Richie,' the group responded.

'I'm pleased I've been asked to share tonight. I don't always talk as much as I know I ought to, but I really do need to share something. I've been holding onto it for the last six months, and unless I deal with it, I know I'll never be able to stay away from coke and the bottle.'

The group waited.

'I'm grandiose, like we all are, right, but not so much that I'd argue that mine is an original problem. You know what I'm talking about – *money*.' They all laughed. 'Yeah, right. Most alkies I know couldn't organise their finances if their lives depended on it, but if I'm not the worst in the room, then I'd be very fuckin' surprised, excuse my French. I lost my job a year ago for the usual reasons – attendance was shitty, and when I did turn up, I was either drunk or thinking about getting drunk – and instead of taking the hint, I decided it'd be a much better idea to get drunk every day for the next month. By the end of that little binge, the savings I had managed to keep were all gone, and the landlord started making threats about throwing me onto the street. I couldn't work; no one would even look at me, not least give me a job. If I got evicted, it was gonna get a hundred times worse, so I thought the only thing I could do was borrow some money from this dude that I had heard would give me credit. But he's not like the bank, you know? He's not on the level, not the kind of dude you'd want to be in hock to, but it wasn't like anyone legit was about to give me credit, and my folks are dead, so the way I saw it, I didn't have much of a choice. I went and saw him and took his money, and after I dropped a couple of Gs on a massive bender – the one that took me to rock bottom – then I found the Rooms, and I haven't drunk or drugged since.'

A round of warm applause was punctuated by whoops from the eager alkies in the front row.

'I know, it's good, best thing I've ever done, but despite it being his cash that allowed me to stay in my place, give me somewhere to anchor myself, the stability I need to try to do all this stuff, he don't necessarily share the sentiment. He's not into community outreach, know what I mean? So he sent a couple of guys around yesterday. They made it clear that I'm running out of rope. He wants his money back. With interest and "administration charges" and all that shit, I'm looking at the thick end of six grand.'

He laughed at this as if it was a particularly funny joke, then put his head in his hands and started to sob. His shoulders quivered, and Milton watched him awkwardly until one of the other guys shuffled across the seats and put his arm around him.

There was silence for a moment until Richie recovered himself. 'I got a job now, like you all know about, but even though it's the best thing that's happened to me for months, it still barely covers my rent and groceries, and if I can save twenty bucks a month, then I reckon I'm doing well. That don't even cover the interest on the loan, not even close. I don't expect any of you to have any clever ways for me to fix this. I just wanted to share it because, I gotta be honest, I've felt the urge to go and buy a bottle of vodka and just drink myself stupid so I can forget all about it. But I know that'd be a crazy idea, worst thing I could do, and now, especially after I've shared, I think maybe I can keep it behind me, at least for the time being. But I've got to get this sorted. The more it seems like a dead end, the more I want to get blasted so I can forget all about it.'

16

Milton was stacking the chairs at the end of the meeting, hauling them across the room to the walk-in cupboard, when he noticed that the woman he knew as Eva was waiting in the entrance hall. She was sitting against the edge of the table, her legs straight, with one ankle resting against the other, and a copy of the Big Book held open before her. Milton watched her for a moment, thinking, as he usually did, that she was a good-looking woman, before gripping the bottom of the stack of chairs, heaving it into the air and carrying it into the cupboard. He took the cloth cover from the table, tracing his fingers over the embroidered A.A. symbol, and put that in the cupboard, too. He shut the cupboard, locked it, then went through. Eva had stacked all the dirty cups in the kitchen sink.

'Hello,' she said, with a wide smile.

'Hello. You all right?'

'Oh, sure. I'm great. Just thought you could do with a hand.'

'Thanks.'

She stood and nodded down at the table. 'Where does that go?'

'Just over there,' Milton said. 'I've got it.' He lifted the table, pressed the legs back into place, picked it up and stacked it against the wall with the others. He was conscious that she was watching him and allowed her a smile as he came back to pick up the large vat, the water inside cooling now that the element had been switched off. She returned his smile, and he found himself thinking, again, that she was very attractive. She was slim and petite, with glossy dark hair and a Latino complexion. Her eyes were her best feature: the colour of rich chocolate, smouldering with intelligence and a sense of humour that was never far from the surface. Milton didn't know her surname, but she was a voluble sharer during the meetings, and he knew plenty about her from the things that she had said. She was a lawyer, used to work up in Century City in Los Angeles doing clearance work for the networks. Now she did medical liability work at St Francis Memorial. She was divorced with a young daughter, her husband had been an alcoholic too, and it had broken their relationship apart. She had found the Rooms; he hadn't. She shared about him sometimes. He was still out there.

'Enjoy it tonight?' she asked.

'*Enjoy* might not be the right word.'

'Okay – get anything from it?'

'I think so.'

'Which other meetings do you go to?'

'Just this one. You?'

'There's the place on Sacramento Street. Near Lafayette Park?'

Milton shook his head.

'I do a couple of meetings there. Mondays and Fridays. They're pretty good. You should— well, you know.'

He turned the urn upside down and rested it in the sink.

'How long is it for you?' she asked.

'Since I had a drink?' He smiled ruefully. 'One thousand and fifty days.'

'Not that you're counting.'

'Not that I'm counting.'

'Let's see.' She furrowed her brow with concentration. 'If you can manage to keep the plug in the jug for just a little while longer, you'll be three years sober.'

'There's something to celebrate,' he said with an ironic smile.

'Are you serious?' she said, suddenly intense. 'Of course it is. You want to go back to how it was before?'

He got quick flashbacks. 'Of course not.'

'Fucking right. Jesus, John! You have to come to a meeting and get your chip.'

Anniversaries were called birthdays in the Rooms. They handed out little embossed poker chips with the number of months or years written on them, all in different colours. Milton had checked out the chip for three years: it would be red. Birthdays were usually celebrated with cake, and then there would be a gathering afterwards, a meal or a cup of coffee.

He hadn't planned on making a fuss about it.

He felt a little uncomfortable with her focus on him. 'You've got more, don't you?'

'Five years. I had my last drink the day my daughter was born. That was what really drove it home for me – I'd just given birth, and my first thought was, God, I really need a gin. That kind of underlined that maybe, you know, maybe I had a bit of a problem with it. What about you? You've never said?'

He hesitated and felt his shoulders stiffen. He had to work hard to keep the frown from his brow. He remembered it very well, but it wasn't something that he would ever be able to share in a meeting.

'Difficult memory?'

'A bit raw.'

The flashback came back. It was clear and vivid, and thinking about it again, he could almost feel the hot sun on the top of his head. Croatia. Zagreb. There had been a cell there, laid up and well advanced with their plan to blow up a car loaded with a fertiliser bomb in the middle of the Ban Jelačić square. The spooks had intercepted their communications, and Milton had gone in to put an end to the problem. It had been a clean job – three shots, three quick eliminations – but something about one of them had stayed in his head. He was just a boy – the intel had said sixteen, but Milton had guessed younger, fourteen or fifteen at the outside – and he had gazed up at him and into his eyes as he levelled the gun and aimed it at his head and pulled the trigger. Milton was due to extract immediately after the job, but he had diverted to the nearest bar and had drunk himself stupidly, horribly, awfully, dangerously drunk. They had just about cashiered him for that. Thinking about it triggered the old memories, and for a moment, it felt as if he was teetering on the edge of a trapdoor that had suddenly dropped open beneath his feet.

He forced his thoughts away from it, that dark and blank pit that fell away beneath him, a conscious effort, and then realised that Eva was talking to him. He focused on her instead.

'Sorry,' she was saying, 'you don't have to say if you'd rather not, obviously.'

'It's not so bad.'

'No, forget I asked.'

A little brightness returned, and he felt the trapdoor close.

'It's fear, right?' she said.

'What do you mean? Fear of what?'

'No, F.E.A.R.' She spelt it out.

He shrugged his incomprehension.

'You haven't heard that one? It's the old A.A. saying: Fuck Everything And Run.'

'Ah,' Milton said, relaxing a little. 'Yes. That's exactly it.'

'I've been running for five years.'

'You still get bad days?'

'Sure I do. Everyone does.'

'Really? Out of everyone I've met since I've been coming to meetings, you seem like one of the most settled.'

'Don't believe it. It's a struggle just like everyone else. It's like a swan, you know: it looks graceful, but there's paddling like shit going on below the surface. It's a day-to-day thing. You take your eye off the ball and, bang, back in the gutter you go. I'm just the same as everyone.'

Milton was not surprised to hear that – it was a comment that he had heard many times, almost a refrain to ward off complacency – but it seemed especially inapposite from Eva. He had always found her to have a calming, peaceful manner. There were all sorts in the Rooms: some twitchy and avid, white-knuckling it, always one bad day from falling back into the arms of booze; others, like her, had an almost Zen-like aspect, an aura of meditative serenity that he found intoxicating. He looked at them jealously.

'What are you doing now?' she asked him impulsively.

'Nothing much.'

'Want to get dinner?'

'Sure,' he said.

'Anywhere you fancy?'

'Sure,' he said. 'I know a place.'

* * *

They were the only people in Top Notch. Julius took their order and set about it with a cheerful smile, and soon, the aroma of cooked meat filled the room. He brought the burgers over on paper plates and left them to get on with it, disappearing into the back. Milton smiled at his discretion; there would be wry comments when he came in tomorrow.

The food was as good as ever, and the conversation was good, too, moving away from A.A. to range across work and family and life in general. Milton quickly found himself relaxing.

'How are you finding the Steps?'

'Oh, you know . . .' he began awkwardly.

'Which one are you on?'

'Eight and Nine.'

'Can you recite them?'

He smiled a little ruefully. '"We made a list of all persons we had harmed and became willing to make amends to them all."'

'And?'

'"We made direct amends to such people wherever possible, except where to do so would injure them or others."'

'Perfect,' she said. 'My favourites.'

'I don't know. They're hard.'

'You want my advice? Do it in your own time. They're not easy, but you do feel better afterwards. And you want to be careful. Plenty of people will be prepared to take your amends for you—'

'—And they can, too, if they're prepared to *make* my amends.'

'You heard that one before?'

He smiled. 'A few times. Where are you? Finished them?'

'First time around. I'm going back to the start again now.'

'Step Ten: "We continued to take a personal inventory."'

'Exactly. It never stops. You keep doing it, it stays fresh.'

Eva was an easy talker, something she affably dismissed as one of her faults, but Milton didn't mind at all; he was happy to listen to her, her soft West Coast drawl smoothing the edges from her words and her self-deprecating sense of humour and easy laughter drawing him in until it was just the two of them in an empty restaurant with Julius turning the chairs upside down on the tables, a hint that he was ready to call it a night and close.

'That was really nice,' she said as they stood on the pavement outside.

'It was.'

'You wanna, you know – you wanna do it again next time?'

'I'd love to.'

'All right, then, John.' She took a step towards him, her hand on his shoulder as she raised herself onto tiptoes and placed a kiss on his cheek. She lingered there for a moment, her lips warm against his skin, and as she stepped back, she traced her fingertips across his shoulder and down his arm to the elbow. 'Take it easy, all right? I'll see you next week.'

Milton smiled, more easily and naturally than was normal for him, and watched her turn and walk back towards where she had parked her Porsche.

17

Peter Gleason was the park ranger for the Golden Gate National Recreation Area. He had held the job for twenty years, watching all the communal spaces, making sure the fishermen and water-sports enthusiasts observed the local regulations, keeping an eye on the wildlife. Peter loved his job; he was an outdoorsman at heart, and there couldn't be many places that were as beautiful as this. He liked to say that he had the best office in the world; his wife, Glenda, had heard that quip about a million times, but he still said it because it was true and it reminded him how lucky he was.

Peter had been a dog-lover all his adult life, and this was a great job to have a hound. It was practically a require-ment. He had had four since he had been out here. They had all been Labradors. Good dogs, obedient and loyal; it was just like he always said, you couldn't go far wrong with a Lab. Jethro was his current dog. He was two years old and mongrel – part Labrador and part pointer. Peter had picked him out as a puppy and was training him up himself. He had the most even temperament out of all the dogs, and the best nose.

It was an early Tuesday morning when Peter stopped his truck in the wide, exposed and bleak square of ground that served visitors to Headlands Lookout. It was a remote area, served by a one-track road with the waters of Bonita Cove at the foot of a sheer drop on the left. He stepped carefully; yet another dense bank of fog had rolled in overnight and visibility was down to twenty yards. It was cold and damp, the curtain of solid grey muffling the sound. The western portion of San Francisco was just on the other side of the bay, usually providing a splendid vista, but it was invisible today. The only sign that it was there was the steady, eerie boom of the foghorns, one calling and the other answering.

There were only two other cars in the lot. Fishermen still visited with reels to try to catch the abundant fish, and as Peter checked, he noticed that a couple of them had followed the precarious path down the cliff face to get to the small beach. Oystermen came, too, even though the oyster beds, which had once been plentiful, had grown more scarce. Others came with binoculars to watch the birds and the seals. Kayakers, clad in neoprene wetsuits, cut across the waves.

The margins between the road and the cliff had grown too wild in places for a man to get through, but the dog was keen to explore today, and Peter watched as he forced himself into thickets of bramble. He walked on, following the headland around to the west. He watched the dog bound ahead, cutting a line through the poison oak and salt hay that was as straight as an arrow.

Peter lived on the other side of the bay, in Richmond, and he had always had a keen interest in the local flora and fauna. He found the rough natural world interesting, which was reason enough, but it was also professionally useful to have some knowledge of the area that you were working in. As he followed Jethro through the salt hay that morning, he found himself thinking that this part of the world would not have changed much in hundreds of years. Once you were down the slope a ways and the city was out of sight, the view would have been unchanged for millennia.

He stepped carefully through the bracken, navigating the thick clumps of vegetation before breaking into the open and tramping down the suddenly steep slope to the water's edge. All along the beach were stacks of rocks brought over from Tiburon. They had been piled into makeshift breakwaters to help combat the constant erosion, and the salty bite of the tide had caused them to crumble and crack.

The dog paused for a moment, frozen still, his nose twitching, and then as Peter watched with a mixture of curiosity and anticipation, he sprinted towards the deep fringe of the undergrowth. He got six feet in and stopped, digging furiously. Peter struggled across the soft, wet sand as the dog started to bark. When he got there, the dog had excavated the sand so that a flap of canvas sacking had been exposed. He called for Jethro to stay, but he was young and excited and knew he was onto something, so he kept digging, wet sand spraying out from between his hind legs.

By the time the ranger had fastened the lead to the dog's collar, he had unearthed a skull, a collarbone and the start of a ribcage.

PART II

MEG GABERT

Meg Gabert had always wanted to run track. She was a born ath-lete. She hadn't decided exactly what her talents best suited – long distance or sprints, she could do both – but there was no question about it in her mind: she was going to go to the Olympics and she was going to win gold. It wasn't in doubt.

When she was in seventh grade, she had started running at a local club. She decided that she was going to concentrate on long distance; she was tall and lithe, and, as she went farther and farther in her training, she found that she had plenty of endurance. She ran her first half-marathon when she was fifteen and then finished Boston the next year in a very competitive time. Her coach said that she had real talent, and she believed him. It was some-thing she would never forget: the excitement she felt as she ran the final few hundred yards, the crowd hollering their encouragement, the older runners struggling to get over the line while she still felt she had more in the tank. If she had needed any confirmation about the course she had chosen for herself, this was it.

But things got harder as she got older. She wasn't great at school and left without any real qualifications. Running was expensive, and she knew that it would take time before she was able to support herself through athletics. Until that happened, she had paid her way with a little hooking. It had started with web-cams, but then she had realised there was more to be made by going further. She had posted an ad on the Fresno/Adult Services page of Craigslist a year after she graduated from high school. She had a killer photo that an ex-boyfriend had taken of her, and the replies had been instantaneous.

Eventually, she moved from Illinois to San Francisco. The johns there were of a different class; they had more money, and she found that she could clear five hundred a night with no problem. The cash got to be addictive, and, as she enjoyed buying herself new clothes and fancy holidays, she forgot all about her running. Her track shoes started to gather dust in the back of her closet.

* * *

Meg heard the Cadillac before she saw it. It backfired loudly from a couple of blocks away, the noise carrying down the street and around the corner to where she was waiting at Sixth and Irving. The engine sounded throaty and unhealthy, as if it was about to expire, and she was nonplussed as it pulled over to stop at the edge of the sidewalk opposite her. The man she had spoken to on the phone had said that he was an executive from a company that dealt in cattle all the way across the south-west. He certainly had the accent for it, a mild Southern burr that lent his voice a musical quality. She hadn't expected him to be driving a beat-up car like this, but as she crossed the sidewalk to the open window, she chided herself for jumping to conclusions.

A bum begging for change next to the entrance to the department store watched as the door was opened for her. He watched as she carefully slid into the car, her hands pressing down her skirt as she lowered herself into the seat. The man didn't think twice about it, and she hardly registered; he was hungry and more interested in adding to the couple of bucks in change that had been tossed into the cap on the sidewalk before his folded legs. If he had paid attention, perhaps he would have noticed the confusion on the girl's face as she looked, for the first time, at the man who had picked her up. He might have remembered more if he had known that he would be the last person to see the girl alive.

18

Milton leant back and traced his fingers against the rough vinyl surface of the table. It had been marked by years of graffiti: gang tags, racial epithets and unflattering remarks about the police, some of them quite imaginative. There was a dirty glass of water, an ashtray that hadn't been emptied for days and, set against the wall, a tape recorder.

He crossed his arms and looked up at the police officers who were sitting opposite him. The first was a middle-aged man with several days of growth on his chin, an aquiline face and a lazy left eye. The second was a little older, a little more senior, and from the way the two of them had behaved so far, Milton could see that he was going to keep quiet while his partner conducted the interview.

The younger of the two pressed a button on the tape recorder and it began to spool.

'Just to go through things like we mentioned to you, we're gonna do a taped interview with you.'

'That's fine,' Milton said.

'There's my ID. And there's my partner's.'

'Okay.'

'So I'm Inspector Richard Cotton. My colleague is Chief of Detectives Stewart Webster.'

'I can see that.'

'Now, first of all, can you please state your name for me?'

'John Smith.'

'And that's S-M-I-T-H.'

'Correct.'

'Your date of birth, sir?'

'Thirty-first of October, 1968.'

'That makes you forty-five, right?'

'It does.'

'And your address at home?'

'259 Sixth Street.'

'What's that?'

'A hotel.'

'An SRO?'

'That's right.'

'Which one?'

'The El Capitan.'

'How are you finding that? Bit of a dive, right?'

'It's all right.'

'If you say so. Phone number?'

He gave them the number of his mobile.

'Are you all right for water?'

'Yes.'

Cotton tossed a packet of cigarettes on the table. 'Feel free to light up. We know this can be stressful.'

Milton had to stifle a long sigh of impatience. 'It would be stressful if I had something to hide. But I don't, so I'll pass, but thanks anyway. Now, please – can we get started? There's already been too much waiting around. Ask me whatever you like. I want to help.'

Cotton squinted one eye, a little spooky. 'All right, then. John Smith – that's your real name, right?'

'It is.'

'And you're English, right?'

'That's right.'

'I've been to England. Holiday. Houses of Parliament, Buckingham Palace, all that history – one hell of a place.'

Milton rolled his eyes. Was he serious? 'Just ask me about Madison.'

'In a minute, John,' the man said with exaggerated patience. 'We just want to know a little bit about you first. So how come you ended up here?'

'I've been travelling. I was in South America for a while, and then I came north.'

'Through Mexico?'

'That's right.'

'How long you been here?'

'Six months. I was here once before, years ago. I liked it. I thought I'd come back and stay a while.'

'How have you been getting by?'

'I've been working.'

Cotton's good eye twitched. 'You got a visa for that?'

'Dual citizenship.'

'How's that?'

'My mother was American.' It was a lie, but it was what his passport said. Dual citizenship saved unnecessary nonsense that would have made it more difficult for him to work. Being able to claim some connection to the United States had also proven to be useful as he worked his way north up the continent.

'All right, John. Let's change the subject – you want to talk about Madison, let's talk about Madison. You know we've dug up two bodies now, right?'

'I've seen the news.'

'And you know neither of them are her?'

That was news to him. 'No. I didn't know that.'

'That's right – neither of them. See, Madison had a metal pin in her hip. Fell off her bike when she was a girl, messed it up pretty good. They had to put one in to fix it all together. The remains in the morgue are all whole, more or less, and neither of them have anything like that.'

Milton felt a moment of relief but immediately tempered it; it was still surely just a matter of time.

'That doesn't mean we won't find her,' Cotton went on. 'If you've been watching the news, you'll know that we're still searching the beach, and we're very concerned that we're gonna find more. So, with all that being said, let's get down to meat and potatoes, shall we?'

'Please.'

'Why'd you do it, John?'

Milton wasn't surprised. 'Seriously?'

'What did you do with her body?'

'You've got to be kidding.'

'I'm not kidding, John.'

'No, you've got to be. It's nothing to do with me.'

'Answer the question, please.'

He looked dead straight at the cop. 'I just answered it. I didn't do it. I have absolutely no idea where she is.'

'So you say. But on your own account a few months back, you were the last person to see her alive.'

He clenched his fists in sudden frustration. 'No – that's not what I said.'

'You got a temper, John?'

'I don't know that she's dead. I hope she isn't. I said that I was one of the last people to see her before she *disappeared*. That's different.'

'We know the two girls we've got in the morgue were both hookers. Madison was hooking when she disappeared. It's not hard to join the dots, is it?'

'No, it isn't. But it has nothing to do with me.'

'All right, then. Let's change tack.' Cotton took a cigarette from the packet and lit it, taking his time about it. He looked down at his notes. 'Okay. The night after she disappeared – this is the Sunday – we've got a statement from Victor Leonard that says you went back to Pine Shore. He said he saw you coming out of the garden of the house where the party was the night before. Is that right?'

'Yes.'

'We checked the security camera, Mr Smith. There's one on the gate. We looked, and there you are, climbing over the wall. Why'd you do something like that?'

Milton gritted his teeth. The camera must have run off rechargeable batteries that would cut in if the power went out. 'The gate was locked,' he said.

'Why didn't you buzz to get in?'

'Because someone had changed the code to the gate after Madison disappeared. Rather than wasting your time with me, I'd be asking why that was. A girl goes missing, and the next day the code to the gate is changed? Why would they want to keep people out? Don't you think that's a little suspicious?'

'We'll be sure to bear that in mind. What were you looking around for?'

'Anything that might give me an idea what caused Madison to be so upset that she'd run away.'

'You spoke to Mr Leonard?'

'Yes.'

'Why?'

'Madison went to his house. I wanted to know what she said to him.'

'He say anything useful?'

Milton thought of Brady. 'Not really.'

'And you don't think all this is something that the police ought to do?'

'Yes, I do, but Madison's boyfriend had already reported her missing and he got the cold shoulder. Most crimes are solved in the first few hours after they happen. I didn't think this could wait.'

Cotton chain-smoked the cigarette down to the tip. 'Know a lot about police work, do you, John?'

'Do you have a sensible question for me?'

'Got a smart mouth, too.'

'Sorry about that. Low tolerance level for idiots.'

'That's it, John. Keep giving me attitude. We're the only people here keeping you from a pair of cuffs and a nice warm cell.'

Milton ignored the threat.

Cotton looked down at his notes. 'You said she was frightened?'

'Out of her mind.'

'That's not what security at the party said.'

'What did they say?'

'Said you barged in and went after her.'

'I heard her screaming.'

'How'd you explain how one of them ended up with a concussion and a broken nose?'

'He got in my way.'

'So you broke his nose and knocked him out?'

'I hit him.'

'It raises the question of that temper of yours again.'

Milton repeated himself patiently. 'I heard Madison screaming.'

'So?'

'So I went in to see if she was all right.'

'And?'

'I told her I'd take her home.'

'And?'

'She got around me and ran.'

Cotton got up and started to circle the table. 'You mentioned Madison's boyfriend' – he consulted his notes – 'Trip Macklemore. We've spoken to him. He said you had Madison's bag in the back of your taxi.'

'I did. I gave it to him afterwards.'

'What was it doing in your car?'

'She left it there.'

'But you'd already taken her where she needed to go. Why would she have left it?'

'I said I'd wait for her.'

'You didn't have another job to go to?'

'She was nervous. I didn't think it was right to leave her there, on her own, with no way to get back to the city.'

'You were going to charge her for that?'

'I hadn't decided. Probably not.'

'A favour, then? Out of the goodness of your heart?'

'It was the right thing to do.'

'He's English,' the other man, Webster, offered. 'What is it you call it?'

'Chivalry?'

'That's right, *chivalry*.'

'Don't know about that, boss. Doesn't strike me as all that likely. Taxi drivers aren't known for their charity.'

'I try to do the right thing,' Milton said.

Cotton looked down at his notes. 'You work for Vassily Romanov, too, right? Mr Freeze – the ice guy?'

'Yes.'

'We spoke to him. He had to have words with you the afternoon after she went missing. That right?'

'I dropped an ice sculpture.'

'He says you were agitated.'

'Distracted. I knew something was wrong.'

'Tell me what happened.'

'I already have.'

Cotton slapped both hands on the table. '*Where* is she?'

Milton stared at him and spoke calmly and carefully. 'I don't know.'

He drummed the table. 'What did you do with her body?'

'It's got nothing to do with me.'

'Is she on the headland?'

'I don't know.'

'Let me share a secret with you, John. The D.A. thinks you did it. He thinks you've got a big "Guilty" sign around your neck. He wants to throw the book at you.'

'Knock yourself out.' Milton calmly looked from one man to the other. 'We can go around the houses on this all day if you want, but I'm telling you now, if anything has happened to Madison, it has absolutely *nothing* to do with me, and it doesn't matter how you phrase your questions, it doesn't matter if you shout and scream, and it doesn't matter if you threaten me – the answers will always be the same. *I didn't do it*. It has nothing to do with me. And I'm not a fool. You can say what you want, but I know you don't think that I did it.'

'Really? How would you know that, John?'

'Because you would have arrested me already and this interview would be under caution. Look, I understand. I know you need to eliminate me. I know that I'm going to be a suspect. It stands to reason. I'll do whatever you need me to do so that you can be happy that I'm not the man you want. The car I was driving that night is parked outside. Get forensics to have a look at it. You can do it without a warrant – you don't need one, you have my authorisation. If you want to search my room, you've just got to ask.' He reached into his pocket and deposited his keys on the table. 'There. Help yourself.'

'You're awfully confident, John.'

'Because I have nothing to hide.' Webster was fingering the cigarette packet. Milton turned to him. 'You're the ranking officer here, right? I'm not going to tell you your job, but you've got to put a lead on your friend here and get off this dead end – right now. You're wasting time you don't have. If Madison is still alive, every minute we're doing this makes it less likely she'll be alive when you find her.'

Webster cocked an eyebrow. 'You like telling us what we should be doing so much, Mr Smith – what would you be doing?'

'I'd be looking at the footage from that CCTV camera. Maybe you'll see what happened. And everyone who went to the party that night will have gone through the gate. You should start looking into them.'

'The footage has been wiped,' he said.

'What?'

'There's nothing from the Saturday night.'

'Who wiped it?'

'We don't know.'

'You need to talk to whoever did that, then. Right?'

Cotton took over. 'Let's put that aside for the moment. You got anything to tell us, John?'

Milton thought about the two men in the house after the party. He would have told the cops what had happened, what he had overheard, but how could he do that without telling them that he had broken in? Why would he have done something like that? It wasn't going to be possible. That was a lead that he would have to follow for himself.

'All right, officers. Is there anything else?'

They said nothing.

'I'm going to be on my way. You know where I am, and you've got my number. If you want me to stay, you're going to have to arrest me.'

He pushed the chair away and stood up from the table.

19

Milton needed a meeting. As he drove across town, he felt as if he needed one even more than usual. He wasn't overly worried – he knew he would be able to run rings around the police – but the interview had still left him angry and frustrated. He had known that the police would treat him as a suspect – he would have done the same, if the roles had been reversed – but they seemed fixated. The longer they wasted on him, the worse it would be for Madison. And also, for a man in his particularly precarious position, there was the overriding need to be careful. More than careful. An arrest, his fingerprints and mugshot taken, metadata passing between anonymous servers – he knew that was all the spooks at GCHQ or the NSA would need to pin him down, and then it would all kick off again. The firestorm that had blazed around him in Juárez would spark back to life. Worse this time. He knew the prudent thing to do would have been to jump town the moment that there had been even a sniff of trouble. The day after Madison had disappeared. Now, though, he couldn't. The city had closed around him like a fist. If he ran, the police would see it as a sign of guilt. They would have all the evidence they needed to push their suspicions about him up a notch. There would be a manhunt. His name would be in the papers. His picture on the internet.

He might as well telephone Control.

I'm in San Francisco.

Come and get me.

No, he thought, as he drove across town. He had to stay and see this through until the end.

He gripped the wheel tightly and concentrated on the pattern of his breathing. The Rooms had taught him that anger and frustration were two of his most delicate triggers. A good meeting was like meditation, and he knew that it would help him to put the lid back on his temper.

Eva was waiting for him, leaning against the wall by the door. She was wearing a woollen jumper, expensive, long enough to reach well down beyond her waist, a pair of jeans and chunky leather boots. She had a black felt beret on her head. She looked supremely cute.

'Hello, John.'

'You're early.'

She leant forward, pressing herself away from the wall. 'Thought maybe I'd give you a hand. That all right?'

'Course,' he said.

They worked quickly and quietly: preparing the room, setting up the table with the tea and coffee, washing the crockery. Milton's thoughts went back to the meeting with the police. He thought about everything he knew. Two escorts found dead on the same stretch of headland. Madison going missing just five miles from the same spot. It looked bad for her. Maybe there was another explanation for what had happened, but then again, maybe there wasn't. The most obvious explanation was often the right one.

'You all right?' Eva asked him.

'I'm fine,' he said.

'Looks like you're a thousand miles away.'

'Sorry,' he said. 'I've got some stuff on my mind.'

'A problem shared is a problem halved.'

'I know.'

The regulars started to arrive twenty minutes before the meeting was scheduled to begin. Milton went behind the table and made their coffees. The room was quickly busy. Eva was waylaid by a young actor who obviously had a thing for her. She rolled her eyes, and as he nudged her towards the room for the start of the meeting, she paused by the table.

'You want to get dinner?'

'I'm not sure I'll be the best company tonight.'

'I'll take the risk.' She looked straight at him and winked.

'Okay.' He smiled. 'That'd be great.'

The room emptied out as it got closer to the top of the hour, and Milton quickly poured himself a coffee.

Smulders hijacked him as he was about to go inside.

'About time you opened that mouth of yours in a meeting, John.'

'Do I get to say no?'

Smulders looked at him with an intense sincerity. 'Man, you need me to remind you? You need me to explain? You're *sick*. And the cure for your sickness, the best cure I ever found, is to get involved and *participate*.' He enunciated that last word carefully, each syllable pronounced slowly, and then pressed a pamphlet into his hands. The title on the pamphlet was THE TWELVE PROMISES. 'Here they are, Smith. Read them out when I tell you and think on them when you do. All right?'

'Fine.'

Milton sat down as Smulders brought the gavel down and opened proceedings. He had recruited a speaker from another meeting that he attended, a middle-aged woman with worry lines carved in deep grooves around her eyes and prematurely grey hair. She started to speak, her share focusing on the relationship with her ex-husband and how he had knocked her around. It was worthy, and she was a powerful speaker, but Milton found his thoughts turning back to the interview and the police. They had already wasted too much time, and now they threatened to waste even more.

Milton didn't know if Madison was still alive, but if she was, and if she was in danger, the longer they wasted with him made it less likely that they would be able to help her.

The speaker came to the end of her share, wiping away the tears that had fallen down her cheeks. Smulders thanked her, there was warm applause, and then the arms went up as men and women who had found similarities between the speaker's story and their own – that was what they were enjoined to look for, not differences – lined up to share their own feelings. Milton listened for ten minutes but couldn't help zoning out again.

Richie Grimes put his hand up. He had come into the room late, and Milton hadn't noticed him. He looked now and saw, with shock, that the man's face was badly bruised. His right eye was swollen and almost completely shut, a bruise that ran from black to deep purple all the way around it. There was a cut on his forehead that had been sutured shut and another beneath his chin. Milton watched as he lowered his arm again; he moved gingerly, pain flickering on his face. Broken ribs.

'My name is Richie, and I'm an alcoholic.'

'Hi, Richie,' they all said.

'Yeah,' he said. 'Look at the fucking state of me, right? It's like what I've been sharing about the past few months, you know, the trouble I'm in? I guess maybe I was hoping it was all bluster, that it'd go away, but I always knew that was just wishful thinking. So I was coming home from work last night, and – *boom* – that was it, I got jumped from behind by these two goons with baseball bats. Broken nose, two broken ribs. I got a week to pay back all the money that I owe or they're coming back. I'd tell the police, but there's nothing they can do – what are they gonna do, put a man on me twenty-four hours? Nah' – he shook his head – 'that ain't gonna happen. If I can't find the money, I'm gonna get more of the same, and now, with the ribs and everything, I'm not sure I can even work properly. I gotta tell you, I'm closer to a drink today than I have been for months. I've been to two other meetings today already. Kinda feel like I'm hanging on by my fingertips.'

The others nodded their understanding and agreement. The woman next to him rested her hand on his shoulder, and others used his story to bounce off similar experiences of their own. If Richie was looking for advice, he didn't get any – that was "grandiose" and not what you came to A.A. to find – but he got sympathy and empathy and examples that he could use as a bulwark against the temptation of getting drunk.

Milton listened to the simple tales that were told, his head down and his hands clasped tightly on his lap. The meeting drew towards a close, and Smulders looked over to him and nodded. It was time. Milton took the pamphlet that his fingers had been fretting with all meeting and cleared his throat.

"'If we are painstaking about this phase of our development, we will be amazed before we are halfway through. We are going to know a new freedom and a new happiness. We will not regret the past nor wish to shut the door on it.'" He cleared his throat awkwardly. "'We will comprehend the word serenity and we will know peace. No matter how far along scale we have gone, we will see how our experience can benefit others. The feeling of uselessness and self-pity will disappear. We will lose interest in selfish things and gain interest in our fellows. Self-seeking will slip away. Our whole attitude and outlook upon life will change. Fear of people and of economic insecurity will leave us. We will intuitively know how to handle situations which used to baffle us. We will suddenly realise that God is doing for us what we could not do for ourselves. Are these extravagant promises?'"

The group chimed back at him, 'We think not.'

"'They are being fulfilled among us – sometimes quickly, sometimes slowly. They will always materialise if we work for them.'"

Peace.

Serenity.

We will not regret the past nor wish to shut the door on it.

We will *not* regret?

Milton doubted that could ever possibly come to pass. Not for him. His transgressions were different to those of the others. He hadn't soiled himself in the office, slapped his wife or crashed his car. He had killed nearly one hundred and fifty men and women. He knew that he would always regret the past, every day for as long as he lived, and what was the point in even trying to shut the door on it? The room behind his door was stuffed full of bodies, stacked all the way up to the ceiling, one hundred and fifty corpses and gallons of blood, and the door wouldn't begin to close.

They said the Lord's Prayer and filed out. Milton put away the coffee and biscuits and started to clean up. The usual group of people were gathering in the lobby to go for their meal together, and Eva was with them, smoking a cigarette and waiting for him to finish up. Milton was turning the tea urn upside down in the sink when the door to the bathroom opened and Richie Grimes hobbled out.

Milton turned to Eva and mouthed that he would be five minutes. She nodded and went outside.

'You all right?' Milton asked Grimes.

'Yeah, man.'

Milton offered the plate that had held the biscuits; it was covered with crumbs and one solitary cookie. 'Want it? Last one.'

'Sure.' Richie reached across and took it. 'Thanks. It's John, right?'

'Right.'

'Don't think I've ever heard you share.'

'I'm more of a listener,' he said. 'How are you feeling?'

'Like I've been ten rounds with Tyson.'

'But it was good to get it off your chest?'

'Sure. Getting rid of the problem's another matter. I ain't barely got a cent to my name. How am I gonna find the money he wants?'

'There'll be a way.'

'I wish I shared your confidence. The only way I can think is to get another loan, but that's just putting it off.' He gave him an underwhelming smile. 'Time to run. See you next week?'

The man looked like a prisoner being led out to the gallows. Milton couldn't let him go like that.

'This guy you owe the money to – who is he?'

'What good's it gonna do, telling you that?'

'Try me. What's his name?'

'Martinez.'

'Works down in the Mission District?'

'That's right. You know him?'

Milton shrugged. 'Heard the name.'

'I should never have gotten involved with him.'

'If it were me, Richie, I'd make sure I stayed in my place apart from when I was at work or at meetings. I wouldn't put myself somewhere where I could get jumped again.'

'How am I gonna get the cash if I hide out at home?'

'Like I say,' Milton said, 'there'll be a way. That's what they tell us, right – we put our faith in a power greater than ourselves.'

'I've been praying for six months, John. If there's a power, it ain't been listening.'

'Keep praying.'

20

Arlen Crawford was nervous. The first debate was two weeks to the day before the primary. It was held in a converted hat factory that had been turned into a new media hub with start-ups suckling the teats of the angel investor who owned the building, offering space in exchange for a little equity. There was a large auditorium that had only recently been done out, still smelling of fresh paint. There was a live audience, card-carrying local party members packed into the cramped seating like sardines in a tin. There was a row at the front – fitted with much more comfortable seating – that was reserved for the heavy-hitters from Washington, who had made the trip west to see the candidates in action for the first time.

Crawford looked down from the back of the room and onto the temporary stage, bathed in the glare of the harsh television lights. Each candidate had a lectern with a name card placed along the top. Governor Robinson's was in the centre; that had been the prize following an hour's horse-trading with the other candidates. The prime position would be fought over for the remaining two debates. Other bargaining chips included the speaking order, whether or not there would be opening and closing remarks, and a host of other ephemera that might have appeared trivial to the unenlightened observer. Crawford did not see them that way at all; to the politicos who were guiding the campaigns of the candidates, they were almost worth dying for. You lose the little battles and you better get ready to lose the war.

Robinson moved among his rivals like a Mafia don, giving them his double-clasped handshake, clapping them on the shoulders, squeezing their biceps, all the while shining out his gleaming smile. He laughed at their jokes and made his own, the consummate professional.

Crawford didn't have that ease with people, and never had. It was an unctuousness that you had to possess if you were going to make it as a player on the national stage. That was fine. He was happy with his strengths, and he recognised his weaknesses. That kind of self-awareness, in itself, was something that was rare to find and valuable to possess.

Robinson had amazing talents, but his instincts were off. Crawford's instincts were feral, animal. He was a strategist, a street fighter, and you needed a whole different set of skills for that. Robinson was surface, but Crawford was detail. He devoured every tiny bit of public life. He hovered above things like a hawk, aware of the smallest nuances yet always conscious of the whole. He could see how one small change might affect things now or eleven moves down the line. It wasn't a calculation he was aware of making; it was something that he processed, understood on a fundamental level.

One of the local party big shots came into the room and announced that it was time. Robinson, who was talking to the senator for New Mexico, wished everyone good luck. Crawford waited at the back, absorbing the energy of the room and the confidence – or lack thereof – that he could see in the other candidates. The retinues filtered into the auditorium. He hooked a doughnut from the refreshment table and followed them.

* * *

The debate couldn't have started any better. Robinson was totally in control, delivering his opening position with statesmanlike charm, so much so that Crawford found himself substituting the drab surroundings of the auditorium for what he imagined the General Assembly of the United Nations might look like with his boss before the lectern, or with the heavy blue drapes of the Oval Office closed behind him during an address to the nation. He was, Crawford thought with satisfaction, presidential.

The first question was posed – something on healthcare reform – and Robinson stayed away from it. The others went back and forth, each of them losing something as they sought to deploy the best lines, the most effective soundbites.

'Next question,' the moderator said.

'Delores Orpenshaw.' A shrew in a green dress and white pearls. 'The way folk around here see it, this country is broken. My question for the candidates is simple: how would they fix it?'

'Governor Robinson?'

Crawford felt the momentary chill of electricity: nerves.

Robinson looked the questioner right in the eye. 'How would I fix it? Well, Delores, there are some pretty fundamental things that we need to do right away. We need to reverse the flood of Third World immigration. We need to stop the flow, and we need to send back the ones who are here illegally.'

Robinson went off on a prepared riff but, as usual, made it look spontaneous. He railed against liberal snowflakes, somehow managed to get onto climate change, jumped across to reviving the manufacturing industry and then bringing glory back to the country. It was a bravura performance; there was a smattering of applause that grew in intensity, triggering more applause and then more, and then, suddenly, it had become a wave as the audience – almost all of them – rose to their feet and anointed the governor with an ovation. The moderator struggled to make her voice heard as she asked the others for their views. None of them looked like they wanted any part of the follow-up.

It went on for another hour in the same vein. Robinson picked his spots and was rewarded volubly every time he finished speaking. Eventually, the moderator brought the debate to an end. They made their way to the spin room, where Crawford and the rest of his team split up and worked the room, buttonholing the hacks from the nationals, talking up the points that Robinson had made that had gone down well and quietly de-emphasising the points that hadn't found their marks. There was no need to spin things.

They had won, and it hadn't even been close.

21

Milton turned the key. The ignition fired, but the engine didn't start. He paused, cranked it again, but still there was nothing. He had serviced the car himself a month ago, and it had all looked all right, but this didn't sound good. He drummed his fingers against the wheel.

Eva paused at the door of her Porsche and looked over quizzically.

He put his fingers to the key and twisted it a final time. The ignition coughed, then spluttered, then choked off to a pitiful whine. The courtesy light dimmed as the battery drained from turning over the engine. He popped the hood, opened the door and went around to take a look.

'Not good?' Eva said, coming over as he bent over the engine.

'Plugs, I think. They need changing.'

Eva had insisted they come back to Top Notch. Julius had never let him down, and the meal had been predictably good. The unease that Milton had felt after reading the Promises had quickly been forgotten in her company. He almost forgot the interview with the police. They had talked about the others at the meeting, slandering Smulders in particular; they agreed that he was well meaning, if a little supercilious, and she had suggested that he had form for coming onto the new, vulnerable male members of the fellowship. She had cocked an eyebrow at him as she had said it. Milton couldn't help but laugh at the suggestion. His troubles were quickly subsumed beneath the barrage of her wit as she took apart the other members of the group. The gossip wasn't cruel, but nevertheless, he had wondered what she might say about him in private. He had said that to her, feigning concern, and she had put a finger to her lips and winked with unmistakeable salaciousness. By the end of the main course Milton knew that he was attracted to her, and he knew that the feeling was mutual.

She watched now as he let the hood drop back into place.

'What are you going to do?'

'Walk, I guess.'

'Where's your place?'

'Mission District.'

'That's miles.'

That much was true. He wouldn't be home much before midnight, and then he would have to come back out in the morning – via a garage – to change the plugs. He was a little concerned about his finances, too. He had been planning to go out and drive tonight. He needed the cash. That obviously wasn't going to happen.

'Come on – I'll give you a ride.'

'You don't have to do that.'

'You're not walking,' she said with a determined conviction.

Milton was going to demur, but he thought of the time and the chance to get some sleep to prime him for the day tomorrow, and he realised that would have been foolish. 'Thanks,' he conceded as he locked the Explorer and walked over to her Cayenne with her.

The car was new and smelt it. It wasn't much of a guess to say that her job paid well – her wardrobe was as good a giveaway as anything – but as Milton settled back in the leather bucket seat, he thought that perhaps he had underestimated how well off she really was.

She must have noticed his appraising look as he took in the cabin. 'I've got a thing for nice cars,' she said, a little apologetically.

'It's better than nice.'

'Nice cars and nice clothes. It used to be Cristal and coke. The way I see it, if you're going to have an addiction, it better be one that leaves you with something to show for it.'

She put on an old Jay-Z album as she drove him across town. Milton guided her into the Mission District, picking the quickest way to his apartment. The area was in poor condition; plenty of the buildings were boarded up, others blackened from fire or degraded by squatters with no interest in maintaining them. The cheap rents attracted artists and students, and there was a bohemian atmosphere that was, in its own way, quite attractive. But it felt even cheaper than usual tonight, and as Milton looked out of the window of the gleaming black Porsche, he felt inadequate. He and Eva shared a weakness for booze, but that was it; he started to worry that there was a distance between the way they lived their lives that would be difficult to bridge.

The El Capitan Hotel and Hostel was a three-storey building with eighty rooms. The frontage was decorated with an ornate pediment and a cinema-style awning that advertised 'OPEN 24 HOURS A DAY' and 'PUBLIC PARKING – OPEN 24 HOURS'. It was a dowdy street, full of tatty shops and restaurants. To the left of the hotel was the Arabian Nights restaurant and, to the right, Modern Hair Cuts. Queen's Shoes and Siegel's Fashion for Men and Boys were opposite. There were tall palm trees, and the overhead electricity lines buzzed and fizzed in the fog.

'This is me,' Milton said.

Eva pulled up outside the building.

She killed the engine. 'Thanks for dinner.'

'Yeah,' he said. 'That was fun.'

There was a moment's silence. 'So – um . . . ?' she said.

He looked at her with an uncertainty that he knew was ridiculous.

'You gonna invite me up?'

'You sure that's a good idea?'

She smiled. 'What do you mean? Two recovering addicts? What could possibly go wrong?'

'That's not what I meant.'

'Really?'

'Maybe it was.'

'So?'

He paused, couldn't find the words, and laughed at the futility of it. 'Come on, then. It's at the top of the building, so you're going to have to walk. And I'll warn you now, save the view, it's nothing to write home about. It's not five-star.'

'Not what I'm used to, you mean?' She grinned. 'Fuck you, too.'

She locked the Cayenne and followed him to the door of the building. The narrow heels of her shoes clacked against the pavement as she took his arm and held it tightly. He was aware of the powerful scent of her perfume and the occasional pressure of her breast against his arm. He opened up and accepted her hand as she pressed it into his.

The reception was incredibly bright; the fluorescent tubes did not flicker, shining down harshly. The night manager nodded at them from behind the glass enclosure. There were all manner of people here. For some, it was a permanent residence, and for others, a room for the night. Many of the residents had mental-health problems, and Milton had seen plenty of disturbances in the time he had been there. No one had ever bothered him – the cold lifelessness behind his eyes was warning enough – and the place had served him well.

They climbed the stairs together, and he gently disengaged as he reached into his pocket for the key to his door. Milton opened the door. Inside was simple and ascetic, but it was all he could afford. The owner was happy enough to take cash, which saved him from the necessity of opening a bank account, something he was very reluctant to do.

Milton's apartment was tiny, an eight-by-twelve room that was just big enough for a double bed with a chair next to it and a small table next to that. There wasn't much else. The bathroom and kitchen were shared with the other rooms on the floor. Milton had always travelled light, so storing clothes wasn't an issue; he had two of everything, and when one set was dirty, he took it down to the laundromat around the corner and washed it. He had no interest in a television, and his only entertainment was the radio and his books: several volumes of Dickens, Greene, Orwell, Joyce and Conan Doyle.

'What do you think?' he said, a slightly bashful expression on his usually composed face.

'It's . . . minimalist.'

'That's one way of describing it.'

'You don't have much . . . *stuff*, do you?'

'I've never been much of one for things,' he explained.

She cast a glance around again. 'No pictures.'

'I'm not married. No family.'

'Parents?'

'They died when I was a boy.'

'Sorry.'

'Don't be. It was years ago.'

'Siblings?'

'No. Just me.'

He had a small pair of charged speakers on the windowsill; he walked across and plugged these into his phone, opening the radio application and selecting the local talk radio channel. The presenter was discussing the Republican primary; the challengers had just debated each other for the first time. The candidates were trying to differentiate themselves from their rivals. J.J. Robinson, the governor of Florida, was in the lead, by all accounts. They were saying that the primary was his to lose. Milton killed the radio app and scrolled through to his music player. He selected *Rated R* by the Queens of the Stone Age and picked out the slow, drawled funk of 'Leg of Lamb'.

'Good choice,' she said.

'I thought so.'

The room was on the third floor, and the window offered a good view of the city. She stood and looked out as he went through the affectation of boiling the kettle for a pot of tea. It was a distraction; they both knew that neither would drink a drop.

Milton took the pot to the table and sat down on the edge of the bed; she sat on the chair next to him. She turned, maybe to say something, maybe not, and he leant across to press his lips gently to hers. He paused, almost wincing with the potential embarrassment that he had misjudged the situation even though he knew that he had not, and then she moved towards him and kissed harder. He closed his eyes and lost himself for a moment. He was only dimly aware of the physical sensations: her breath on his cheek, her arms snaked around his shoulders as her mouth held his, her fingers playing against the back of his neck. She pulled away and looked into his face. Her fingers reached up and traced their way along the scar that began at his cheek and ended below his nose. She kissed it tenderly.

'How'd you do that?'

'Bar fight.'

'Someone had a knife?'

Milton had no wish to discuss the events of that night – he had been drunk, and it had ended badly for the other guy – so he reached for her again, his hand cupping around her head and drawing her closer. Her perfume was pungent, redolent of fresh fruit, and he breathed it in deeply. He pulled off her sweater and eased her back onto the bed with him. They kissed hungrily. He cupped her neck again and pulled her face to his while her hands found their way inside his shirt and around, massaging his muscular shoulders. They explored their bodies hungrily, and Milton soon felt dizzy with desire. Her lips were soft and full; her legs wrapped around his waist and squeezed him tight; her underwear was expensively insubstantial, her breasts rising up and down as she gulped for air. He kissed her sweet-smelling neck and throat as she whispered out a moan of pleasure. He brushed aside the hair that framed her face. They kissed again.

His mobile buzzed.

She broke away and locked onto his eyes with her own.

Her eyes smiled.

'Don't worry. I'm not answering.'

The phone went silent.

He kissed her.

Ten seconds later, it rang again.

'Someone wants to speak to you.'

'Sorry.'

'Who is it? Another woman?'

He laughed. 'Hardly.'

'Go on – the sooner you answer, the sooner they'll shut up. You're all mine tonight.'

Milton took the call.

'Mr Smith?'

The boy's voice was wired with anxiety. 'Trip – is everything all right?'

'Did you see the police today?'

'Yes,' he said.

'They say you're a suspect?'

'Not in as many words, but that's the gist of it. I'm one of the last people to see her before she disappeared. It stands to reason.'

'They had me in, too. Three hours straight.'

'And?'

'I don't know. I think maybe they think I'm a suspect, too.'

'Don't worry about it. They're doing what they think they have to do. Standard procedure. Most murders are committed by— well, you know.'

'People who knew the victim? Yeah, I know.'

Milton disentangled himself from Eva and stood. 'You haven't done anything. They'll figure that out. This is all routine. Ticking boxes. The good thing is that they're taking it seriously.'

'Yeah, man – like, finally.'

Milton took out his cigarettes and shook one out of the box. He looked over at Eva. She was looking at him with a quizzical expression on her face. He held up the box, and she nodded. He tossed it across the room to her, pressed the cigarette between his lips and lit it. He threw her the lighter.

'There was another reason for calling.'

'Go on.'

'I had a call ten minutes ago. There's this guy, Aaron; he says he was the driver who usually drove Madison to her jobs. He was the guy who didn't show the night she went missing, so she called you. He heard about what's happened on the TV.'

'How did he get your number?'

'Called the landline. Madison must've given it to him.'

'You need to tell him to go to the police. They'll definitely want to talk to him.'

'He won't, Mr Smith. He's frightened.'

'Of what?'

'He knows the agency she was working for. He says they're not exactly on the level. If he rats them out, they'll come after him.'

'You need to tell the police, Trip.'

'I would, Mr Smith, but this guy, he says he'll only speak to me. He says he'll tell me everything.'

'When?'

'Tomorrow morning. I said I'd meet him at Dottie's. Nine.'

Milton knew it. Dottie's was a San Francisco institution, and conveniently enough, it was right at the top of Sixth Street, just a couple of minutes from the El Capitan. Milton yanked up the sash window and tossed the cigarette outside. 'I'll be there.'

The relief in Trip's thanks was unmistakeable.

'Don't worry. Try to sleep. We'll deal with this tomorrow.'

Milton ended the call.

'What was that?'

Milton hadn't told Eva anything about Madison, but he explained it all now: the night she disappeared, Trip and the days that he had helped him to look for her, the dead bodies that had turned up on the headland, the interview with the police.

'Did you have a lawyer there?' she said. There was indignation in her voice.

'I didn't think I needed one.'

'They spoke to you without one?'

'I haven't done anything.'

'Are you an idiot?' she said angrily. 'You don't speak to the police investigating a *murder* without a lawyer, John.'

'Really,' he said, smiling at her. 'It was fine. I know what I'm doing.'

'No,' she insisted, sitting up. 'You don't. Promise me, if they bring you in again, you tell them you're not speaking until I get there. All right?'

'Sure,' he replied. 'All right.'

'What did he want?'

Milton related what Trip had told him.

'All right, then. This is what we're going to do. I'm taking tomorrow morning off. I'll drive you so you can get your car fixed and then you can go and see him.'

'You don't have to do that.'

'You don't listen much, do you, John? This isn't a democracy. That's what we're doing. It's not open to debate.'

22

Eva drove Milton to the garage to pick up a new set of spark plugs and then they returned to Top Notch. She waited while he changed the plugs and until the engine was running again.

He went over to the Porsche. They hadn't said much during the ride across town to his car, and he felt a little uncomfortable. He had never been the best when it came to talking about his feelings. He had never been able to afford the luxury before, and it didn't come naturally to him.

'Thanks for the ride,' he said.

'Charming!'

He laughed, blushing. 'I didn't mean—'

'I know what you meant,' she said, the light dancing in her eyes. 'I'm joking.'

The words clattered into each other. 'Oh – never mind.'

'You're a funny guy, John,' she said. 'Relax, all right? I had a nice night.'

'*Nice?*'

'All right – better than nice. It was *so nice* that I'd like to do it again. You up for that?'

'Sure.'

'Be at the next meeting. My place for dinner afterwards. Now – come here.'

He leant down and rather awkwardly kissed her through the window.

'What's up?'

'I was wondering,' he said. 'Could you do me a favour?'

'Sure.'

He told her about Doctor Andrew Brady and his potential involvement on the night that Madison went missing. He explained that he had worked at St Francis, like she did, and asked if she could find out anything about him.

'You want me to pull someone's personnel file?' she asked with mock outrage. 'Someone's *confidential* personnel file?'

'Could you?'

'Sure,' she said. 'Can you make it worth my while?'

'I can try.'

'Give me a couple of days,' she said.

'See you,' he said.

'You will.'

* * *

Trip was waiting outside Dottie's, pacing nervously, catching frequent glances at his watch. He was wearing a woollen beanie, and he reached his fingers beneath it, scratching his scalp anxiously. His face cleared a little when he saw Milton.

'Sorry I'm late. Traffic. Is he here?'

'Think so. The guy at the back – at the counter.'

'All right. That's good.'

'How we gonna play this?'

'I want you to introduce yourself and then tell him who I am, but it might turn out best if I do the talking after that, okay? We'll play it by ear and see how we get on.'

'What are we going to do?'

'Just talk. Get his story.'

'And then the police?'

'Let's see what he's got to say first – then we decide what we do next.'

The café was reasonably large, with exposed beams running the length of the ceiling with a flat glass roof above. The brick-work was exposed along one side, there was a busy service area with a countertop around it, and the guests were seated at free-standing tables. Blackboards advertised breakfast and a selection of flavoured coffees. A counter held home-made cakes under clear plastic covers, and wooden shelving bore crockery and condiments. A single candelabra-style light fitting hung down from the ceiling, and there were black-and-white pictures of old Hollywood starlets on the walls. The room was full.

Milton assessed the man at the counter automatically: the clothes were expensive, the empty mug suggested that he was nervous, the Ray-Bans he still hadn't removed confirming it. He was sitting so that he could see the entrance, his head tilting left and right as he made constant wary assessments of the people around him. Milton paused so that Trip could advance a step ahead of him and then followed the boy across the room.

'Aaron?' Trip asked.

'Yeah, man. Trip, right?'

'Yes.'

He looked up, frowned and stabbed a finger at Milton. 'He with you?'

'Yes.'

'So who is he?'

'It's all right. He's a friend.'

'Ain't my friend, bro. I said just *you*. Just you and me.'

'He was driving Madison the night she went missing.'

That softened him a little. 'That right?'

'That's right,' Milton said.

'I don't like surprises, all right? You should've said.'

'Shall we get a table?'

A booth had emptied out. Aaron and Trip went first; Milton bought coffees and followed them.

'Thanks,' Aaron said as Milton put the drinks on the table. 'What's your name, man?'

'I'm Smith.'

'You a driver, then?'

'That's right.'

'Freelance or agency?'

'Mostly freelance, bit of agency.'

'Police been speaking to you?'

'All afternoon yesterday.'

The hardness in his face broke apart. 'I'm sorry about you being involved in all this shit. It's my fault. It should've been me that night, right? I mean, I'd been driving her for ages. The one night I didn't turn up, that one night, and . . . I can't help thinking if it had've been me, she'd still be here, you know?'

There was an unsaid accusation in that, too: if it were me, and not you, she would still be here. Milton let it pass. 'You were good friends?'

'Yeah,' he said with an awkward cough. 'She's a good person. Out of all the girls I've driven, she's the only one I could say I ever really had any kind of fun with.' He looked at Trip and, realising the implication of what he had just said, added, not persuasively, 'As a friend, you know – a good friend.'

Milton found himself wondering if that disclaimer was insincere – the way his eyes flicked away from Trip as he delivered it – and whether Aaron and Madison had been sleeping together. The boy was certainly all broken up about what had happened. Milton wondered whether Trip had started to arrive at the same conclusion. If he had, he was doing a good job of hiding it.

'What do the police think has happened to her?'

'They've got no idea,' Trip said. 'It took them finding the bodies on the headland for them to start taking it seriously. Up until then she was just a missing person, some girl who decided she didn't want to come home, nothing worth getting excited about.'

'Jesus.'

'Why didn't you call before?' Milton asked him.

'I don't know,' he said. 'I felt awkward about it, I guess, you being her boyfriend and all.'

'Why would that matter?' Trip said tersely.

'No, of course, it wouldn't—'

Milton nudged Trip beneath the table with his knee. 'You said you could tell us who Madison was working for.'

'Yeah,' Aaron said vaguely. 'Same agency I work for, right?'

'Has it got a name?'

'Fallen Angelz. It's this Italian guy, Salvatore something, don't know his second name. I was out of work, got fired from the bar I was working at; I had a friend of a friend who was driving for them. I had no idea what it was all about until he explained it to me. I had no job, no money, not even a car, but I had a clean licence, and I thought it sounded like an easy way to make a bit of cash, maybe meet some people, a bit of fun, you know? Turns out I was right about that.'

'How did it work?'

'Straightforward. The girls get a booking, some john all on his own or a frat party or something bigger – some rich dude from out of town wants company all night, willing to pay for a girl to come to his hotel room. Celebrities, lawyers, doctors – you would *not* believe some of the guys I drove girls to see. Each girl gets assigned a driver. If it's me, the dispatcher in the office calls me up on my cell and tells me where I have to go to pick her up. They gave me a sweet whip, a tricked-out Lexus, all the extras. So I head over there, drive her out to wherever the party's at, then hang around until the gig's finished and drive her back home again or to the next job, whatever's happening. It's a piece of cake; the more girls I drive, the more money I make.'

'You get a slice of their takings?'

'That's right. When you've got a girl charging a grand for an hour and she's out there for two, maybe three hours, well, man, you can imagine, you can see how it can be a pretty lucrative gig, right? I was getting more money in a night than I could earn in two weeks serving stiffs in a bar.'

'What about drugs?' Milton asked.

Trip shot a glance at him.

'What about them?' Aaron said.

'They ever involved?'

He shifted uncomfortably. 'Sure, man, what do you think? These girls ain't saints. The agency offered it to customers as an extra and I'd bring it along. Sometimes I'll get some to sell myself. I've lived here my whole life; it's not like I don't know the right guys to ask, you know what I'm saying?' He delivered that line with a blasé shrug of his shoulders, like it was no big thing, but Milton wasn't impressed and fixed him in a cold stare. 'I ain't *endorsing* it,' Aaron backtracked. 'Can't say I was ever totally comfortable with having shit in the car, but the money's too good to ignore. You can make the same on top as you do with the girls.'

'What about Madison?' Milton asked. 'Does she use at all?'

'Yeah, man, sure she does.'

'*Bullshit*,' Trip said.

Aaron looked at Trip with a pained expression. 'You don't know?'

'She doesn't.'

'It's the truth, dude, I swear. They use, all of them do.'

Trip flinched but held his tongue.

'What does she use?' Milton asked.

'Coke. Weed.'

'Anything hallucinogenic?'

He shook his head. 'Never seen that.'

'All right. Tell us about her.'

Aaron shifted uncomfortably. 'What do you want to know?'

'Everything.'

He shrugged again. 'I don't know, man. I'd driven her before, this one time, maybe a year ago. We hit it off right away. She's a great girl, a lot of fun – the only girl I ever drove who I looked forward to seeing. Most of them— well, most of them, let's just say they're not the best when it comes to conversation, all right? A little dead behind the eyes, some of them; not the smartest cookies. But she's different.'

'Go on.'

He looked over at Trip and then back to Milton. He looked pained. 'Is this really necessary?'

'Come on,' Trip insisted. 'Don't pussy out now.' He must have known where this was going, but he was tough, and he wasn't going to flinch.

Aaron sighed helplessly. 'All right, man. I guess this was seven, eight months ago, before she went missing. The dispatcher said it was her, and I was happy about it. I'd had the same girl for a week, and she was driving me crazy. I went over to Nob Hill and picked Madison up in the Lexus. She talked and talked, told me everything that was going on in her life. Turns out that they put us together for two shifts after that. That's like almost two whole days and nights. The third time out, it was quiet, just two or three gigs, and we talked more. The next night was the same. I found a place to park the car and we had a drink. I had a wrap of coke in the glove compartment, and we ended up doing bumps of that, too. She said things about the work that I hadn't heard from the other girls.'

Aaron cleared his throat and looked down at the table.

'Keep going,' Milton said, knowing what was coming next and hating himself for pressing, hating what it was going to do to Trip.

'Then – I guess it just sort of happened. We had sex.'

'And?'

'She said she liked it. I didn't really believe it, but then, the next time I was driving her, like a couple of days after that, it happened again.'

Trip stood abruptly. Without saying a word, he turned on his heel and stalked out of the café.

'I'm sorry, man,' Aaron said helplessly. 'I didn't want to say—'

Milton stared at him. 'Keep going.'

He frowned, his eyes on the table again. 'I had a girlfriend then, but I ended it. I couldn't stop thinking about Madison. I knew it wasn't right. My girl was cut up, and I knew Madison had a guy, but I couldn't help it – neither of us could help it. I was getting pretty deep into working for the agency then, and my girl had always been jealous about that, the girls I was driving, but Madison didn't have any of that. No jealousy, just totally cool about it all. She got me, totally, understood where I was coming from. Sometimes I drove her, and sometimes I didn't, but it didn't matter. We were both cool with how it was. When I drove her, we slept together between calls. Sometimes she'd pretend to be on call during the day, but she'd meet me, we'd check into a hotel and stay there all day.'

'What was she like?'

'How do you mean?'

'Ever think she was depressed?'

'She had her moments, like all the girls, but no – I don't think so. If you mean do I think she's run away or done something worse, then, no, I'd say there was no chance. That'd be completely out of character. You want my opinion, I'd say that something bad has happened. No way she stays out of touch this long. She says nothing to me, nothing to your friend – no, no way, I ain't buying that.'

'You know you have to tell the police, don't you?'

'About us?'

'Yes, and about the agency.'

His eyes flickered with fear. 'No way, man. Talk to the cops? You mad? Salvatore, he's connected, you know what I mean? *Connected*. It's not like I know everything about how it works, but my best guess, the things I heard from the girls and the other drivers, he's fronting it for the Lucianos. You know them, man? The fucking *Lucianos*? It's fucking Mafia, right? The *Mafia!* Ain't no way I'm getting myself in a position where they might think I was ratting them out to the cops. No way. You know what happens to guys they reckon are rats, right?'

'Your name doesn't have to come out.'

'Fuck that shit, man! What you been smoking? That kind of stuff don't ever stay under wraps. They got cops on the payroll; everyone knows it. My name would be on the street in minutes, and then they'll be coming over to talk to me about it, and that ain't something that I want to think about. Next thing, I'd be floating in the bay with my throat cut. Fish food, man.'

'All right,' Milton said, smiling in the hope that he might relax a little. 'It's okay. I understand.'

Aaron looked at him suspiciously. 'You're just a driver, right?'

'That's right.'

'So why you asking all the questions, then?'

He spoke with careful, exaggerated patience. 'Because I'm one of the last people to have seen Madison before she disappeared. That means I'm a suspect, and I'd rather that I wasn't. Trip is a suspect now, too, and it'll probably get worse for him when the police find out that you were sleeping with his woman. Jealousy, right? That's a good motive. The more information you can give us, maybe that'll make it easier for us to find out what happened to her, and then maybe the police will realise me and him had nothing to do with it. Understand?'

'You wait for her that night?'

'Yes.'

'Why didn't you help her, then? If it was me out there, I guarantee nothing would've happened.'

Milton looked at him dead straight, staring right into his eyes; the boy immediately looked down into the dregs of his coffee. 'She didn't give me a chance,' Milton said sternly. 'Something happened to her at that party, and there wasn't anything I could do about it. By the time I got to her, she was already in a mess.'

'So where is she?'

'She ran. That's all I know.'

Aaron gestured towards the door. 'That dude – you tell him I'm sorry, will you? I didn't want to say anything, and you know, muscling in on another guy's girl, that ain't the way I do things, that ain't my style at all, you know what I'm saying?'

'I'm sure it isn't,' Milton said.

'All right,' he said. 'I'm done.'

'The agency. How can I get in touch with them?'

'What are you gonna do?'

'I'm going to visit them.'

'And?'

'And get as much information as I can.'

'No way, man. I *can't*. That shit's gonna come back to me, right? They'll figure out I've been talking. I don't know. I don't know at all.'

Aaron got up quickly, the chair scraping loudly against the floor. He made to leave, but Milton reached out a hand, grabbed the boy around the bicep and squeezed.

'Shit, dude!' he exclaimed. 'That hurts.'

Milton relaxed his grip a little, but he didn't let go. 'Have a think about it,' he said, his voice quiet and even. 'Think about Madison. If you care about her at all, you give me a call and tell me how I can get in touch with the agency. Don't make me come and find you. Do we understand each other?'

'Shit, man, yeah – all right.'

Milton took a pen from his pocket, pulled a napkin from the chrome dispenser and wrote his number on it. 'This is me,' he said, putting it in the boy's hand. 'Take the rest of the day to think about it, and call me. Okay?'

The boy gulped down his fear and nodded.

Milton released his grip.

23

Milton drove them as near to Headlands Lookout as he could get. Trip was nervous, fidgeting next to him, almost as if he expected them to find something. The police had blocked the road a hundred yards from the car park, a broad cordon cutting from the rocky outcropping on the right all the way down to the edge of the cliff on the left. Half a dozen outside-broadcast trucks had been allowed down to the lot, and they were crammed in together, satellite dishes angled in the same direction and their various antennae bristling.

Milton slowed and pulled off the narrow road, cramming the Explorer up against the rock so that there was just enough space for cars to pass it to the left. The sky was a slate grey vault overhead, and rain was lashing against the windscreen, pummelling it on the back of a strong wind coming right off the Pacific. Visibility was decent despite the brutal weather, and as Milton disembarked, he gazed out to the south, all the way to the city on the other side of the bay.

They made their way through the cordon and down to the car park. There were several dozen people there already, arranged in an untidy scrum before a man who was standing on a raised slope where the cameras could all get a decent view of him. Milton recognised him. It was Commissioner William Reagan, the head of the local police. He was an old man, close to retirement, his careworn face chiselled by years of stress and disappointment. The wind tousled his short shock of white hair. He pulled his long cloak around him, the icy rain driven across the bleak scene. An officer was holding an umbrella for him, but it wasn't giving him much shelter; he wiped moisture from his face with the back of his hand.

'Ladies and gentlemen,' he said into the upheld microphones, 'before I get into my remarks, let me identify those who are here with me. I got Chief of Detectives Stewart Webster – everyone knows the chief – and I got Inspector Richard Cotton.' He cleared his throat and pulled out a sheet of paper. 'As you know, we've found two bodies along this stretch of the headland. I wish we hadn't, but that's the sad fact of it. It appears that they were taken down from the road into the foliage and hidden there so that they wouldn't be seen. We're assuming they were dumped here by the same person or persons.'

A brusque man from cable news shouted loudest as he paused for breath. 'You identified them yet?'

'No,' Reagan said. 'Not yet.'

'So you're saying you've got a serial killer dumping victims along this stretch of land?'

'It would be a big coincidence if it was two separate people.'

'You expect to find anyone else?'

'That's impossible to say. But we're looking.'

'So are you, or are you not, looking at it being the same guy?'

'Well, you know, I'm not gonna say that, but, certainly, we're looking at that.'

*   *   *

The press roadshow decamped and moved to Belvedere. A slow crawl of traffic worked sluggishly along the narrow road, with Milton and Trip caught in the middle of it. Their purpose in driving out of the city had been to go and speak to Brady, but Milton had not anticipated all this extra company. It made him nervous. The vehicles turned left and headed north, taking the right and doubling back to the south.

Milton gripped the wheel tightly and ran the morning's developments through his mind. It wasn't surprising that they had reached the conclusion that Madison's disappearance must have been connected. Why not? Two working girls turning up murdered just a few miles away, another working girl goes missing: it was hardly a stretch to think that she was dead, too, and dead at the hands of the same killer.

As they reached Pine Shore, it was obvious that the prospect of a community of potential suspects was just too tempting to ignore. The gates stood open – it looked as if they had been forced – and the cavalcade had spilled inside. Reporters and their cameramen had set up outside the two key properties: the house where the party had taken place and Dr Brady's cottage. Police cars were parked nearby, but the cops inside seemed content to let them get on with things.

Milton parked the Explorer and joined Trip at the front of the car. They watched as two reporters for national news channels delivered their assessments of the case so far – the discovery of the two bodies, the fact that a third girl had gone missing here – and suggested that the police were linking the investigations.

Milton looked at the cameras.

'We shouldn't be here,' he said, more to himself than to the boy.

'What are they doing outside his place?' Trip said, his eyes blazing angrily as he started up the street towards Brady's cottage.

'Trip – stop.'

'They think *he* did it, right? That must be it.'

Milton followed after him and took him by the shoulder. 'We need to get back in the car. They'll be all over us if they see us and figure out who we are.'

Trip shook his hand away. 'I don't care about that. I want to speak to him.'

He set off again.

Milton paused. He knew he should leave him, get back into the car and drive back to the city. He had been stupid to come up here. He should have guessed that it would be swarming with press. It stood to reason. He didn't know if they would be able to identify him, but if they did, if he was filmed and if the footage was broadcast? *That* would be very dangerous indeed.

Milton's phone vibrated in his pocket.

'Hello?'

'Mr Smith?'

'Speaking.'

'It's Aaron Pogue – from this morning.'

Milton put his hand over the microphone. 'Trip!'

He paused and turned. 'What?'

'It's Aaron.'

The boy came back towards him.

'You there?' said Aaron.

'Yes, I'm here. Hello, Aaron.'

'I've been thinking about what you said.'

'And?'

'And I'll tell you what you need. The agency, all that.'

'That's good, Aaron. Go on.'

'I don't have a number for the agency – the number they use when they call, it's always blocked, so there's nothing I can do to help you there. But Salvatore, the guy who runs it, I know he owns the pizza house in Fisherman's Wharf. That's just a cover – the agency is his main deal, that's his money gig; he runs it from the office out back. That's it.'

'Thank you.'

'You'll keep my name out of it?'

'I'll try.'

'I hope you find her.'

Milton ended the call.

'What did he say?'

'He told me where to find the agency.'

The thought of confronting Brady seemed to have left Trip's mind. 'Where?'

'It's in the city,' Milton said. 'Want to come?'

24

Milton parked the car on the junction of Jefferson and Taylor. He had explained his plan to Trip during the drive back into the city and persuaded him that it was better that he go in alone. Trip had objected at first, but Milton had insisted and, eventually, the boy had backed down. Milton didn't know what he was going to find, but if the agency was backed by the Mafia, what he had in mind was likely to be dangerous. He had no intention of exposing Trip to that.

'I won't be long,' he said as he opened the door. 'Wait here?'

'All right,' Trip said.

Milton stepped out and walked beneath the huge ship's wheel that marked the start of Fisherman's Wharf. He passed restaurants with their names marked on guano-stained awnings: Guardino's, The Crab Station, Sabella & LaTorre's Original Fisherman's Wharf Restaurant. Tourists gathered at windows, staring at the menus, debating the merits of one over another. A ship's bell clanged in the brisk wind that was coming off the ocean, the tang of salt was everywhere, and the clouds pressed down overhead. It was a festival of tacky nonsense, as inauthentic as it was possible to be. Milton continued down the road.

The Classic Italian Pizza and Pasta Co. was between Alioto's and The Fisherman's Grotto.

He climbed the stairs to the first floor and nodded to the maître d' as he passed him as if he were just rejoining friends at a table.

It was a decent place: a salad and pasta station, tended to by a man in a chef's tunic and a toque, was positioned beneath a large Italian tricolour; string bags full of garlic and sun-dried tomatoes hung from a rack in the area where food was prepared; a series of tables was arranged on either side of an aisle that led to the bar; the tables were covered with crisp white tablecloths, folded napkins and gleaming cutlery and glassware. Two sides of the restaurant were windowed, the view giving out onto the marina beyond on one side and the wharf on the other. It was busy. The smell of fresh pizza blew out of the big wood kiln that was the main feature of the room.

Milton went into the kitchen. A man in grimy whites was working on a bowl of crabmeat.

'I'm looking for Salvatore.'

The man shifted uncomfortably. 'Say what?'

'Salvatore. The boss. Where is he?'

'Ain't no one called Salvatore here.'

Milton was in no mood to waste time. He stalked by the man and headed for the door at the end of the kitchen. He opened the door. It was a large office. He surveyed it carefully, all eyes. First, he looked for an exit. There was one on the far wall, propped open with a fire extinguisher. There was a window, too, with a view of the wharf outside, but it was too small to be useful. There was a pool table in the middle of the room and a jukebox against the wall. There was a desk with a computer and a pile of papers. A man was sitting at the computer. He was middle-aged, burly, with heavy shoulders, biceps that strained against the sleeves of his T-shirt and meaty forearms covered in hair. Both arms were decorated with lurid tattooed sleeves, the markings running all the way down to the backs of his hands and onto his fingers.

The man spun around on his chair. 'The fuck you want?'

'Salvatore?'

He got up. 'Who are you?'

'My name is Smith.'

'And?'

'I want to talk to you.'

'You think you can just bust into my office?'

'We need to talk.'

'Then make an appointment.'

'It's about your other business.'

The man concealed the wary, nervous turn to his face behind a quick sneer. 'Yeah? What other business?'

Milton looked at him with dead eyes. He had always found that projecting a sense of perfect calm worked wonders in a situation like this. It wasn't even a question of confidence. He knew he could take Salvatore, provided there were no firearms involved to even the odds. Milton couldn't remember the last time he'd lost a fight against a single man. He couldn't remember the last time he'd lost a fight against two men, either, come to that.

'Your escort business, Salvatore.'

'Nah.'

'Fallen Angelz.'

'Never heard of it.'

'It would be better to be honest.'

'I don't know nothing about it, friend.'

Milton scanned for threats and opportunities. There were drawers in the desk that might easily contain a small pistol. No way of knowing that for sure, though, so he would just have to keep an eye on the man's hands. There was a stack of cardboard trays with beer bottles inside, still covered by cellophane wrap, but Milton wasn't worried about them. A bottle wouldn't be all that useful as a weapon, and, in any case, it would be necessary to tear through the cellophane wrap to get at them. No time for that. He glanced at the pool table. That would work. There were the balls, good for throwing or for using as blunt weapons in an open fist. There were the cues held in a vertical rack on the nearest wall. Any of those would make a decent weapon.

Milton watched the Italian carefully. He could see from the way that the veins were standing out in his neck and the clenching and unclenching of his fists that it would take very little for things to turn nasty.

'So – let's talk about it.'

'Don't you listen? I don't know what you're talking about.'

'So I wouldn't find anything in those papers if I were to have a look?'

'Reckon that'd be a pretty dumb thing to go and try to do.'

Salvatore reached down slowly and carefully pulled up the bottom of his T-shirt, exposing six inches of tattooed skin and the stippled grip of a Smith & Wesson Sigma. He rested the tips of his fingers against it, lightly curling them around the handle.

'This isn't the first time I've seen a gun.'

'Could be your last.'

Milton ignored that. 'Let me tell you some things I know, Salvatore. I know you run girls out of this office. I know you distribute drugs on the side. And I know you sent Madison Clarke to a party at the house in Pine Shore.'

'Yeah? What party was that?'

'The one where she went missing.'

He stared at him. A flicker of doubt. 'Madison Clarke? No. I don't know no one by that name.'

'I don't believe you.'

'You think I care what you believe?' He stood up now, his right hand curled more tightly around the grip of the handgun. He pointed to the telephone on the desk with his left hand. 'You know who I'm gonna call if you don't start making tracks?'

'I've no idea.'

'I'm gonna call an ambulance. I'm telling you, man, straight up, you don't get out of here right now, you won't be leaving in one piece. I'm gonna fucking shoot your ass.'

'I tell you what – you tell me all about the escorting business and maybe I won't break your arm. How's that sound?'

Salvatore slapped his hand against the gun. 'You miss this, man? Who the hell are you to tell me what to do?'

'Let's say I'm someone you don't want to annoy.'

'What's that supposed to mean?'

'I'm a concerned member of the public. And I don't like the business you're running.'

Milton assessed the distance between them – eight feet – and couldn't say for sure that he would be able to get all the way across the room before the man could draw and shoot. And if Salvatore could get the gun up in time and shoot, it would be point-blank and hard to miss.

That wasn't going to work.

Plan B.

Milton stepped quickly to the table, snatched up the eight-ball and flung it. His aim was good, and as Salvatore turned his head away to avoid it, the ball struck him on the cheekbone, shattering it.

Milton already had the pool cue, his fingers finding the thin end.

Salvatore fumbled hopelessly for the gun.

Milton swung the cue in a wide arc that terminated in the side of Salvatore's head. The wood crunched and splintered and blood splashed over the computer monitor. Salvatore slid off the chair and onto the floor. He stayed down.

Milton discarded the remains of the cue and started to look through the papers on the desk.

* * *

Trip was listening to the radio when Milton reached the Explorer again. He opened the door and slid inside, moving quickly. He started the engine and pulled away from the kerb.

'You get anything?'

'Nothing useful.'

'So it wasn't worth coming down here? We should've stayed in Belvedere?'

'I wouldn't say that. I made an impression. There'll be a follow-up.'

25

Milton heard the buzzer as he was cleaning his teeth. He wasn't expecting a delivery, and since very few people knew where he lived, he was about as sure as he could be that whoever it was who had come calling on him at eight in the morning wasn't there for the good of his health. He put the brush back in its holder and quietly opened the window just enough that he could look downwards. The window was directly above the entrance to the building, and he could see the three men who were arrayed around the door. There was a car on the corner with another man in the front. It was a big Lexus, blacked-out windows, very expensive.

Four men. An expensive car. He had a pretty good idea what this was.

Milton toggled the intercom. 'Yes?'

'Police.'

'Police?'

'That's right. Is that Mr Smith?'

'Yes.'

'Could we have a word?'

'What about?'

'Open the door, please, sir.'

'What do you want to talk to me about?'

'There was an incident yesterday. Fisherman's Wharf. Please, sir – we just need to have a word.'

'Fine. Just give me five minutes. I work nights. I was asleep. I just need to get changed.'

'Five minutes.'

He went back to the window and looked down at them again. There was no way on earth that these men were cops. They were dressed too well in expensive overcoats, and he saw the grey sunlight flickering across the caps of well-polished shoes. And then there was the car; the San Francisco Police Department drove Crown Vics, not eighty-thousand-dollar saloons.

He waited for the men to shift around a little and got a better look at them. Three of the men he had never seen before. The fourth, the guy waiting in the car, he recognised. Milton looked at him as he wound down the window and called out to the others. It was Salvatore. His face was partially obscured by a bandage that had been fixed over his shattered cheek. Milton waited a moment longer, watching as the men exchanged words, their postures tense and impatient. One of them stepped back, and the wind caught his open overcoat, flipping his suit coat back, too, revealing a metallic glint in a shoulder holster.

That settled it.

The three guys at his door were made guys; that much was for sure. So what to do? If he let them in, then the chances were they'd come up, subdue him and Salvatore would be called in to put the final bullet in his head. Or if he went down to meet them, maybe they would take him somewhere quiet, somewhere down by the docks, perhaps, and do it there. Milton had known exactly what he was doing when he beat Salvatore, and the way he saw it, he hadn't been given any other choice. There was always going to be consequences for what he'd done, and here they were, right on cue. An angry Mafioso bent on revenge could cause trouble. *Lots* of trouble.

So maybe discretion was the better part of valour this morning. Milton dropped his mobile in his jacket pocket and went through into the corridor. There was a window at the end; he yanked it up. The building's fire escape ran outside it. He wriggled out onto the sill, reached out with his right hand, grabbed the metal handrail and dropped down onto the platform.

He climbed down the stairs and walked around the block until he had a clear view onto the frontage of the El Capitan. The Lexus was still there, and the three hoodlums were still waiting by the door. One of them had his finger on the buzzer; it looked like he was pressing it non-stop.

Milton collected the Explorer. It was cold. He started the engine and then put the heater on max. He took out his phone and swiped his finger down, flipping through his contacts. He found the one he wanted, pressed call and waited for it to connect.

26

The sign in the window said 'BAXTER BAIL BONDS'. The three words were stacked on top of one another so that the three Bs, drawn so they were all interlocked, were the focus that caught the eye. The shop was in Escondido, north of San Diego, and Beau Baxter hardly ever visited it these days. He had started out here pretty much as soon as he had gotten out of the Border Patrol down south. He had put in a long stint, latterly patrolling the Reaper's Line between Tijuana, Mexicali, Nogales and, worst of them all, Juárez. Beau had run his business from the shop for eighteen months until he came to the realisation that it was going to take years to make any serious coin, and, seeing as he wasn't getting any younger, he figured he needed to do something to accelerate things. He had developed contacts with a certain Italian family with interests all the way across the continental United States, and he started to do work for them. It paid well, although their money was dirty and it needed to be laundered. That was where having a ready-made business, a business that often ran on cash and dealt in the provision of intangible services, sometimes anonymously, came in very handy indeed.

So Beau had kept the place on and had appointed an old friend from the B.P. to run it for him. Arthur 'Hank' Culpepper was a hoary old goat, a real wiseacre they used to call 'PR' back in the day because he was the least appropriate member of the crew to send to do anything that needed a diplomatic touch. He had always been vain, which was funny because he'd never been the prettiest to look at. That didn't stop him developing a high opinion of himself; Beau joked that he shaved in a cracked mirror every morning because he thought of himself as a real ladies' man. His airs and graces might have been lacking, but he had made up for that by being a shit-hot agent with an almost supernatural ability to nose out the bad guys.

He wasn't interested in the big game that Beau went after nowadays; there was a lot of travel involved in that, and there was the ever-present risk of catching a bullet in some bumble-fuck town where the quarry had gone to ground. Hank was quite content to stick around San Diego, posting bond for the local scumbags and then going after them whenever they were foolish enough to abscond. He had his favourite bar, his hound and his dear old wife (in that order), and anyways, he had a reputation that he liked to work on. Some people called him a local legend. He was known for bringing the runners back in with maximum prejudice, and stories of him roping redneck tweakers from out of the back of his battered old Jeep were well known among the Escondido bondsmen. It was, he said, just something that he enjoyed to do.

Beau pulled up and took a heavy black vinyl sports bag from the rear of his Cherokee. He slung it over his shoulder, blipped the lock on the car, crossed the pavement and stopped at the door. He unlocked it, pushed down the handle with his elbow and backed his way inside. The interior was simple. The front door opened into the office, with a desk, some potted plants, a standard lamp and a sofa that had been pushed back against the wall. There was a second door, opposite the street door, that led to a corridor that went all the way to the back of the building. There was a kitchenette, a bathroom and, at the end, a small cell that could be locked.

The safe was in the kitchen, the kettle and a couple of dirty mugs resting atop it. Beau spun the dial three times – four-nine-eight – and opened the heavy cast-iron door. He unzipped the bag and spread it open. It was full of paper money.

Fifteen big ones.

The smell of it wafted into the stuffy room. Beau loved that smell.

He took out the cash, stacked the fifties in neat piles and locked the safe.

He locked the front door, got back into his Cherokee and headed for the hospital.

* * *

Hank was sitting up in bed, his phone pressed between his head and shoulder while his right hand was occupied with tamping tobacco into the bowl of the pipe in his left hand. He was in his early sixties, same as Beau was, and lying there in bed like that, he looked it. Man, did he ever look *old*. The whole of his right side was swathed in bandages, and there was a drip running into a canula in the back of his hand. He hadn't shaved for a couple of days, and that added on a few extra years. He wasn't wearing anything above the waist, and his arms – Beau remembered them when they were thick with muscle – looked withered and old. The tattoo of the snake that he had had done in Saigon was wrinkled and creased where once it had been tightly curled around his bicep.

Old age, Beau thought. That was the real reaper. Coming for all of us. Still, he thought, I'd rather eat five pounds of cactus thorns and shit-sharp needles than look like *that*.

He raised a hand in greeting, and Hank reciprocated with a nod, mouthing that he would be two minutes, before speaking into the receiver again: 'I'm telling you, Maxine, the judge don't give a sweet fuck about that. What he's gonna get now ain't a pimple on a fat man's ass compared to what he's gonna get. If he don't make it for the hearing tomorrow, the judge'll make an example out of him. I'm telling you, no shit, he's looking at five years before he even gets a sniff of parole. *Five.* Is that what you want for him? No? Then you better tell me where he's at.'

Beau could hear the buzz of a female voice from the receiver.

There was a coffee machine in the hall, and Beau went outside for two brews in white Styrofoam cups. He searched the small wicker basket next to the machine for a packet of Coffee-mate, came up empty, went back through into the room and found a bowl of sugar instead. He spooned a couple into both cups, stirring the sludgy brown liquid until it looked a little more appealing.

'Fine. Where – Pounders? All right, then. I'm gonna send someone to go and get him.'

Beau sat down and stared at his old friend. He thought about the first time they had met – 1976. They'd graduated from the Border Patrol Academy and been posted up in Douglas at about the same time. Hank had been a uniformed cop near the border in El Centro, California, before coming on duty with the B.P.

'I'm serious, Maxine,' Hank was saying. 'If he comes back, you call me right away. He really doesn't want to rile me up right now. I'm not in the mood to go chasing him down all over the state, and if he makes me do that, I ain't promising he don't get brought back in cuffs and with a bloody nose. You hearing me straight, darling? I ain't messing. Don't you dare make me look like a fool, now.'

He ended the call.

'You ain't chasing anyone tonight, partner,' Beau said.

'She don't know that.'

'Who is it?'

'Fellow named George Bailey. Been stealing cars. This time, though, the dumb fuck had a pistol on him while he was doing it. "Possession of a concealed weapon" – he's looking at five, minimum, probably seven or eight depending on which judge he gets. He decided he'd take his chances on the road; I'm trying to persuade his lovely *girlfriend*' – that word was loaded with sarcasm – 'otherwise. He's out getting drunk, so I'm going to send George McCoy to go pick him up. Unless you wanna do it?'

'Uh-huh,' Beau said with a big smile, shaking his head. 'I'm not into that no more.'

'Only the big game for you now, partner?'

'That's right.'

'What was the last one?'

'Mexican.'

'And?'

'Not so bad.'

Beau had finished the job the night before. It had been an easy one by his usual standards. The Lucianos had interests in a couple of big casinos in Vegas, and one of their croupiers, this wiry beaner by the name of Eduardo del Rio, had entertained the thought that he could run south with fifty grand of their money. The Lucianos had sent Beau after him. He must have been the most dumbshit robber in the Mexican state of Sonora that night, and it had been a simple bust. He had run straight home to his wife, and Beau just had to wait there for him. He'd been a little punchy when Beau confronted him, but his attitude had adjusted just as soon as he started looking down the barrel of Beau's 12-gauge pump.

'Boy was as dumb as you like,' Beau said. 'Dumb as a box of rocks.' He sipped his coffee; it was foul. 'All right.' Beau crossed his legs, the hem of his right trouser leg riding up a little to show more of his snakeskin cowboy boot. 'Now then. You wanna tell me what in God's name has been going down round here?'

'Meaning what?'

'Meaning *what*? Which sumbitch shot you up, Hank?'

'Ever heard of Ordell Leonard?'

Beau shook his head. 'Can't say I have.'

'Big brother from 'Bama. Quiet fella until he gets on the drink, then you never know what you're gonna get. They had him for driving under the influence and resisting arrest. All he was looking at was a couple of months, but he reckons they're prejudiced against black men from the South round here, so he decides he's gonna take his chances and takes off. I ended up in Arkansas before I could catch him. Fucking Little Rock, can you believe that shit? Two thousand miles, man. It took me three days there and three days back, although, course, he was in the back coming home, so I had to listen to his goddamn problems the whole way. The whole experience made me think I ain't getting a good enough shake out of this here thing we got going on.'

He was grinning as he said it; Beau knew he was fooling around.

'And then?'

'And then I got lazy, I guess. We was right back up at the store when I let him out. I was going to put him in the cell until I could transfer him to the courthouse. He'd been on best behaviour for the whole trip, and I'd taken off his cuffs. Clean forgot. Dude cold-cocks me, knocks me down, then gets my shotgun from the front and fires off a load. I'm not sure how he missed, to be honest with you. Ended up catching me in the shoulder, but it could've been a helluva lot worse.'

'Know where he's headed?'

'Got a brother in Vallejo. I'd bet you a dime to a doughnut that's where he's gone.'

'All right, then. You can leave that one to me.'

'You sure? Not much money in it, Beau.'

Beau looked at Hank again. He was getting on. Couldn't have that many years left in him doing what they were doing. A shotgun at close range? He'd got lucky. Maybe it was time Beau suggested Hank took it easy. Maybe it was a message. 'Ain't about money all the time, partner. Dude shot you all up. I can't stand for that. Bad for our reputation.'

'Ah, shit – I'll be fine. I was gonna enjoy seeing him again.'

'How long they going to keep you in?'

'Couple more days.'

'By which time he'll be long gone. Nah, Hank, don't worry about it. Leave him to me.'

Hank sucked his teeth and, eventually, nodded his assent. 'Shit,' he said. 'I remembered something; you had a call back at the office. Jeanette took the details down and told me about it.'

Jeanette was the secretary who kept things ticking over. 'Who from?'

'She said he called himself Smith. Sounded like he was English, she said; he had that whole accent going on. She says you weren't around and could she take a message for you, and he says yes, she could, and he tells her that he wants you to call him pronto. He gave her a number – I've got it written down in my pants pocket.'

'He say what he wanted to speak to me about?'

'Nope,' Hank said, shaking his head, 'except it was urgent.'

27

Beau drove north. It took him eight hours on the I-5, a touch under five hundred miles. He could have flown or caught a northbound Amtrak from San Diego, but he liked the drive, and it gave him some time to listen to some music and think.

He spent a lot of time thinking about duties and obligations. He had always lived his life by a code. It wasn't a moral code because he couldn't claim to be a particularly moral man; that would be fatuous, given the profession he had latterly chosen for himself. It was more a set of rules that he tried to live his life by, and one of those rules insisted that he would always pay his debts. It was a matter of integrity. Beau's father had always said that was something you either had or you didn't have, and he prided himself that he did. Getting the Mexican journalist away to safety had been the right thing to do, but he couldn't in all honesty say that he thought it had completely squared the ledger between them. He figured the Englishman had done him two solids down in Mexico: he had saved him from *Santa Muerte* and then drew the fire of whoever it was who'd hit *El Patrón*'s mansion so that he and the girl could get away. Helping the girl had paid back only half of the debt. At the very least, he could drive up to San Francisco and hear what the Englishman had to say. If it wasn't something Beau could help him with, then he would book into a nice hotel for a couple of nights and enjoy the city. He really had nothing to lose.

And if nothing else, he could find out how on earth Smith had gotten out of Mexico. It hadn't looked so good for him when Beau and the girl had made tracks. That guy, though – he was something else.

Beau could mix in a spot of business, too. Ordell Leonard was up there, and there was no way on God's green earth Beau was going to let him have even an extra second of liberty. He would never have admitted it to another person, but seeing Hank in the hospital like that, old and shot up, had reminded him of his own advancing years. He had been thinking about his own mortality a lot recently. He was sixty-two years old. Every morning, he seemed to wake up with another ache. Everyone came to the end of the road eventually, that was the one shared inevitability, but Beau was determined that he wasn't there yet. The more he thought about it, the more he understood his own reaction: Ordell Leonard was a bad man, a dangerous man, and he would have been a challenge to collar ten years ago, when he and Hank were fitter and meaner than they were now. Bringing him in now would be his way of thumbing his nose at the notion that he was ready to retire.

Ordell would be the proof that Beau wasn't ready to hang it up just yet.

* * *

Beau booked a suite at the Drisco, and five minutes before the time that they had agreed to meet, he was waiting in the bar downstairs.

John Smith was right on time.

'Beau,' he said, sitting down opposite him.

'All right, English,' Beau said. 'Didn't think I'd ever be seeing you again.'

'I guess you never know what's around the corner.'

'I guess you don't.'

'What happened to the girl?' Smith asked.

'As far as I know, she's safe and sound.'

'As far as you know?'

'That's all I can say. The man who makes people disappear, this guy my employers use when they need to send someone out of harm's way, the arrangement is strictly between him and the client. No one else gets to know anything about it. She could be in Alaska for all I know. She could be back in Mexico, although I hope for her sake she ain't. But what I can say for sure is that I got her into the country like I said I would, and she was just fine and dandy when I dropped her off.'

Smith nodded at that. 'You get paid for the job?'

'Sure did,' Beau said.

He had delivered the body of Adolfo González to the Lucianos nine months ago. The job had been to bring him in dead or alive, yet there had been consternation that it was in the former condition that *Santa Muerte* was delivered. Beau had explained what had happened – that the girl journalist from Juárez had put a bullet in the Mexican's head while he

227

was outside their motel room getting ice – but his honesty had led to recriminations. The awkwardness had been underscored by the requirement, stipulated by Beau, that the girl was to be given a new identity and kept hidden from the cartels. There had been a moment when Beau had been unsure that they were going to let her leave in one piece, but he had stuck to his guns and, eventually, they had conceded. Beau didn't necessarily care about her either way – she wasn't his problem, after all – but he had promised Smith that he would get her out of Mexico and set up in the States, and Beau wasn't the sort of man who went back on his word. Doing the right thing had eventually lightened his payment by fifteen grand; the Italians docked ten from his bounty for spoiling the fun they had planned for González and the other five went to pay the fee of the professional who made people disappear.

Fifteen.

Beau hadn't been happy with that, not at all.

'I appreciate it,' Smith said.

'No sweat, English. Least I could do, circumstances like they were.' He paused and lit up a smoke. 'So – how'd you get out alive?'

'There was a lot of confusion. I took advantage of it.'

'Who were those dudes?'

'Best not to ask.'

'What about *El Patrón*?'

'What about him?'

'He got himself shot dead a couple of days later. That wouldn't have been anything to do with you, would it?'

'Me? No,' Smith said. 'Course not.'

Beau laughed and shook his head. The Englishman was something else. Quiet and unassuming for the most part, but when he got all riled up, there weren't many people who would have concerned Beau more. He remembered the way he had strode through *El Patrón*'s burning mansion, offing gangsters just like he was shooting fish in a barrel. He had been ruthlessly efficient. Not a single wasted shot and not a moment of hesitation. The man was private, too, and Beau knew that there was no point in pushing him to speak if he didn't want to.

'You said you needed a favour,' he said instead. 'What can I do for you?'

'The syndicate you've been working for – it's the Lucianos?'

Beau paused and frowned a little. He hadn't expected that. 'Could be. Why?'

'I have a problem – you might be able to help.'

'With them? What kind of problem?'

'I put one of their men in the hospital.'

'Why would you want to do a crazy-assed thing like that?'

'He pulled a gun on me. I didn't have much choice.'

'By "hospital" – what do you mean?'

'He's not dead, Beau. Broken nose, broken ribs. I worked him over with a pool cue.'

'Jesus, English.'

Smith shrugged.

'You wanna tell me why he was going to pull a gun on you?'

'They're running an escort business. This man fronted it for them. I had some questions about it, and he didn't like them.'

'What were they?'

'They sent a girl to a party. She hasn't been seen since, and I was one of the last people to see her. Apart from anything else, the police have got me down as a suspect.'

'For what?'

'You hear about those dead girls up north?'

'Sure.'

'The party was right around there. I'd say there's a good chance her body'll be the next body they find.'

'Murder, then.'

'I'm not concerned about me, I know I didn't do it, and I know they're just going through the motions.'

'Kicking the tyres.'

He nodded. 'Exactly. But I got talking to her before.'

'An escort?'

'I was driving her. I have a taxi.'

'Chef. Cab driver. You're full of surprises.'

Smith brushed over that. 'She's a nice girl. And her boyfriend's a good kid. When the police realise I don't have anything to do with it, they're going to go after him, and maybe he isn't quite as single-minded as me, maybe they need a conviction, and he looks like he could be their guy. Maybe they *make* him their guy. I'd like to get to the bottom of what happened, one way or another.'

Beau shook his head. 'You've got yourself in a mess over another woman? You got a habit for that. What is it with you, English?'

'I need to talk to them, Beau, but at the moment, I think they'd rather put a bullet between my eyes. I was hoping you might be able to straighten things out.'

'Put a good word in for you, you mean?'

'If you like.'

Beau couldn't help but chuckle. 'You're unbelievable. Really – you're something else.'

'Can you do it?'

'Can I ask them not to shoot you? Sure I can. Will they listen? I have absolutely no idea.'

'Just get me in a room with whoever it is I need to speak to. It might not look like it, but we both have a stake in this. If she's dead, I'm going to find out who killed her. It's in their best interests that I do. Because if I don't, there's going to be a whole lot of heat coming their way. You'd be doing them a favour.'

'Well,' Beau said, 'you put it like that, how can I possibly refuse?'

28

'I know you've got a temper,' Beau said to him as he reverse-parked his Jeep into a space next to the bowling alley, 'but you'll want to keep it under wraps today, all right? Apart from the fact that I vouched for you, which means it'll be me who gets his ass kicked if you start getting rambunctious, these aren't the kind of dudes you want to be annoying, if you catch my drift.' He paused. 'You *do* catch my drift, John, don't you?'

'Don't worry, Beau,' Milton said. 'I'm not an idiot.'

'One other thing, let me do the talking to start with. Introduce you and suchlike. Then you can take the conversation whichever way you want. If you get off on the wrong foot with them, you'll get nowhere – you might as well just pound sand up your ass. This has to be done right.'

The car park was half full, mostly with cheap cars with a few dings and dents in the bodywork, nothing too showy, the kind of first cars that kids new to the business of driving would buy with the money they had managed to scrape together. Beau had parked next to the most expensive car in the lot. It was a Mercedes sedan with darkened windows and gleaming paint-work. There was a driver behind the wheel. Milton could only

233

just make him out through the smoked glass, but there he was; it looked like he was wearing a uniform, the cap of which he had taken off and rested against the dash. He had reclined the seat, and he was leaning back, taking a nap.

They got out of the car and Milton followed Beau inside.

He looked around. It was a scruffy dive, dirty around the edges and showing its age, staffed by kids in mismatched uniforms trying to make beer money. There were two exits. One was the door they had just come through; the other was at the end of a long, dark bathroom corridor all the way in back. An air-conditioning unit over the door was on its last legs, running so hard that it was trembling and rattling, but it wasn't making much difference to the humidity in the air. Seven bowling lanes had been fitted into what might once have been a large warehouse. It was a generous space, the roof sloping down towards the end of the lanes with dusty skylights at the other end. There was a bar at the back with ESPN playing on muted TVs, then some upholstered benches, then a cluster of free-standing tables and then the lanes. There were computerised scoring machines suspended from the roof. All sorts of bottled beers behind the bar. The place was loud. Music from a glowing jukebox was pumped through large speakers, but that was drowned out by the sound of balls being dropped onto wood, falling into the gully and smashing into the pins. The machinery rattled as it replaced the pins, and the balls rumbled as they rolled back to the players.

'What is this place?'

'What's it look like?'

'Looks like a bowling alley.'

'There you go.'

'The family owns it?'

'Sure they do. They own lots of things: pizza parlours, nail bars, couple of hotels.'

'All useful if you've got money you need to wash.'

'Your words, John,' he said, with a big smile that said it was all the way true.

Milton checked the clientele, counting people, scanning faces, watching body language. Kids, mostly, but there were a few others that caught his eye. At a table in a darkened corner away from the bar were two guys talking earnestly, their hands disappearing beneath the table, touching, then coming back up again. A dealer and his buyer. There were two guys further back in the room, sat around a table with a couple of bottles of beer. Big guys, gorillas in sharp suits. The first was a tall, wide man with collar-length hair and a black T-shirt under a black suit. The second was a little smaller, with a face that twitched as he watched the action on the nearest lane. They were a pair. Milton pegged them as bodyguards. Operators. Made men, most likely. He'd seen plenty of guys like that all around the world. They'd be decent, dangerous up to a point, but easy enough to take care of if you knew how to do it. There would be a point beyond which they were not willing to go. Milton had their advantage when it came to that; he didn't have a cut-off. The men were sitting apart from each other, but their twin gazes were now trained on the table in a private VIP area that was raised up on a small platform accessed by a flight of three steps and fenced off from the rest of the room.

A further pair of men were sitting there.

'Is that them?'

Beau nodded. 'Remember – I'll do the introductions, and for God's sake, show them a little respect. You're not on home territory here, and I don't care how tough you think you are, they won't give two shits about that. Wait here. I'll go and speak to them.'

Milton sat down at the bar. One of the televisions was tuned to CNN. They had a reporter out at Headlands Lookout, ghostly in the thick shroud of fog that alternated between absorbing and reflecting the lights for the camera. The man was explaining how the police had set out the large area that they would search, breaking it down into smaller areas that were then administered by several officers. The item cut to footage of the search. The narrow road he had previously driven down was marked with plastic signs pointing to where remains had been found. Marker flags had been driven into the scrub and sand on each of the sites. Officers were working in the bramble, using the flags as their reference points.

Beau came back across. 'All right,' he said. 'They'll see you. Remember, play nice.'

'I always do.'

Milton approached the two men. One was older, wrinkled around the eyes and nose. He had a full head of hair, pure black, the colour obviously out of a packet. There was a beauty spot on his right cheek, and his right eyelid seemed to be a little lazy, hooding the eye more than the other. He was wearing a shirt with a couple of buttons undone, no tie, with a jacket slung over the back of the chair. The second man was younger. He had a pronounced nose with flared nostrils, heavy eyebrows and beady eyes that never stayed still.

Beau sat down on one of the two empty seats.

Milton sat down, too.

'This is Mr Smith,' Beau said.

'How are you doing?' the older man said, nodding solemnly at him. 'My name is Tommy Luciano.'

He extended his hand across the table. Milton took it. His skin was soft, almost feminine, and his grip was loose. He could have crushed it.

'And my friend here is Carlo Lucchese.'

Lucchese did not show the same hospitality. He glowered at him across the table, and Milton recognised him; he was the one who had been on the intercom to him at the El Capitan, one of the four who had come to kill him.

He didn't let that faze him. 'Thank you for seeing me.'

'Beau said it was important. That wouldn't normally have been enough to interrupt my afternoon, but he told us that you were *very* helpful with a small problem we had over in Juárez.'

'That's good of him to say.'

'And so that's why we're sitting here. Normally, with what you've done, you'd be dead.'

Lucchese looked on venomously.

'Perhaps,' Milton said.

'You had an argument with one of my men.'

'I'm afraid I did.'

'Want to tell me why?'

'I have some questions that I need to have answered. I asked him, and they seemed to make him uncomfortable. He threatened me with a gun. Not very civil. I wasn't prepared to stand for that.'

'Self-defence on your part, then?'

'If you like.'

Beau put a hand down on the table and intervened: 'John's sorry, though – right, John?'

Milton didn't respond. He just kept his eye on the older man.

'He don't look sorry,' Lucchese said.

'Carlo . . .'

'This douche broke Salvatore's face. Messed him up real good. And we're *talking* to him? I don't know, Tommy, I don't, but what the goddamn fuck?'

'Take it easy,' the old man said, and Milton knew from the way that he said it that he was about to be judged. The next five minutes would determine what came after: he was either going to get the information he wanted, or he was going to get shot. 'These questions – you wanna tell me what they are?'

He didn't take his eyes away from the older man. 'There was a party in Pine Shore. I drove a girl up there.'

'You drove her?'

'I'm a taxi driver.'

Luciano laughed. 'This gets better and better.'

Milton held his eye. 'Something happened at the party, and she freaked out. She ran, and she's not been seen since.'

'Pine Shore?'

'That's right. Near where the two dead girls turned up.'

'I know it. And you think this girl is dead?'

'I think it's possible.'

'And what's any of it got to do with us?'

'Fallen Angelz. She was on the books.'

He looked at him with an amused turn to his mouth. 'Fallen Angelz? That supposed to mean anything to me?'

Milton didn't take his eyes away. 'You really want to waste my time like that?'

Beau stiffened to Milton's right, but he said nothing. The younger man flexed a little. Milton stared hard at Luciano, unblinkingly hard. The old man held his glare steadily, unfazed, and then smiled. 'You have a set of balls on you, my friend.'

'Aw, come on, Tommy – you can't be serious. You said—'

'Go and do something else, Carlo. I don't need you around for this.'

'Tommy—'

'It wasn't a suggestion. Go on – fuck off.'

Lucchese left the table, but he didn't go far. He stopped at the bar and ordered a beer.

Milton didn't relax, not even a little. He was very aware of the two bodyguards at the table across the room.

'All right,' Luciano said. 'So suppose I said I do know about this business. What do you want?'

'A name – the person who booked the girls that night.'

'Come on, Mr Smith, you know I can't give you that. That business only works if it's anonymous. We got some serious players on the books. Well-known people who would shit bricks if they knew I was letting people know they took advantage of the services we offer. They need to trust our discretion. I start spilling their names, there are plenty of other places who'll take their money.'

'You need to think bigger than that, Mr – Luciano. Telling me who booked her that night is the best chance you've got of keeping the business.'

'That so? How you figure that?'

'One of your drivers told me that the girl was sent by the agency. You could say he's had a crisis of conscience about it. He knows he ought to be telling the police. So far, that hasn't been strong enough to trump the fact that he's terrified that talking is going to bring him into the frame. That's his worst-case scenario.'

'No, Mr Smith. His worst-case scenario is that *I* find out who he is.'

'But you won't find out, not from me.'

'So what's his worry?'

'If he goes to the cops? That he gets charged with procuring prostitution.'

'So he's not saying anything.'

'Not yet. But you know the way that guilt is. It has a way of eating away at you. I'm betting that he's feeling worse and worse about what happened every single day, and the longer the police dig away without getting anywhere, the harder it's going to be for him to fight off going to them and telling them everything he knows. And if she turns up dead? I reckon he calls them right away. The first thing that's going to happen after that is that Salvatore gets a visit about the murders. The second thing is that he gets arrested and charged. The police need to be seen to be doing something. They'll go after the low-hanging fruit, and three dead prostitutes linked – rightly or wrongly – to an illegal agency like Fallen Angelz would be a perfect place to start. And, without wanting to cast aspersions, Salvatore didn't strike me as the kind of fellow with the character to stand up to the prospect of doing time when there's a plea bargain on the table. I don't need to go on, do I?'

'You sure Salvatore would flip? Just like that?'

'Are you sure he won't?'

'You saying you can help me?'

'I've got a few days' head start on the police. Maybe that's enough time for me to find out what happened. Maybe my girl isn't linked to the other two. Maybe something else has happened to her. And maybe, if I can find some answers, the driver decides he doesn't have to say anything.'

'And if this girl is dead?'

'Provided it had nothing to do with you, maybe I can find a way that leaves you out. That agency's got to be valuable to you, right? It's got to be worth giving me the chance to sort things out. What have you got to lose?'

Luciano looked at him shrewdly. 'I could speak to the driver myself. Find out what he knows.'

'You don't know who he is.'

'*You* do. You could tell me.' He smiled thinly, suggestively.

'Forget it,' Milton said, smiling back. 'I'm not frightened of you.'

'What did you do before you drove cabs, Mr Smith?'

'I was a cook,' he said.

'A cook?'

'He was working in a restaurant when I met him,' Beau said.

'You think he's a cook, Beau?'

'No.'

Luciano sucked his teeth.

Milton clenched his fists beneath the table.

'All right – let's say, just for the sake of discussion, that I give you what you want. Why are you so interested? What does it have to do with you?'

'The police have me down as a suspect, and it's not in my interest for my name to come out. The sooner I can clear this up, the better.'

'Publicity is bad for you?'

'Very bad.'

Luciano shook his head, a small smile playing on his lips. 'You're a very interesting man, Mr Smith. That's all I need for now. I'll speak to Beau. You can wait outside.'

*　*　*

Milton made his way down from the raised area and across the wide room. As he passed the bar, he saw Carlo with another man. The newcomer held himself at an odd angle, his left arm clutched to his side as if he was in pain, and he had a huge, florid bruise on his cheek. There were purples and blues and greys in the bruise, and the centre was pure black and perfectly rounded, as if it had been caused by a forceful impact with something spherical. The nose was obscured by a splint.

Salvatore glared at Milton as he crossed in front of him, his eyes dripping with hate. Milton nodded once, a gesture he knew he probably shouldn't have made but one that he just couldn't resist. The injured man lost it, aggrieved at the beating that he had taken, aggrieved at seeing Milton walk out of the bowling alley with impunity, not a scratch on him, and he came in at an awkward charge, moving painfully and with difficulty, his right fist raised. Milton feinted one way and moved another. The Italian stumbled past, Milton tapped his ankles, and Salvatore tripped and fell. He grimaced as he pushed himself to his feet again, but by then Milton had backed off and turned around and was ready for the second go-around. Salvatore came at him again, his fist raised, lumbering like a wounded elephant. Milton ducked to one side and threw a crisp punch that landed square on his nose, crunching the bones again. Salvatore's legs went, and he ate carpet. He stayed down this time, huffing hard.

Milton raised his hands helplessly and looked over at the VIP area, wondering whether things were going to get heated. Beau looked anxious, but neither Tommy Luciano or Carlo Lucchese did anything. Milton turned to look at Luciano, then to Lucchese, then to Salvatore; then he pushed out of the door and went outside to wait for Beau in the cold, bright afternoon sun.

29

Milton had gone to a meeting that evening. It wasn't his usual, and Eva wasn't there. He had gone out for dinner afterwards with a couple of the guys, and by the time he returned to his flat, it was midnight. He was reasonably confident that there would be no more issues with the Lucianos – at least for the moment – but he couldn't completely rule out that Lucchese might ignore his boss and come at him again, so he had driven around the block twice before going inside. He saw nothing to make him anxious, and there was nothing in the blindingly bright lobby to suggest that his visitors had returned or that they intended to. He climbed to the third floor. He knew exactly where the light switch was, and it was with a single blur of motion that he opened the door, flicked it on – and stood in the threshold with the door open wide, scanning the room with practised eyes. Everything looked as if it was in order.

He stepped forward and locked himself inside, bending down to examine one of his own black hairs, which still lay undisturbed where he had left it before going out, placed carefully across the drawer of the coffee table. He had left a faint trace of talcum powder on the handle of the bedroom door and that, too, had not been disturbed. These were, he knew, extravagant measures to confirm his safety, but years in a business as dangerous as his had hardwired him with caution. Paying heed to that creed, and to his instincts, was the reason he was still alive. The precise application of a routine like this had saved his life on several occasions. The Mafia was a blunt instrument compared to the secret services of the countries that he had infiltrated – a cudgel as to a scalpel – but that was no reason to treat them with any less respect. A cudgel was still deadly.

Milton propped a chair beneath the door handle, locked the window that faced the fire escape and slept with his fingers wrapped around the butt of the Smith & Wesson 9mm that he kept under the pillow.

* * *

He rose early the next morning. There was a lot to do. First, though, he dressed in his running gear, pulled his battered trainers onto his feet and went downstairs. It was a crisp, bright day, the sun's cold rays piercing the mist that rose off the bay. Milton ran south on Mason Street, turned onto Montgomery Street and ran until he reached the Embarcadero, the piers, the bridge to Oakland and, beyond it, the greenish-blue of the ocean. He ran north, following the road as it curved to the west, listening to the rhythmic cadence of his feet and clearing his mind. This had always been his preferred way to think. It was his meditation before he found the sanctuary of the Rooms, a peaceful retreat where he had the time and the luxury to let his thoughts develop at their own speed, without even being conscious of them.

He ran onto Jefferson, turned left inside Aquatic Park and then followed Hyde to Broadway and then, finally, Mason Street and home.

He passed through the lobby and took the stairs at a jog.

There were two men waiting outside the door to his room.

He recognised them both.

'Inspector Cotton. Detective Webster.'

'Mr Smith.'

'How can I help you?'

'We're going to need to talk to you.'

'Again? Really?'

'A few more questions.'

'I answered them before. Is there anything else?'

'I'm afraid there is. We found another body this morning.'

PART III

MILEY VAN DYKEN

Miley Van Dyken had been having second thoughts about how she had chosen to live her life. She'd told friends about them, how she was thinking about getting out. She knew that turning tricks could be a dangerous business, but it seemed to her that there had been more stories of psychos preying on working girls recently. There had been all those poor girls down on the beach, for one, and the police still had no idea who was responsible for their deaths.

But still she carried on. There were plenty of benefits that came from doing what she did; the money, obviously, but the freedom of working to your own schedule was another that other girls often overlooked. That was true, but it had been getting to the stage that her doubts and fears were starting to get so bad that she couldn't ignore them.

Her latest john had hired a room in The Tuscan on North Point Street in North Beach, five minutes from Pier 39. Miley usually preferred to sort the room herself, charging a little extra as expenses so that she still cleared her two hundred per hour, but the guy had apologised that he couldn't very easily leave the hotel and, when he had sensed her reluctance, had offered to pay a further fifty bucks on top to 'make up for her inconvenience'. He sounded nice enough, kind, speaking with a lilting Southern accent that put her in mind of that guy Kevin Spacey played in the Netflix thing, and even though she had initially turned him down and hung up, she stewed on it for fifteen minutes and changed her mind. She didn't have another job booked, he had been polite on the phone, and most importantly, she needed the money.

She tried not to think about her fears as she rode the bus. The driver smiled at her as she disembarked outside the hotel.

He was the last person to see her alive.

It was a small hotel that catered to travelling business people. It was a two-storey building surrounded by a parking lot. It didn't appear to be very busy; the lot was almost empty, save for a couple of rentals and a beaten-up Cadillac Eldorado. She went around the car on the way to the lobby when the driver's-side door opened and a man got out. He was tall and skinny, dressed in a white T-shirt, jeans and a pair of cowboy boots. He said her name. She recognised his voice.

30

Cotton and Webster didn't sit, so neither did Milton. Webster wandered absently to the window and looked down onto the street below. Cotton took a book from the shelf – it was *The Unbearable Lightness of Being* – made a desultory show of flicking through the pages and then put it back again. He looked around, his face marked by a lazy sneer.

'Nice place you got here,' he said.

'It suits me very well.'

'I don't know, Mr Smith. We get called out to places like this all the time. Don't you find it a bit tawdry?'

'You didn't come here to critique my accommodation.'

'No.'

'And I have things to do. What do you want?'

The cop took out his phone and selected a picture. He slid it across the table. Milton looked at it; it was a picture of a woman, white, slender with a short-cropped elfin hairstyle. Very pretty. 'Recognise her?'

Milton looked at the picture. 'No.'

'You sure about that? Swipe right for the next one.'

Milton did as he was told. It was the same girl, this time in some sort of prom dress. She looked young. 'No,' he said. 'I've never seen her before. Who is she?'

'Her name is Miley Van Dyken.'

'I don't know her, detective.'

'Where were you three weeks ago last Wednesday?'

'I'd have to check.'

'Like I say, it's a Wednesday. Think.'

Milton sighed exasperatedly. 'I would've gone to work in the afternoon and driven my car at night.'

'We can check the afternoon. What about the night – can anyone prove you were driving?'

'If my calls were from the agency, then maybe. If they came straight through to me, then no, probably not.' He slid the phone back across the table to him. 'Who is she? Number three?'

'That's right, Mr Smith. We found her this morning. Same place as the other two.'

'There's only so many times I can say it – I've got nothing to do with this.'

'Can I ask you something else?'

'Please do.'

'You own any firearms?'

Milton felt his skin prickle. 'No.'

'So if we looked around, we wouldn't find anything?'

'Help yourself. I don't have anything to hide.'

'Reason I'm asking, that guard you put on the ground at the party, he said you took his gun from him. Smith & Wesson. Pro Series, 9mm – very nice gun.'

Milton concentrated on projecting a calm exterior. He had left the gun under the bed. It wasn't even well hidden, all they would need to do would be to duck down and look. 'No,' he said. 'I don't know anything about it. I don't own a gun. To be honest, I doubt I'd even know what to do with one.'

'All right, then.'

'Is that it?'

'No,' Webster said from the window. 'There is one more thing you can help us with.'

'Please.'

'When we spoke to you before, you said you came across the border from Mexico. Six months ago. February. That's right, isn't it?'

'Yes.'

'Where did you cross?'

Milton started to feel uncomfortable. 'Juárez into El Paso.'

'That's weird,' Webster said. 'You know, there are forty-six places where you can legally cross over from Mexico. We spoke with Immigration. We checked El Paso, Otay Mesa, Tecate, Nogales. Hell, we even tried Lukeville and Antelope Wells. We found a handful of John Smiths who came across the border around about then. That's no surprise, really, a common name like that, but the thing is – the thing I just can't get my head around is – that when we looked at their pictures, none of them looked anything like you.'

That, Milton thought, was hardly surprising. He had crossed the border illegally, trekking across country east of Juárez into the Chisos Mountains and then Big Bear National Park. The last thing he had wanted to do was leave a record that would show where he had entered the country. He had not been of a mind to give the agents pursuing him any clue at all as to his location.

'Mr Smith?' Webster and Cotton were eyeing him critically.

Milton shrugged. 'What do you want me to say to that?'

'Can you explain it?'

'I was working in Juárez. I crossed into El Paso. I can't explain why there's no record of it.'

'Do you mind if we take your passport for a couple of days?'

'Why?'

'We'd just like to have a look at it.'

Milton went over to the bedside table and took his passport from the drawer. He could see the dull glint of the brushed steel on the handgun, an inch from his toe. He handed the passport to Webster. 'There you are,' he said. 'I've got nothing to hide.'

'Thank you.'

'Anything else?'

'Nah,' Cotton said. 'We got nothing more for you now.'

'But don't leave town without telling us,' Webster advised. 'I'm pretty sure we'll want to talk to you again.'

31

Milton had a lock-up at Extra Space Storage at 1400 Folsom Street. He had hired it within a couple of days of arriving in San Francisco and deciding that it was the kind of town he could stay in for a few months. The lock-up was an anonymous place, a collection of industrial cargo crates that had been arranged in several rows. Each crate had been divided into two or four separate compartments, and each was secured with a thick metal door padlocked top and bottom.

It cost Milton twenty dollars a week, and it was easily worth that for the peace of mind that it bought. He knew, eventually, that Control would locate him again and send his agents to hunt him down. He didn't know how he would react to that when it happened – he had been ready to surrender in Mexico – but he wanted the ability to resist them if that was what he chose to do. More to the point, he knew that his assassination of *El Patrón* and the capture of his son would not be forgotten by La Frontera. There would be a successor to the old man's crown – a brother or another son – and then there would be vengeance. They would have put an enormous price on his head. If they managed to find him, he certainly did not want to be unprepared.

Milton took out his key and unfastened the locks. He checked again that he was alone in the facility and, satisfied that he was, opened the door. He had stocked the storage crate with everything he would need in an emergency. There was a change of clothes, a cap, a packet of hair dye and a pair of clear-lensed spectacles. There was a go-bag with three false passports and the money he had found at *El Patrón*'s super-lab before he had torched it. Five thousand dollars, various denominations, all used notes.

At the back of the crate, hidden beneath a blanket, was a Desert Eagle .50 Action Express with a picatinny rail. It had been *El Patrón*'s weapon, and like everything else in his comic-book life, it had been tricked out to clichéd excess. The gun was gold-plated with diamonds set into the butt. Milton had no idea how much it was worth – thousands, obviously – but he didn't really care about that. The semi-automatic was one of Milton's favourite weapons. It was gas-operated with a firing mechanism usually found in rifles as opposed to the more common short recoil or blowback designs. The mechanism allowed for far more powerful cartridges, and he had purchased a box of Speer 325-grain .50 AE ammunition for it the day after he had arrived in town. He tore back the cardboard and tipped the bullets onto the floor of the unit; they glittered in the light of the single naked bulb that had been fitted to the roof of the crate. Lethal little golden slugs.

Milton detached the magazine and thumbed seven into the slot.

He slid the Desert Eagle into his jeans, his belt pressing it against his skin. The golden barrel was icy cold, the frame flat against his coccyx. He filled his pockets with the rest of the bullets. He dropped the Smith & Wesson 9mm into the go-bag and slung it over his shoulder.

He shut and locked the crate.

He wouldn't be coming back again.

Things were already too hot for him in San Francisco. He hadn't been named in any of the newspaper reports that he had read about the missing girls, but that was probably just a matter of time. It was a little irrelevant, too; his name would have been recorded by the police, and Control would sniff that out soon enough. They could be here tomorrow or next week; there was no way of knowing when, except that they were coming. Under normal circumstances, he would have moved on already, but he didn't feel able to leave until he had tried a little harder to find Madison. Trip would have no chance without him, and besides, he had a lead now. He would find out what he could and then disappear beneath the surface again.

The Explorer was parked close to the entrance to the facility.

He nodded to the attendant and made his way out to his car.

* * *

A short detour first. Manny Martinez ran his operation out of a grocery shop in the Mission District, not far from Milton's place. Milton had called ahead to make an appointment, and when he arrived, he was ushered all the way to the back of the store. There was a small office with a desk and a computer. A clock on the wall. Martinez was a big man, wearing an old pair of cargo pants and a muscle top that showed off impressively muscled biceps and sleeves of tattoos on both arms. His head was shaved to a furze of rough hair, and he had a tattoo of a tear beneath his right eye. Prison ink. Milton checked the office; his eye fell on the cudgel with a leather strap that was hanging from a hook on the wall.

'You Smith?'

'That's right. Thank you for seeing me.'

'How much you want?'

'I don't want anything.'

'You said—'

'Yes, I know – and I'm sorry about that. It's something else.'

He sat up, flexing his big shoulders. 'That right?'

'One of your customers – Richie Grimes?'

'Yeah,' he said. 'I know Richie. Fucking reprobate. Drunk.'

'How much does he owe you?'

'What's it got to do with you?'

'I'd like to buy his debt.'

'Just like that?'

'Just like that.'

'What if I don't wanna sell?'

'Let me make you an offer – if you don't want to sell after that, that's fair enough.'

Martinez swivelled the chair so that he was facing the computer and clicked through a series of files until he found the one he wanted. 'He's in the hole for fifty-eight hundred. He wanted four, and the vig was ten per cent.'

'How'd you get to fifty-eight from there?'

'Compound interest, buddy. Interest on top of interest.'

'Hardly ethical.'

'*Ethical*? These are the streets, buddy. *Ethics* don't get much play here.'

'I'll give you five.'

Martinez shook his head. 'No.'

'Debt's only worth what someone'll pay for it.'

'What are you? An economist?'

'Five. That's a grand clear profit.'

'I can get seven.'

'Not from him.'

'Don't have to be from him, does it?'

The second hand on the clock swept around the dial. Milton opened his bag and reached for the stolen drug money inside. He would put it to good use. He took out the five bundles, each secured by an elastic band around twenty fifties, and put them on the desk.

'Five thousand. Come on, Mr Martinez – it's right there.'

Martinez looked up at him with an amused cast to his face. 'I said no.'

'What's the point in dragging this out? He's got nothing.'

'He told you that? Guy's an addict, like I said. You can't believe a thing they say.'

'I believe him,' Milton said. 'He can't pay.'

'Then he's got a problem.'

'Is that your final word?'

'That's right.'

Milton nodded. He picked up the money and put it back into his bag.

'Come back with seven, maybe we can talk.'

Milton looked at him, then the cudgel. He was a big man, but he was lounging back in his chair. He was relaxed. He didn't see Milton as a threat, but Milton could have killed him, right there and then. He could have done it before the second hand on the clock had skirted another semicircle between the nine and twelve. Fifteen seconds. He thought about it for a moment, but that wouldn't solve Richie's problem. The debts would be taken over by someone else, and that person might be worse. There would have to be another way.

'See you around,' Martinez said. A gold tooth in his mouth glittered as he grinned at him.

'You will,' Milton said.

* * *

Milton called Beau Baxter as he drove to the airport.

'Morning, English. What can I do for you?'

'Did you get a name for me?'

'I did. You got a pen and paper?'

'Go on.'

'You want to speak to Jarad Efron. You know who that is?'

'I've heard the name before.'

'Not surprising. He's a big noise on the tech scene.'

'Thanks. I'll find him.'

'Goes without saying that you need to leave the Italians out of this.'

'Of course. Thanks, Beau. I appreciate it.'

'Anything else?'

'There is, actually. One other thing.'

'Shoot.'

'Do our friends have an interest in the lending business?'

'They have interests in lots of things.'

'So I'll assume that they do. There's a loan shark in the Mission District. A friend of mine owes him money. I just made him a very generous offer to buy the debt.'

'And he turned you down?'

'Thinks he can get more.'

'And how could our friends help?'

'I get the impression that this guy's out there all on his own. A lone operator. I wondered, if that's something they're involved in, whether the competition is something they'd be happy about. You think you could look into it for me?'

'What's this dude's name?'

'Manny Martinez.'

'Never heard of him. I can ask around, see what gives. I'll let you know.'

Milton thanked him and said goodbye, ended the call and parked the Explorer. He took his go-bag and went into the terminal building. He found the Hertz desk and hired a Dodge Charger, using one of the false passports and paying the three hundred dollars in cash. He drove it into the long-stay car park, put the go-bag in the boot, locked it and then found his way back to the Explorer.

He felt better for the preparation. If he needed to get out of town on short notice, he could.

He put the car into gear and drove away.

There was someone he wanted to see.

32

The man was in his early forties, in decent shape, just a little under six foot tall and with the kind of naturally lean frame that has gone a little soft with the onset of middle age. He had dark hair with flecks of grey throughout it, and the expensive glasses he wore were borne a little uncomfortably. His clothes were neat and tidy – a crisp polo shirt, chinos and deck shoes – the whole ensemble marking him out as a little vain.

Milton had parked in the car park for thirty minutes, the angle good enough for him to see the place side on, and to see all the comings and goings. It was more like a campus than an office. It looked like a busy place. The car park was full, and there had been a steady stream of people going in to start their working day. He had been waiting for one man in particular, and now, here he was. Milton eyed him as he opened the passenger door of his red Ferrari Enzo and took out a rucksack.

Milton looked at the scrap of paper that he had stuck to the windscreen of the Explorer.

It was a picture.

The man in the Ferrari and the man in the picture were the same.

Jarad Efron.

Milton got out of his car, locked the door and followed the man as he exited the car park and started towards the office. The campus was in the hills outside Palo Alto, surrounded by a lush forest bisected by streams, hiking paths and mountain-bike trails. The wildness of the landscape had been transplanted here, too, with grasses and wildflowers allowed to grow naturally. Purple heather clustered around the paths, and coneflowers, evening primroses and asters sprouted from natural rock gardens. Milton quickened his pace so that he caught up with Efron and then overtook him. He gave him a quick sidelong glance: he had white iPhone earbuds pressed into his ears, something upbeat playing; his skin was tanned; his forehead was suspiciously plump and firm; and there was good muscle tone on his arms. He was gym fit.

Milton slowed a little and entered the lobby just behind him.

After he had spoken with Beau yesterday morning, he had spent the afternoon doing research. Three hours at the local library. They had free internet and cheap coffee there, and he had had plenty of things that he wanted to check.

Jarad Efron was familiar to him from the news, and a quick Google search filled in the details: the man was CEO of StrongBox, one of the survivors of the first dotcom bubble that had since staked a claim in the cloud storage market. He was a pioneer. The company owned a couple of massive data farms in South Carolina, acres of deserted farmland rammed full of servers that they rented out to consumers and, increasingly, to big tech companies who didn't want to build facilities of their own. They offered space to Netflix and Amazon, among others. The company was listed on the NASDAQ with a price of $54 per share. Another search revealed that Efron had recently divested himself of five per cent of the company, pocketing thirty million dollars. He still owned another two million shares.

A paper fortune of $108,000,000.

Milton looked around quickly, taking everything in. The lobby was furnished sparsely, minimally, but every piece of furniture – the leather sofas, the coffee table – looked exceedingly expensive. Two security guards wore light blue uniforms and well-shined shoes, big boys with a stiff posture. They both had holstered .45s hanging from their belts. The staff behind the reception desk looked like models from a high-end catalogue, with glossy, airbrushed skin and preternaturally bright eyes.

Milton knew he only had one opportunity at this, and straightening his back and squaring off his shoulders, he followed right alongside Efron as the man beamed a bright smile of greeting to the girls and headed for the lifts. One of the girls looked past him at Milton, a moment of confusion breaking across her immaculate face, but Milton anticipated it and shone out a smile that matched Efron's for brightness and confidence. Her concern faded, and even if it was with a little uncertainty, she smiled right back at him.

Milton dropped back again and let Efron summon a lift. There were six doors; one of the middle ones opened with a pleasant chime, and Efron went inside.

Milton stepped forwards sharply and entered the lift as the doors were starting to close.

'Which floor?' Efron asked him absently.

Milton looked: ten floors, and Efron had hit the button for the tenth.

'Five, please.'

Efron pressed the button and stood back against the wall, leaving plenty of space between them.

The doors closed quietly, and the lift began to ascend.

Milton waited until they were between the second and third floors and hit the emergency stop.

The lift shuddered and came to a halt.

'What are you doing?' Efron protested.

'I've got a few questions. Answer them honestly.'

'Who are you?'

Efron's arm came up and made a sudden stab towards the button for the intercom. Milton anticipated it, blocked his hand away with his right, and then, in the same circular motion, jackhammered his elbow backwards into Efron's gut. It was a direct hit, just at the right spot to punch out all the air in his lungs, and he staggered back against the wall of the lift with his hands clasped impotently to his sternum, gasping for breath. Milton grabbed the lapels of his jacket, knotted his fists into the fabric and heaved Efron backwards and up, slamming him into the wall so that his feet were momentarily off the ground. Then he dropped him.

'Hello?' said a voice through the intercom speakers.

Efron landed on his behind, gasping. Milton lowered himself to the same height, barred his forearm across the man's throat and pressed, gently.

'It's in your best interests to talk to me.'

'They'll call . . . the police.'

'Probably better for you if they didn't. The police are going to want to talk to you soon anyway, but you'll do better with a little time to prepare. If they show up now, they'll ask me what I was doing here. And I'm going to tell them all about the party you had in Pine Shore.'

'What party?'

'I was there, Mr Efron. I drove Madison Clarke. You remember – the missing girl? I went inside. I saw it all. The drugs. The people. I recognised some of them. I have an eye for detail, Mr Efron, and I have a very good memory. You want the police to know that? The press? I know a man like you, in your position, you definitely don't want this in the papers. Bad publicity. It'd be a scandal, wouldn't it? So we can speak to them if you want – go right ahead. I'll wait.'

Milton could see him working out the angles, a frown settling over his handsome face.

'Fuck,' he cursed angrily, but it was from frustration backed by resignation; there was no fight there.

'Better sort that out.' Milton indicated the intercom. 'You hit the button by mistake. Tell them it's all right.'

He stood aside.

Efron's breath was still a little ragged. He pushed the button to speak. 'It's Jarad,' he said. 'I pressed the wrong button. Sorry. Can you reset it, please?'

'Yes, sir,' the girl said.

The lift started to rise again.

It reached the fifth floor. The doors opened, no one got on, the doors closed and the lift continued upwards.

'Is your office on the tenth?'

'Yes.'

'We'll go inside and shut the door. Don't do anything stupid, and I'll be gone in five minutes.'

They reached the tenth floor, and the doors opened again. Efron stepped out first, and Milton followed. The floor must have been reserved for StrongBox's executive team. Milton looked around. The big lobby was bright, daylight streaming in through huge floor-to-ceiling windows. One of the windows was open, leading out to a terrace area. The room was airy and fresh, very clean, the furniture and décor obviously chosen with great care and a generous budget. Efron led the way to an office with a wide picture window that framed the gorgeous landscape beyond: the deep green of the vegetation, the brown flanks of the distant mountains, infinite blue sky and crisp white clouds. There was a leather sofa, and Milton indicated that Efron should sit. He did as he was told. Milton shut the office door and sat on the edge of the desk.

'Don't get too comfortable,' Efron said. 'You're not staying.'

'You better hope not. Tell me what I want to know, and I'll be on my way.'

'What's your name?'

'You can call me Smith.'

'So what do you want?'

'Just to find the girl.'

'What girl?'

'The girl who went missing after the party.'

'I really have no idea what you're talking about.'

'Playing dumb is just going to mean this takes longer, Mr Efron. And I'm not the most patient man in the world.'

'What's her name?'

'Madison Clarke.'

His shrug didn't quite mask a flicker of disquiet. 'I don't know anyone by that name.'

'But you own a house in Pine Shore.'

'No, I don't. The *company* owns it. We're expanding. Hiring a lot of new talent. Time to time, we have new executives stay there while they're looking for places of their own. It's not mine.'

'There was a party there.'

'Okay. So there was a party there. Your point?'

'Madison is a prostitute. She was hired to be there.'

'You're fucking crazy. We're gearing up for an IPO. Do you know how stupid it'd be to invite a hooker onto company property?'

'You weren't there?'

'I was in Boston.'

'That's strange.'

'Come on, man. Enough with this shit!'

'No, it's strange, Mr Efron, because you hired her.'

'What?'

Milton saw him swallow.

'I didn't!'

'You've never used Fallen Angelz?'

'No.'

'Yes, you have. You paid, in advance, with a credit card registered to your company.'

He was starting to panic. 'Someone used a StrongBox credit card?' he gasped. 'So? Maybe they did. Lots of people have a company card.'

'Including you?'

'Of course. I'm the CEO. But it wasn't me.'

'I thought you might say that, Mr Efron, so I did a little extra checking. The things you find out when you speak to the right people, know what I mean? Here's what I know: I know it's not the first time you've used that agency. I know you're a valued customer. One of the regulars. I know the girls speak highly of you. A good payer, they said. A nice guy.'

He swallowed again, harder.

It was a bluff. Milton looked at Efron, setting aside the bland mask and letting him see him as he really was: a seasoned, iron-willed operative. 'Now,' he said. 'Bearing that all in mind, you want to reconsider?'

'Okay.'

'Okay what?'

'Okay, yes. I hired her. All right?'

'Better. Keep going. And you were there.'

'Yes.'

'You saw her.'

'Only briefly. I was hosting.'

'What happened to make her so upset?'

'I didn't know she was – not until afterwards.'

'You know she hasn't been seen since the party?'

'Yes – but only because the police said.'

'Have they spoken to you?'

'Not to me, but to a couple of guys who work for me. We said it was their party, and that's how it needs to stay. The IPO is everything, man. I got three hundred people working here. Their jobs depend on getting it right. If I get involved in a scandal now, we'll have to pull it.'

'I don't care about that, Mr Efron. I just want to find out what happened to Madison.'

'And I told you I don't know.'

'Someone who was there does know.'

'Maybe it was nothing to do with the party at all.'

'Give me a list of the people who were there.'

'You're kidding?' He shook his head. 'No way.'

'Last chance. Don't make me ask you again.'

'I can't do that.'

Milton got up and walked straight at Efron. The man scrabbled backwards, into the chair, and held up his hands to ward him away. Milton swatted them aside, hauled him out of the chair and dragged him across the room to the terrace. He struggled, guessing what Milton had in mind, but his right arm was jacked up behind his back with the fingers splayed, almost pointing all the way up. The more he tried to free himself, the harder Milton pushed his palm, flattening it, each added ounce of pressure closer to breaking Efron's wrist and fingers.

'Last chance.'

'I can't tell you.'

'Your choice.'

Milton shoved him up against the wooden balustrades, the rail at waist height, then forced him over it until his feet were raised off the floor. He fixed his right hand in the waistband of Efron's trousers, locking his bicep to bear the weight, and used his left to press him down. Efron's head went almost vertical, looking straight into the ten-storey drop.

Milton kept his voice calm. 'Who was there?'

'Jesus!'

'Who was there, Jarad?'

'Shit, man, please! I'll tell you, *I'll fucking tell you!*'

* * *

Milton took the lift back down to the ground floor. He had a sheet of A4 paper that Efron had printed for him; he halved it, then quartered it and slipped it into his inside pocket. He waited patiently as the lift descended, the floors ticking off with the same pleasant chime as before. He reached the ground floor, and the doors parted. He wasn't particularly surprised to see the two security guards waiting for him.

'It's all right, boys,' he said. 'No need for any trouble. Your boss is fine, and I'm leaving.'

They each had their hands resting on the butts of their identical Colt .45s.

'Don't move,' the nearest one ordered. He was a big boy – bigger than Milton – and stood with the kind of lazy confidence that a guy gets from being young, a little stupid, six-three and two-ten. The other one had a similar stance: quarterback type, jock, used to getting whatever he wanted. At that age, Milton thought, they'd probably tried out for the police but been shit-canned because they weren't bright enough. They didn't fancy shipping out to the desert in the army, so private security was their best chance to wear a uniform – they probably thought they looked cute doing it – and to wield a little authority.

'You sure you want to do this?'

'Turn around.'

Milton shrugged, made it look like he was resigned to doing as they asked, but as he turned he flung out his right hand in a streaked blur of motion, his fingers held straight with his thumb supporting them beneath. The jab caught the first guard above the larynx, hard and sharp enough to dent his windpipe; he fell backwards, his mouth open in a wide 'O' of surprise, his hands flapping impotently, gasping for breath that wasn't getting into his lungs as easily as it had done before. The second man went for his holstered .45. Milton hit him high on the cheekbone with his right fist, rocking him back, fired in a left jab, then shoved the guy in the chest to bounce him off the wall, and as he came back toward him, he delivered a headbutt straight to his nose. He caught the man's wrist in his hand, yanked his arm around and pivoted so that all of his weight propelled him back into the lift. He bounced face-first off the wall of the lift and landed on his knees. Milton caught the second man by the belt and collar and boosted him into the lift after his friend, reaching around the corner and slapping the button for the tenth floor.

'Tell your boss if he does anything stupid like that again, I'll be back.'

He stepped back as the doors closed and the lift began to ascend.

Then he turned. The two receptionists and the handful of staff in the lobby were all gawping helplessly at him. Milton pulled at his jacket to straighten it out, squared his shoulders again, wished them all a good morning and then walked calmly and purposefully into the car park to his car.

33

Arlen Crawford sat at the desk in the hotel room with policy papers scattered around him. There was a stack on the desk, three distinct piles on the carpet by his feet, and a pile – ready to be read, digested and sorted – spread out across the bed. The speech at the Moscone Center that afternoon was starting to look a whole lot like a coronation, and he wanted to make sure that everything about it was perfect. He had *CNN* on the flat-screen TV that had been fixed to the wall inside a frame to make it look like a painting – it didn't work – and he was drinking from a glass of orange juice, staining a paper on fiscal prudence with wet, concentric circles.

He looked up at the TV. The newscaster was introducing a panel discussion on the San Francisco killings. A third girl had been found and the show featured three specialists who had been brought on to discuss the case. They discussed the findings so far, agreeing that the police didn't appear to have very much to go on. Eventually, and egged on by the host, they diverted to a discussion about the name that should be given to the killer. They looked back through history: BTK,

Zodiak, the Green River Killer, and settled on the Headlands Lookout Killer.

Crawford was roused from his distraction by a soft knocking at the door.

He got up, took a sip of the orange juice and padded across the room in his stockinged feet. It was just after breakfast, and he wasn't expecting anyone.

He opened the door. Karly Hammil, the young female staffer who had been with Robinson after the speech in Woodside, was on the other side.

'What is it, Karly?'

She was anxiously chewing her bottom lip. 'Could I have a word?'

'Yes, of course. Come in.'

He stood back, and she came into the room, closing the door behind her.

'What is it?'

'This is difficult, Mr Crawford.'

'Call me Arlen.' He felt a moment of apprehension. He pointed to the opened minibar. 'You want anything? Water?'

'No, I'm fine.'

'Want to sit?'

'I'd rather stand if that's all right.'

'Well, I'm going to sit.'

She stammered. 'I-I—'

She was nervous, and that made him nervous, too.

'You better tell me what it is.'

She drew a breath. 'There's no point sugar-coating this, I guess. All right, then. Okay.' Another breath. 'Okay. I guess you know some of this already. Five weeks ago, the governor made a sexual advance to me. I know he has a reputation, everyone knows that, but I couldn't believe it. And I resisted it at first; I told him to forget about it, it was a crazy idea, but then he tried again the day after that. I told him no again, but he was more persistent. You know what he can be like, so persuasive, that feeling you get when he fixes his attention on you, like you're the most important person in the world. Well, that's what he made me feel like, and he persuaded me that he really meant all those things he was telling me.'

Crawford felt himself deflate, the air running from his lungs.

'We've been sleeping together once or twice a week ever since.'

'You *have been* – this is past tense?'

'He's stopped it. I saw him last night after the speech. He said he couldn't do it anymore. Something about his wife. It's bullshit, obviously. I guess he's just had what he wanted. He doesn't need me anymore. He's probably already onto the next one.'

Crawford tried to marshal himself. He needed to deal with this. He needed to be diplomatic. He needed her to think that he was sympathetic and understanding. He had experience with this kind of motherfucking nonsense – *plenty* of experience – and he knew what he needed to do. 'I'm sure it isn't like that, Karly. You know what he's like.'

'He's unsafe for a woman to work around is what he is,' she said angrily.

'Why are you telling me? What do you want me to do?'

She looked at him as if he was stupid. '*Seriously?*'

'Tell me.'

'You need to look after me.'

'Of course you'll be looked after. I'll make sure you get an apology. And it'll never happen again.'

'Not like *that.*'

'Then like what?'

'Come on, Mr Crawford. You want me to spell it out?'

'Money?'

'Maybe I should sit tight, wait until he's better known. A story like this, what kind of book deal do you reckon I'd get if I waited until later? His inauguration, maybe? The day before the election?'

Crawford felt the familiar, cold knot of anger tightening in his gut. 'All right, I get it. I get it. How much do you want?'

'I don't know.'

'You have to give me a number.'

'Okay. Fifty thousand – that's what I would've earned this year.'

'Fifty.' He felt his temperature rising.

She hesitated uncertainly. 'What do we do now?'

'First time you've shaken somebody down?' he spat sarcastically.

Her eyes flashed. 'You're angry with *me*? Maybe you ought to think a little about him, Mr Crawford.'

He tried to defuse the tension. 'Arlen – call me Arlen, please.'

She ignored the attempt at conciliation. 'You don't know how close I was to putting this out there. A man like him, a weak man – how is that good for our country to have him in high office?'

Crawford forced himself to take a breath, to regain a little composure. 'No, you're right. Quite right. I'm sorry, Karly. It'll take me a little while to sort this out. It's not quite as straight-forward as you think, that much money. It needs to be done quietly. Is that all right?'

'Of course.'

She exhaled.

He had a moment of empathy; it had probably been one of the most difficult conversations she had ever had. She didn't deserve his anger. It wasn't her fault. Robinson, on the other hand, *did* deserve it. His behaviour kept putting him in intolerable situations. Robinson was irresponsible and child-ish, ignoring his clear instructions that he had to put this behind him and keep it zipped. Cleaning up the mess that he left in his wake was becoming a full-time job. An *expen-sive* full-time job.

Crawford told the girl that she just had to be patient, that he would sort it all out for her, and then he showed her to the door of his room. He switched channels on the television, lay back on his bed and stared at the ball game that was playing on repeat for five minutes, not paying any attention to it, running the situation around in his head and wondering if there was any other way it could be resolved.

He decided that there was not.

He picked up his phone from the bedside table and called the usual number.

34

Milton was headed to the Moscone Center when his mobile buzzed in its cradle. He glanced at the display; Trip Macklemore was calling. He pulled out of the traffic, parked and called him back.

'Have you heard?' Trip said as soon as he accepted the call.

'Heard what?'

'They've found another body – it's on the news.'

'It isn't Madison.'

'How do you know that?'

'The police turned up again.'

'You're kidding?'

'It's just routine. It's nothing.'

'It might not be her now, but it's just a matter of time, isn't it? You know that – she'll be next.'

'We don't know that.'

'*I* do.'

Milton thought he could hear traffic on the call. 'Where are you?'

'In a cab. I'm going up there.'

'What for?'

'To see Brady.'

'No, Trip—'

'Yes, Mr Smith. He did it. It's fucking obvious. It's *him*. We know he's been lying to us right from the start. What else has he been lying about? I'm gonna make him admit it.'

'How are you going to do that?'

'It's all right. I'll take it from here.'

Milton gripped the wheel. 'Don't,' he said. 'Turn around and come back. We just need to wait. Getting into an argument up there will make things worse.'

'I'm sick of waiting. Nothing's happening. They're not doing shit.'

Milton was about to tell him about Efron and what he had learnt, but the call went dead.

He redialled, but there was no answer.

Dammit.

The boy had sounded terrible, wired, his voice straining with stress, as if at his breaking point. Milton had to stop him before he did something stupid, something that would wreck his life. He put the Explorer into gear, pulled out into traffic and swung around.

He drove as fast as he dared. Trip was already on the way. Where was he? The traffic was mercifully light as he accelerated across the Golden Gate Bridge, and it stayed clear all the way to the turning onto Tiburon Boulevard. He swung to the south, still clear, and reached Pine Shore without seeing the boy.

He drove inside the gates. There was an outside-broadcast truck parked across the pavement and a reporter delivering a piece to a camera. Great, Milton thought. He was hoping the media would all have moved on by now, but the new body had juiced the story again, and with the police still floundering, they were going to focus on the place where the next presumed victim went missing. There was nothing else for them to go on.

An empty San Francisco cab was coming the other way.

Too late?

Milton parked outside Brady's cottage and hurried up the steps. The door was ajar, and he could hear raised voices from inside.

He made out two bellowed words: '*Tell me!*'

He pushed the door and quickly followed the corridor through into the living room. Brady was on one side of the room, next to the wide window with the view down to the bay. Trip was opposite him.

'I know she was in here!' Trip said, angrily stabbing a finger at the doctor.

'No, she wasn't.'

'Don't fucking lie to me!'

'Get out of my house!'

'I'm not going anywhere. What did you do to her?'

Milton was behind Trip, and it was Brady who noticed him first. 'Get this meathead out of here,' he ordered. 'You got ten seconds, or I'm calling the cops.'

'Go ahead and call them,' Trip thundered back at him. 'Maybe they'll finally ask *you* some questions.'

'I've told you – I had nothing to do with whatever it was that happened to your girlfriend. You know what? Maybe you want to stop harassing me and start thinking that maybe if you'd done something to stop her from going out hooking, then none of this would have happened.'

That really pushed Trip's buttons; he surged forward, knocking a chair out of the way. Brady's face registered stark fear as Trip raised his fist and drilled him in the mouth. The doctor stumbled backwards, overbalanced and slammed against the low wooden coffee table, the impact snapping one table leg and tipping a fruit bowl onto the floor.

'Where is she?' Trip yelled.

Brady shuffled away from him on the seat of his pants. 'I don't know,' he stammered, blood dribbling out of the corner of his mouth.

'Trip!' Milton said. 'Calm down.'

'Fuck that. What's that got us so far? Nothing. We need to *do* something.'

'We are doing something.'

'Yeah? What are you doing? I don't see anything happening. Doing things your way hasn't got us anywhere, has it? It's my turn now. I'm telling you, man, this piece of shit is going to tell me what happened to my girl.'

The boy reached down with his right hand, and Milton saw, just in time, the glint of silver that emerged from the darkness of his half-open jacket. He thrust his own arm out, his hand fastening around Trip's wrist.

'No,' the boy said, struggling, and he was young and strong, but Milton knew all kinds of things that the boy could only dream about, and he slid his index and forefinger around to the inside of his arm, down until it was two fingers up from the crease of his wrist, and squeezed. The pressure point was above the median nerve, and Milton applied just enough torque to buckle the boy's knees with the unexpected shock.

'Don't,' Milton said, looking at him with sudden, narrow-eyed aggression.

Trip gritted his teeth through the blare of pain. 'He did it.'

Milton kept the pressure on, impelling Trip back towards the hallway. 'No, he didn't.'

He looked at Milton in fuming, helpless entreaty. 'Then who did?'

'I have a better idea,' he said.

Confusion broke through the pain on the boy's face. 'Who?'

'You're going to go outside now,' Milton said in a firm voice that did not brook disobedience. 'There's a reporter out there, down the road, so you need to be calm, like nothing's going on – we don't want there to be a scene. Understand?'

'*Who* is it?'

'I'll tell you on the way back. But you have to tell me you understand. Do you understand?'

Trip's eyes were red-raw, scoured and agitated. He looked as if he had gone without sleep. 'Fine.'

Milton gave him the keys to the car. 'I'll be right after you.'

'What are you going to do?'

'Just go.'

Milton waited until he heard the squeak of the front door as Trip opened it.

He went across the room and offered a hand to Brady. The man took it, and Milton helped him back to his feet.

Brady went to the galley kitchen, picked up a dishcloth and mopped the blood from his face. 'If you think that's the end of this, you're out of your mind.'

'It *is* the end of it,' Milton said.

'You saw – he sucker-punched me!'

'I know, and he's sorry he did that. So am I. I know you've got nothing to do with what happened to Madison.'

'Damn straight I don't.'

'But I also know that it's better for you to forget that just happened and move on.'

'You reckon? I don't think so.'

'I do. A friend of mine works for St Francis. Legal department. You said you used to work down there, so I thought maybe it was worth getting her to have a look into your record, see if it stacked up like you said it did. And it turns out you have a pretty thick personnel file there.'

'How dare you—'

'Here's what I know: you didn't choose to leave, you were *asked* to go. Two sexual harassment cases. The first one was a nurse, right?'

Brady scowled at him, but said nothing.

'And the second one was a technician. She had to be persuaded from going to the police. You had to pay her a lot of money, didn't you?' Milton was next to the picture of Brady in the desert; he picked it up and made a show of examining it. 'It was an interesting read, Dr Brady. You want me to go on?'

'Get out,' Brady said.

* * *

Trip was waiting in the car. Milton leant across towards him and used his right hand to reach inside his coat. His fingers touched the butt of a small gun. He pulled it out. It was a .25 calibre semi-auto, a Saturday Night Special. Milton slipped the gun into his own pocket.

'You're an idiot,' Milton said. '*What* were you thinking?'

Trip stared out of the window. 'I had to do something,' he said with a surly inflection that made Milton think how young he really was. 'Someone had to do something.'

'And so you were going to threaten him with a gun?'

'You got a better plan?'

'You would've gone to prison.'

'I don't care.'

'Yes, you do. And so do I. And anyway, it would all have been for nothing; he didn't do it.'

The boy frowned, confused. 'How do you know that?'

'Brady is a talker. He likes to be the centre of attention. He has enemies in the neighbourhood, too, and maybe those enemies like other people to believe that he's up to no good. Victor Leonard and Brady hate each other. If you ask me, Leonard put us onto Brady because he wants to see him in trouble. But Brady's got nothing to do with this. If he's guilty of anything, it's being a fantasist and a braggart.'

'I don't buy that,' Trip said, although Milton could see that he was getting through to him.

'So are you going to let me drive you back into town?'

'You said you had something.'

'I do. I have a very good lead.'

'What do you mean?'

'I think I know what happened to Madison.'

35

Arlen Crawford drove around the block three times until he was sure that he was not being followed. It was an abundance of caution, perhaps, but Crawford was an operator, experienced enough to know all the tricks. He knew staffers who had been tailed before, heading to meet a friendly journalist to leak something explosive, only to find that their meeting was photographed and reported, and before they knew it, *they* were the story, not the leak. There was no way that he was going to let that happen to him. He was too good. And the consequences didn't bear thinking about.

Not for this.

The guys operated out of a warehouse in Potrero Hill. It was a low-slung building in the centre of a wide compound surrounded by a perimeter of ten-foot-high wire. Floodlights stood on pylons, and there were security cameras all over. The warehouse was owned by a company that distributed beer, and the compound housed three trucks. Empty kegs had been stacked against the wall of the warehouse, and next to that, four big motorcycles had been parked. An old Cadillac Eldorado had been slotted alongside the bikes.

Crawford drew up against the compound gate and sounded his horn. The single black eye of the security camera gleamed down at him, regarding him, and then there was the buzz of a motor and a rusty scrape as the gate slid aside. Crawford put the car into gear and edged inside. He parked next to the Caddy and went into the warehouse. The main room had been fitted with comfortable chairs, a large television and a sound system that was playing stoner rock. The place smelt powerfully of stale beer; it was strong enough that Crawford felt like gagging.

The four men were arranged around the room. Their leader was a tall, skinny man with prison tattoos visible on every inch of exposed skin. There was a swastika etched onto the nape of his neck, just below the line of his scalp. His name was Jack Kerrigan, but they all referred to him as Smokey. Crawford had been introduced to him by Sidney Packard, their head of security. He had recommended him and his boys as a solution for problems that could only be solved with the radical measures that they could implement. Strong-arm jobs, pressure that needed exerting to shut people up or to get them to do things that they naturally didn't want to do. The others were cut from the same cloth as Kerrigan: tattoos, lank hair worn long, a lot of greasy denim.

Kerrigan got up and stretched, leonine, before sauntering across to him.

'Mr Crawford,' he said, a low Southern drawl.

'Jack.'

The air was heady with dope smoke; Crawford noticed a large glass bong on the table.

'How's our boy doing?'

'He's doing good.'

'Good enough to get it done?'

'He'll win,' Crawford said. 'Provided we keep him on the right track.'

'That's all that matters.'

Crawford nodded at that, then scowled a little; he had forgotten the headache he had developed the last time they had dragged him out here. It was the dope, the droning music, the dull grind of the necessity of making sure the dumbfuck rednecks stayed on the right path.

'Wanna beer?'

'No, thanks.'

He nodded at the bong. 'Smoke?'

'What do you think?'

'Nah, not your scene. All business today, then. I can work with that. What's up?'

'We've got a problem.'

'If you mean the girls – I told you, you need to stop worrying.'

'That's easy for you to say.'

'I have a little update on that, something that'll make you feel better.' Kerrigan stooped to a fridge and took out a bottle of beer. He offered it to Crawford. 'You sure?'

'No,' he said impatiently. 'What update?'

Kerrigan popped the top with an opener fixed to his keychain and took a long swig.

'What is it, Jack?'

'Got someone who knows someone in the police. Friend of our persuasion, you know what I mean. Fellow soldier. This guy says that they have no clue. Those girls have been out there a long time – all that salty air, the animals, all that shit – there's barely anything left of them.'

'Clothes?'

'Sure, but there's nothing that would give them any idea who they were.'

'I wish I shared your confidence, Jack. What about the others?'

'You know, I can't rightly recall how many there were, and I ain't kidding about that.'

'*Four.*'

'It'll be the same. You might not believe it, but we were careful.'

'They're all in the same place.'

'Give or take.'

'You think that's careful?'

'The way I see it, the way we left them girls, all in that spot and all done up the same way, police are gonna put two and two together and say that there's one of them serial killers around and about, doing his business.'

'I heard that on the TV already,' one of the other men, Jesse, chimed in. 'They had experts on, pontificating types. They said they was sure. Serial killer. They was saying Zodiac's come back.'

'Son of Zodiac,' Kerrigan corrected.

Crawford sighed.

'They're gonna say it's some john from the city, someone the girls all knew.'

'The Headlands Lookout Killer. That's what they're saying.'

'Exactly,' Kerrigan said with evident satisfaction. 'And that's what we want them to think.' He took a cigarette from a pack on the table and lit it. 'It's unfortunate about our boy's habits, but if there's one thing we got lucky on, it's who they all were. What they did. In my experience, most hookers don't have anyone waiting for them at home to report them missing. They're in the shadows. Chances are, whoever those girls were, no one's even noticed that they're gone. How are the police going to identify people that they don't know is missing? They ain't. No way on earth. And if they can't identify them, how the hell they gonna tie 'em all back to our boy?'

'I don't know,' Crawford said impatiently.

'I do – I do know. They *ain't*.' Kerrigan said it with a sly leer. 'Make you feel any better?'

'Oh, yes,' Crawford replied, making no effort to hide his sarcasm. 'I can't tell you how relieved I am. I would've felt even better if you'd done what I asked you to and made them all *disappear*.'

'What happened to them, Mr Crawford, it's the same thing. They are disappeared. You've got to relax, man. You're gonna give yourself a coronary if you keep worrying about stuff that don't warrant no worrying about.'

'Someone has to.'

'Fine.' Kerrigan took another long pull of his beer. 'You worry about it as much as you want, but I'm telling you, there ain't no need for it.' He finished the beer and tossed it into an open bin. 'Now then – you didn't come here to bitch and moan at us. What can we do for you?'

'There's another problem.'

'Same kind of problem as before?'

'The exact same kind.'

Kerrigan shook his head. 'Seriously? Number five? You want to get our boy to keep his little man in his trousers.'

'You think I haven't tried? It's not as easy as you think.'

'Who is it? Another hooker?'

'No, not this time. Worse. She's on staff. He's been schtupping her for a month, and now she's trying to shake us down. We either pay up, or she goes public. One or the other. It couldn't be any more damaging.'

'And paying her wouldn't work?'

'What do you think?'

Kerrigan's greasy hair flicked as he shook his head. 'Nah – that ain't the best outcome. She might get a taste for it. You want her gone?'

There it was – the power of life and death in the palm of his hand. It still gave Crawford chills. And what choice did he have? Joseph Jack Robinson II, for all his faults, was still the medicine that America needed. He was the best chance of correcting the god-almighty mess that the country had become, and if that meant that they had to clean up his messes to keep him aimed in the right direction, then that was what they would have to do. It was distasteful, but it was for the greater good. The needs of the many against the needs of the few.

'Sort it,' he said.

'Same as before. No problem.'

'No, Jack. *Not* the same as before. Make it so she disappears. Properly disappears. This stuff on the news—'

'I'm telling you, that was just bad luck is what that was.'

'No, Jack, it's fucking amateur hour, *that's* what it was. I never want to hear about her again. Not next week. Not next month. Not when some mutt puts its snout into a bush on the beach next fucking year. You get me? *Never.*'

'Sure I do.' Kerrigan fixed him with gimlet eyes, and Crawford remembered what the man was capable of; the man was a snake – venomous, lethal – and like a snake, he needed careful handling. 'You got her details? We'll get looking into it right away.'

36

'Thank you so much. Thank you all very, very much. Thank you all. I can't tell you how wonderful that makes me feel.'

The crowd roared. Robinson took the applause, raising his arm above his head and waving broadly, shining his high-beam smile out over the adoring crowd. He walked across to the right-hand side of the stage, paused to bask in the acclaim – occasionally pointing out people in the crowd who he recognised, or those who he wanted to give the impression that he recognised – and then came back to the left, repeating the trick.

Milton was almost entirely apolitical, a personal choice he had made so that he was able to carry out his orders dispassionately and without regard to the colour of the government that he was serving, but even he could feel the electricity in the air. The woman next to him was glassy-eyed and a little unsteady on her feet. The man at her side was booming out the three syllables of Robinson's name with no regard to what the others around him might think (not that it mattered; they were just as fervent as he was). The air thrummed with excitement. It was close to mania.

Robinson came down the steps. A path had been arranged right down the centre of the hall, maintained on either side by metal railings that slotted together to form a barrier. There were photographers there, their cameras ready to take a thousand snaps of the governor in the midst of his people.

Milton knew he would only have one chance to get at him, and he had to move fast. He pushed his way to the front of the crowd, muscling through the throng until he was pressed up against the barrier. Robinson was ten feet away, the crowd swelling until Milton was squeezed even tighter against the metal. He thrust his elbow back to free his right arm and extended it out, over the guardrail, bending his usually inexpressive face into a smile. 'Great speech, Governor.'

'Thank you, sir.'

Robinson bathed him in that brilliant smile and took his hand, emphasising the gesture by placing his left on top of Milton's right. A nearby camera flashed, white streaks blasting across his eyes.

Milton maintained his own smile.

He tightened his grip.

He leant in even closer.

'I need to speak to you, Governor.'

A flicker of concern. 'I'm afraid I'm a little busy.'

Milton didn't release his hand.

'And you need to talk to me. It's very important.'

Robinson tried to pull his hand away, but Milton just tightened his grip, taking the strain easily.

Robinson took his left hand away and tugged again with his right. 'Let go.'

Milton did not. The governor's expression mutated; the fixed grin and the sparkle in his eyes were both washed away by a sudden flush of fear. The security man in the suit, less than five paces away, had noticed what was happening. He started to close in. Milton guessed he had a couple of seconds.

'I know about you and Madison Clarke.'

The fear in Robinson's eyes was subtly altered. It graduated from an immediate fear, a response to the physical threat of the smiling man with the cold eyes who wouldn't let go of his hand, to a deeper fear, more primal, more fundamental, one that required calculation to properly assess.

Milton could see him begin to make that calculation.

'Let go of the governor's hand,' the man in the suit said.

Milton held on.

His mouth was inches from Robinson's ear.

'I *know*, Governor. You need to talk to me. Your campaign is going to end tomorrow if you don't.'

37

Arlen Crawford followed the governor into the back of the building. He was worried. He had seen the man to whom Robinson had been speaking. It could only have been a short conversation, a handful of words, but whatever had been said had spooked Robinson badly. Normally, after a speech that had been as well received as that one had been, the governor would have been exhilarated, anxiously seeking the redundant confirmation from Crawford that it had gone as well as it had appeared. He would have soaked up the acclaim. This was different; his eyes were haunted, there was a sheen of light sweat across his brow, and the tic in his cheek that was only noticeable when he was nervous had started to twitch uncontrollably.

Crawford hurried to catch up. 'What did he say?'

'Something about me and Madison.'

'What about her?'

'That *he knows*, Arlen. He knows about me and her. He said I needed to talk to him, and if I don't, he'll end the campaign.'

Crawford's stomach immediately felt empty. 'Let me handle it.'

'No. Not this time.'

Robinson walked quickly through a service corridor. Crawford had trouble keeping up with him.

'He's a crank. We've had them before, and there'll be more and more of them the better we're doing. Please, sir – let *me* speak to him first. If it's anything we need to worry about, I'll let you know. You speaking to him now is just asking for trouble.'

'No, Arlen.'

'We don't even know who he is!'

'We'll do it in private, out back. I want to hear what he has to say. I don't want you reporting it back to me, pulling your punches – you do that all the time.'

Crawford trailed after him. 'I don't understand. Why are you so worried about him?'

'I told you before – I still don't know what happened with me and Madison.'

'It was nothing.'

'No, Arlen, it was. She just stopped taking my calls. One day, it was great; the next, nothing. It was out of character. I never got an explanation.'

'We spoke about that. It was for the best. If it came out . . . you and her . . . a prostitute . . . Jesus, J.J., that would sink us for good. There's no coming back from a story like that.'

Robinson stopped abruptly and turned to him. 'Do you know what happened to her?'

Crawford took a quick breath and covered his discomfort with a vigorous shake of his head. 'No, sir, I don't. But we've been lucky so far. No one has said anything about the two of you. I just don't see the point in pushing it.'

'Noted.'

'So you'll let me handle this?'

'No. I want to speak to him.'

Robinson pushed through wide double doors and into the kitchen that served the conference centre. The doors banged back against Crawford's shoulders as he followed in his wake. It was a large space, full of scratched and dented metallic work surfaces, large industrial ovens and burners, walk-in fridges and freezers, dinged pots and pans hanging down on racks suspended from the ceiling. Chefs in grubby white jackets were preparing the lunch that would be enjoyed by the governor's guests. The space was filled with noise, warm aromas and clouds of steam.

Robinson walked right into the middle of the busy chaos; the man to whom he had been speaking was waiting for them at the edge of the room, standing next to the two security guards who had brought him back here. Crawford hurried in his wake, straining for a better glimpse of his interlocutor.

He didn't recognise the man. He was a little over six feet tall and slender, at least when compared to the muscular security on either side of him. He had dark hair and a scar across his face. A cruel mouth. His eyes were blue, crystal blue, and they were cold and calm. There was something unsettling about him. He looked perfectly composed, a centre of calm in the frantic activity that clattered and whirled around him. He wasn't fazed by the guards. He wasn't fazed by the governor, either.

'What's your name, sir?' Robinson asked him.

'John Smith.'

'Let's get this over with as quickly as we can.'

'I think that would be best.'

'So – what is it you want to say?'

'Wouldn't you prefer this to be in private?'

Robinson told the security guards to stand aside.

'Who's this?' Smith asked, indicating Crawford.

'This is my chief of staff. I have no secrets from him. Now – please – what do you want to tell me?'

'I know that you were having an affair with her.'

'How do you know that?'

'There was a party in Pine Shore. A fundraiser for your campaign. Jarad Efron hosted it.'

He frowned. 'And? How is that relevant?'

'Madison Clarke was there. Obviously, you know she was an escort.'

'The governor doesn't know that,' Crawford interposed hurriedly. 'And he doesn't know who the girl is, either.'

'It would be better if we didn't waste time,' Smith said, looking straight at Robinson rather than Crawford. 'I spoke to Mr Efron. He said you were at the party. And he said that you and Madison were seeing each other. I understand that he introduced the two of you – he said that he was a client of hers and then you took a shine to her. I believe you had been seeing her for several weeks. He arranged for her to be there.'

Crawford felt a red-hot scorch of anger. Why had Efron said that? What was he thinking? And then, a flash of divination:

there was something about Smith. It was self-evident what had happened. There was a deadness in the man's eyes. It was unnerving, a little menacing. Crawford guessed that he could be very persuasive.

'You *were* seeing her, weren't you?'

'I was,' Robinson confirmed quietly. 'She's special. I'm very fond of her.'

'Did you see her at the party?'

'The governor wasn't at the party.'

'Arlen—'

'You know she went missing afterwards?'

Robinson looked at Crawford, then back at Smith. 'I had no idea.'

Crawford felt a shiver of anxiety. 'She hasn't been seen since.'

Crawford stepped forwards. 'What does this have to do with you, Mr Smith?'

'I drove her to the party.'

'So, what – you're her friend? Her agent?'

'I'm just a driver.'

'And so what's this about? What's it *really* about? You want money or you're going to the papers? They won't believe you, Mr Smith—'

'I don't want money,' he interrupted. 'I want to know what happened to her.'

'Arlen—'

Crawford ignored the governor. 'Let's say he did know her, just for the sake of argument. She was a *prostitute*, Mr Smith. You said so yourself. Maybe she had money problems? Maybe she's hiding from someone? Maybe she had an issue with drugs? There could be any number of reasons.'

'Arlen—'

Smith pressed ahead. 'Those things are all possible, but unlikely, considering the circumstances. I waited for her that night. I was going to drive her back into the city again. But then I heard her screaming.'

'It was *that* party?' Robinson said to Crawford. 'I remember. You dragged me away? She was there?'

Crawford clenched his teeth.

'I went into the house to get her out,' Smith said. 'She was in a terrible state – panicking, she said someone had threatened to kill her.'

'Arlen?'

'This is news to me.'

'She ran away and disappeared,' Smith said.

'So she's hiding somewhere,' Crawford said sharply. 'Report it to the police.'

'I did that. But now I think she might not be missing. I think she's been murdered. The bodies that have been turning up along the coast road—'

'How on earth is that relevant—'

'—Up on the headland?' Robinson interrupted.

'Yes,' Smith said. 'You know about that?'

'Only vaguely.'

'I think her disappearance might be connected.'

'You think the governor has something to do with that?' Crawford managed to splutter.

Smith shrugged. 'I didn't say that. But he might know something that could help find her, one way or another.'

Crawford felt like he was losing control of the conversation and, beyond that, his tenuous grip on the whole situation. 'That is all speculation,' he protested. 'Dangerous speculation with no basis in fact. And it has nothing to do with the governor.'

'Of course it does, Arlen! I was seeing her, and then she disappears. Maybe something has happened to her. Of course it's relevant. At the very least, I need to speak to the police. Maybe I can help.'

Smith pressed. 'You've no idea what happened?'

'Of course he doesn't know!'

Smith ignored him; he moved around slightly so that he was facing away from him, placing his shoulder between himself and Robinson so that Crawford was temporarily boxed out of the conversation. 'If there's anything you can tell me, sir, I would appreciate it.'

'I can't think of anything. Really – I can't.'

Crawford pressed himself back into the conversation. 'What are you going to do?' he asked Smith.

'That depends. You need to speak to the police. I think you should do it right away. I'm not an expert at these things – crisis management, I suppose you'd call it – but it would probably be best for you and your campaign if you're seen to be volunteering information. Maybe they can keep it confidential, I don't know. But you have to speak to them. I'll wait until tomorrow, and then I'll tell them what I know.'

'We'll tell them,' Robinson said. 'Right away. Thank you for speaking to me, Mr Smith. I really do appreciate it.'

The governor had a dazed look on his face. He shook the man's hand, an automatic reaction after these long months of campaigning, and made his way out of the kitchen. Crawford turned to follow, then paused, turning halfway back again, wanting to say something to the man, something that might make the problem go away, but he didn't look like the kind of person who could be intimidated or bought off or deflected from his course in any way whatsoever. His posture was loose and easy, and he returned Crawford's angry stare with implacable cool. It was unnerving.

Crawford turned back to the door again and hurried after the governor.

He was waiting for him in the service corridor.

'We need to think about this, sir.'

'What's there to think about? It's obvious what we have to do.'

'We mustn't act hastily. Everything is at stake.'

'I have to speak to the police.'

'That's a bad idea. A *terrible* idea.'

'No, Arlen. It's the right thing to do.'

'J.J. please – this doesn't have to be a threat. All he has is what Efron told him.'

'But it's *true*.'

'All he can say is that you were at the same party as she was.'

'And I was seeing her.'

'No one can prove that.'

'It doesn't matter if they can or they can't. She's missing. Those girls have turned up not five miles from there. Maybe this is connected. And maybe there is something that I can help the police with. Don't you think it's possible?'

'No, I don't. But if you're determined, then, all right, fine – but let me speak to them.'

'No,' he said. 'It has to be me.'

38

Milton got into his car and drove. He wasn't sure how to assess the meeting. Had he scared Robinson enough? He was confident that he had. The governor had received the message, but it was obvious that Crawford held significant influence over him. There was a base cunning there, Milton had seen it clearly, and he could see that he would try to limit the governor's exposure. How would he do that? Milton wasn't sure. Would Crawford be able to stop him from going to the police? Perhaps. All he had were guesses about what would happen next. Milton had meant what he said, though; he would give them until tomorrow to do the right thing. If they did not, he would take matters into his own hands and go to the police himself.

He checked his watch: six. He was late for his next appointment. He drove quickly across town to Pacific Heights and parked in a lot near to the Hotel Drisco. It was a boutique place, obviously expensive, everything understated and minimal. Milton climbed the steps to the smart lobby, all oak panelling and thick carpet, a little out of place in his scruffy jeans, dirty shirt and scuffed boots. The doorman gave him a disapproving look, but Milton stared him down, daring him to say anything, then walked past him and into the bar.

Beau was sitting at a table beneath an ornate light fixture, a copy of the *San Francisco Chronicle* spread out on the table before him. His glass was empty, so Milton diverted to the bar, paid for a beer and an orange juice and ferried them across.

'Evening,' Milton said, sitting down.

'Evening, English.'

Milton pushed the beer across the table.

Beau thanked him and drank down the first quarter of the glass. 'That name you got from the Lucianos – you do what you needed to do?'

'Yes.'

'And?'

'And thanks for your help.'

'I should know better than to ask what it was all for?'

'Probably best.'

'You're a secretive fella, ain't you?'

Beau folded the paper but not before Milton saw the news on the front page: an article on the bodies that had been dug up on the headland. He said nothing and watched as Beau drank off another measure of the beer. 'How long are you here for?' he asked him.

'Couple days. I've got some work to attend to.'

'Anything interesting?'

'Not particularly. I ever tell you about my other business?'

'I don't think we ever had the chance.'

Beau put the glass on the table. 'I'm a bail bondsman—well, least I used to be. You have them in England?'

'It doesn't work like that.'

'Guess the whole thing is a little Wild West. I got into it when I got out of the Border Patrol. Probably why I used to like it so much. I don't do so much of that no more, though, but it's still my good name above the door, still my reputation on the line. An old friend of mine who runs the show while I'm away got shot trying to bring a fellow back to San Diego to answer his obligations. This fellow's got family up here, and the word is that he's hiding out with them. Sure as the sun rises in the east and sets in the west, he's coming back down south with me. You calling was good timing – I was going to have to come up here anyways. Two birds with one stone. Now I'm going to have a look and see if I can find him.'

Milton sipped his orange juice. Time to change the subject. 'So – did you speak to the Italians?'

'About the other thing? The loan shark? I did.'

'And?'

'They did a little looking into it. Like you thought – your Mr Martinez has been running his operation without cutting them in. Strictly small-time, just a local neighbourhood kind of deal, but that ain't clever on his part. You want to play in that particular game, you got to pay your taxes, and he ain't been paying. They were unhappy about it.'

'Unhappy enough to do something about it?'

'Oh, sure.'

'What are they going to do?'

'Let's call it a hostile takeover. You just need to tell me where he's at, and I'll see that it gets sorted.'

'I can do that. What about my friend?'

'They'll wipe out the debt.'

'How much do they want for it?'

Beau held up his hands. 'No charge. They'll be taking over his book – that's worth plenty to them. His debt can be your finder's fee. They'll give it to you.'

Milton took his orange juice and touched it against the side of Beau's beer. 'Thanks, Beau,' he said. 'I owe you.'

'Yeah, well, about that. There's maybe something we can do to square that away. This fellow I've come to take back down to San Diego, there's no way he's going to play nice. Some of the runners we go after, they're real badass until it comes down to the nut-cutting, and then, when the moment of true balls comes around, most of them capitulate. This guy, though? There's always one asshole in the crowd who has to be different, and I'm not getting any younger. I was thinking maybe I could use a hand.'

'When?'

Beau finished his beer. 'You doing anything now?'

39

The place was in the hills outside Vallejo. It was a clear evening, and for once, there was a perfect view all the way down to the Golden Gate Bridge and the lights of the city beyond. Beau drove along Daniels Avenue until he found number 225. Hank had given him the address, and Beau had had it checked with an investigator they sometimes used when they had runners in Northern California. It was a small, two-storey house painted eggshell blue. There was a line of red-brick steps that led up from a carport to the first-floor entrance. The brick wall was topped with imitation lanterns on the corners, the garden was overgrown and scruffy, and the car in the driveway was up on bricks. It was down-at-heel, the worst house on the street, and tonight, it looked like it was hosting a party. A couple of men were smoking in the garden, and loud music was coming from inside.

'That the place?'

'It is.' Beau drove on and parked out of sight.

'A busy place, drink, maybe drugs? That'll make things more difficult.'

'I know.'

'Still want to do it?'

'I'm picking him up come hell or high water.'

'How do you want to play it?'

Beau looked at the house, assessing it. 'You got a preference?'

Milton looked at him with a smile. 'Old man like you?' he said. 'You go around the back, and get ready if he runs. I'll go in and flush him out.'

'All right,' he said. 'You know what he looks like?'

Smith had studied Beau's photograph on the drive north from San Francisco. 'Big. Nasty-looking. I'll recognise him.'

'Goes by the name of Ordell,' Beau reminded him.

'Don't worry. I got it.'

Beau held up the cosh. 'Want this?'

'Keep it. I'll give you ten minutes to get yourself around the back, and then I'll go in.'

* * *

Beau rolled the car around the block until he found an access road that ran between the back gardens of Daniels Avenue. It was a narrow street that climbed a hill with broken fencing on both sides, wooden garages that were barely standing and unkempt trees that spread their boughs overhead. A row of cars, covered over with tarps, was parked along one side of the road. He recognised Number 225 from the peeling blue paint and settled into place to wait behind the wing of a battered old Ford Taurus.

He had barely been there a minute when he heard the sound of raised voices and then crashing furniture.

He rose up quickly.

The back door exploded outwards, the limp body of a man tumbling through the splintered shards.

He took a step forward just in time to intercept the big, angry-looking man who was barrelling out of the shattered doorway. He looked madder than a wet hen. He held one hand to his nose, trying unsuccessfully to stem the flow of blood that was running down his lip, into his mouth and across his chin.

Beau stepped into his path.

'Oh, *shit*,' Ordell Leonard said.

Beau swung the cosh and caught him flush on the side of the head. He went jelly-legged and tripped, Beau snagging the lapels of his shirt as he went stumbling past him, heaving his unsupported weight and lowering him down to the road.

He was out cold before his chin hit the asphalt.

Smith came out of the house, shaking the sting out of his right fist.

'That was easy,' he said.

40

Arlen Crawford was working on the preparation for the next debate. They were in Oakland, another anonymous hotel that was the same as all the others. They were all high-end, all luxury. All the same, one after another, after another, a never-ending line of them. The sheets on the bed were always fine Egyptian cotton, the bathrooms were always Italian marble, the carpets were always luxuriously deep. They were all interchangeable. It was easy to forget where you were.

He put down his pen and leant back in his chair. He thought of John Smith and his threats. That certainly was a problem, and if it had been left to metastasise, it would have grown into something much, much worse. But Crawford had it under control. He had been with Robinson when he reported his connection to the girl to the police. They had done it yesterday evening. He had called in a whole series of favours to arrange for a friendly detective to take the statement. The detective had come to them to avoid any whiff of it getting to the press. There would be no shots of the governor on the steps of a police precinct house. The process of the interview looked official, just as it should, but the statement would never see the light of day. It would never be transcribed, and the tapes onto which it had been recorded had already been shredded.

The detective had reassured Robinson that there was little chance that his liaison with Madison had anything to do with her disappearance. He went further, just as Crawford had suggested, saying that there was no evidence to suggest she had anything to do with the dead girls. The governor's conscience was salved, and now they would be able to get back to the business of winning an election.

Some things were just too important to be derailed.

There was Smith himself, of course. He would need to be dealt with, but that was already in hand. The background checks had turned up very little. He wasn't registered to vote. He didn't appear to pay any taxes. A shitty place in an SRO in the Mission District. He worked nights as a cab driver and worked days hauling blocks of ice. He was a nobody. Practically a vagrant. They had two good men on his case now. Good men, solid tails, both with surveillance experience, the sort who could drift in and out of a crowd without being spotted. They had already got some good stuff. The man went to a meeting of Alcoholics Anonymous. That was useful to know. There was no family, but it looked like there was a girl.

That, too, might be helpful.

Leverage.

He turned his attention back to his work. Crawford had just been emailed the latest polling numbers, and the news was good. They were tracking nicely ahead of the pack, and the last debate ought to be enough to nail the lead down. They had blocked out the weekend for preparation. Crawford was going to be playing the role of Robinson's most likely rival, and he was putting together a list of questions that he knew would be difficult if they came up. Forewarned was forearmed, and all that. Fail to prepare, prepare to fail. Crawford knew all the questions and had drilled them into the rest of the team; drilled them into the governor. That was a difficult proposition given his propensity to shy away from preparation and rely upon his instinct. Crawford preferred a balance, but—

There was a fierce knocking on the door of his hotel room.

He put his pen down. 'What is it?' he called.

'Arlen!'

The banging resumed, louder.

He padded across the carpet and opened the door.

It was Robinson.

'Have you seen the news?'

He looked terrible; his face was deathly pale.

'No,' Crawford said. 'I've been working on the debate.'

'Put it on. *CNN*.'

Crawford rescued the remote from the debris on the desk and flipped channels to *CNN*. It was an outside broadcast. The presenter was standing on the margin of a road with scrub and trees. It was heavy with fog, a dense grey curtain that closed everything in. The ticker at the bottom of the screen announced that the police had finally identified all three sets of remains that had been found at Headlands Lookout.

'Turn it up,' Robinson demanded.

Crawford did as he was told.

'. . . the bodies of three women found near Headlands Lookout, just behind me here. The victims are twenty-one-year-old Tabitha Wilson of Palo Alto, twenty-five-year-old Megan Gabert of San Francisco and twenty-one-year-old Miley Van Dyken of Vallejo. A police official has revealed to me that there were substantial similarities in how the women died but declined to reveal their causes of death. The same source suggested that the police believe that the three women were killed at a different location, but then their bodies were dumped here. Lorraine Young, Tabitha's mother, has said that police forensic tests, including DNA, have confirmed that one of the bodies belonged to her daughter. The bodies were found within fifty feet of each other in this stretch of rocky grasslands, hidden by overgrown shrubbery and seagrass.'

Crawford felt his knees buckle, just a little.

'What the fuck, Arlen? What the *fuck*?'

Crawford muted the TV.

The muscles in his jaw bunched as he considered all the possible next moves.

None of them were any good.

'Arlen! Don't play dumb with me.' Robinson stabbed a finger at the screen. 'What the fuck!'

'Calm down, sir.'

'*Calm down*? Are you kidding? Seriously? Those girls – you know who they are. Jesus Christ, Arlen, you remember, I know you do.'

Yes, he thought bitterly, I do remember. There were no next moves now. Checkmate. End of the line. The situation was completely out of control, and it could only get worse before it got better. He had been managing it, carefully and diligently, nudging events in the best direction and very discreetly burying all of this so deep that it would never be disturbed. That, at least, had been his intention. The girls were never supposed to be seen again.

'I do remember,' he said.

And then came the recrimination. He should have seen to this himself rather than trusting others; that was his fault, and now he would have to live with it. He had been naïve to think that those dumbass rednecks could be expected to handle something so sensitive in the way it needed to be handled. The brakes were off now, and momentum was gathering. There was little to be done, and knowing that, Crawford almost felt able to relax. The sense of fatalism was strangely comforting. He had, he realised, been so intent on keeping a lid on events that he had neglected to notice the pressure that was building inside him. The stress and the constant worry. The campaign, twice-daily polling numbers, the places they were strong and the places they were weak, the governor's appeal across different demographics, how was he playing with the party, how would the Democrats go after him?

His erratic behaviour.

The suicidal appetite that he couldn't sate.

Time bombs.

Crawford had done his best for as long as he could, but it was too much for one man to handle.

And he didn't have to handle it anymore.

Maybe this had always been inevitable.

Robinson gaped as if the enormity of what he was discovering had struck him dumb. 'And – I—'

'Yes, Governor. That's right.'

'I—'

'You were seeing them all.'

'But—'

'That'll have to come out now, of course. There will be something that ties them to you, something we couldn't clean up: a text message, a diary entry – anything, really. Nothing we can do about that, not now. That ship has sailed.'

The governor put a hand down against the mattress to steady himself. He looked as if he was just about ready to swoon. 'What happened?'

'You don't recall?'

'What's going on, Arlen?'

'You had your way with them for as long as it suited you, and then you put them aside and moved on to whoever you wanted next. The same way you always do. They all came to me. They were hurt and angry, and they wanted revenge. They threatened to go to the press. They asked for money. The problem with that, though, is that you can't ever be sure that they won't come back for more. They get their snouts in the trough, they're going to think that it's always going to be there. It's not hard to see why they might think that, is it? I would. They still have the story to sell. We can't run a campaign with that hanging over us, let alone a presidency.'

'*You* did this?'

'I arranged for things to be sorted.'

'"*Sorted*?"'

'That's right.'

'You *murdered* them?' Robinson slumped.

'No, sir. *You* did.'

'Don't be—'

'I arranged for things to be sorted. What else could I have done?'

'And Madison?'

He shrugged. 'I shouldn't think it'll be long until she turns up.'

'Oh, Jesus . . .'

'It's a bit late for that.'

'Who did it?'

'Friends who share our cause. It doesn't matter who they are. There are some things that are more important than others, Governor. Country, for one. I love this country, sir. But I look at it, and I can see everything that's wrong: unchecked immigration; drugs everywhere; invasive government; standards through the floor; weak foreign policy; the Chinese and the Russians making us look like fools at every turn. That's not what this country was founded to be. We haven't fulfilled our potential for years. *Decades*. You were the best chance of making this country great again. You are . . . No' – he corrected himself, a bitter laugh – 'you *were* . . . very electable. We would have won, Governor. The nomination, the presidency and then whatever we wanted after that. We could've started the work that needs to be done.'

Robinson was hardly even listening to him. 'You *killed* them.'

There was no anger there, not yet, although that would come. He had been stunned into a stupor. The life had been sucked from him. It was a depressing thing to see; the sight of him on a stage, in full flow, railing against the state of the world and promising that he would make things right – that, Crawford thought, *that* was something special. Something to experience. But it was also a mirage. The man was a fraud. No sense in pretending otherwise. A snake-oil salesman. Joseph Jack Robinson II, the most inspirational politician that Arlen Crawford had ever seen, was just another man selling moonshine.

He went over to his suitcase and opened it.

'Why did you do it, Arlen?'

'What happened was necessary for the greater good, sir. It's regrettable, of course, but what were they? Four prostitutes and an intern. They were expendable.'

'An intern? What? What do you mean? *Karly*?'

'That's in hand.'

Robinson jackknifed over the edge of the bed and, suddenly and explosively, voided his guts. He straightened up, wiping the back of his hand across his mouth.

'It's all over now, sir. You had everything. The charisma, the way you command a room, the good sense to know when to listen and adopt the right ideas. You would have been perfect.

Perfect, Governor, if it wasn't for the fact that you're weak. No discipline. I should have realised that months ago. There was always only ever going to be so much that I could do for you, and now, after this' – he pointed to the TV – 'we've gone past the limit. The only thing we can do now is try to limit the damage.'

The smell of his vomit was strong, acrid and cloying.

Crawford took out a gun with a silencer and pointed it at Robinson.

'Arlen—'

'I'm sorry it's come to this, sir, but I don't see any other way.'

PART IV

KARLY HAMMIL

Mr Crawford had said to meet her at a lookout point in Crissy Field. He had arranged for her to take a temporary leave of absence from the campaign, saying that she had contracted glandular fever and would be out of action for at least a month. That, he said, would be enough time for them to come up with something better, but she knew that she would never be going back. In the meantime, he had promised that he would see to the money, and the rendezvous was so that he could deliver the first instalment to her. She had driven up to the park and sat in her car and watched as the sun went down over the bay. It had been a bright day, and as the sun slipped slowly beneath the horizon, the rusty red metal of the bridge glowed brightly in its dying rays. The lights of Treasure Island and, beyond that, Oakland began to flicker, twinkling in the gloaming, growing brighter.

Karly wound down the window and let the air into the car. She took a pack of cigarettes from the dashboard, held them to her mouth and pulled one out with her lips. She lit it, sucking the smoke into her lungs, closing her eyes and enjoying the hit of the nicotine. The park was empty, save for a couple of joggers who were descending the hill back towards the city. The night grew darker. The last ferry headed back to the mainland from Alcatraz. A jet laid down grey vapour trails as it cut through the star-sprinkled sky overhead. Gulls wheeled on lazy thermals. It was a spectacular view.

She saw the high beams of a car as it turned up the steep road that ended in the vantage point. Karly finished the cigarette and flicked the butt out the window. The car was an old Cadillac, and it was struggling with the incline. As it drew closer, she could see that it was dented on the front-right wing and the number plate was attached to the chassis with duct tape. It slowed and swung into the bay next to her. She squinted through the glare of the headlights, but they were bright and she couldn't make out anything about the driver or the passenger. The door opened, and the driver came over to her side of the car.

41

Julius had a small TV set on a shelf above the door, and he was flicking between channels; they were all running with the same story. Joseph Jack Robinson II, the presumptive candidate as Republican nomination for president, had been found dead in his hotel room. Details were still sketchy, but the early indications were that he had taken his own life. Suicide. There was unconfirmed speculation that he had been found on his bed next to a bottle of Scotch and empty bottles of prescription sleeping tablets. The anchors on all of the channels were reporting the news with the same breathless, stunned sense of disbelief. A major piece in the political life of the country had been swiped from the board. Friends and colleagues were interviewed, some of them fighting back tears. No one could believe that Robinson had killed himself. It didn't make sense, they said. He had been full of life. He had been determined to win the nomination, and now that he had almost achieved that, he was gearing up for election year. To do this, now, to end it all when he had so much to look forward to? It didn't make any sense at all.

There were four other customers in the place today. They were all watching the television.

'*Unbelievable*,' Julius said as he slid a spatula beneath a burger and deftly flipped it. 'Someone like that just topping himself? Don't make no sense.'

'Goes to show,' said one of the others. 'You never know what's in a man's head.'

The coverage switched to an outside broadcast. It was a hotel. Flashbulbs flashed as a figure emerged from the lobby of the hotel and descended until he was halfway down the steps, a thicket of microphones quickly thrust into his face.

'Turn it up, would you?' Milton said.

Julius punched the volume up.

Milton recognised the man. It was Robinson's chief of staff, Arlen Crawford.

'Mr Crawford,' a reporter shouted above the hubbub, 'can you tell us what you know?'

'The governor was found in his room this afternoon by a member of the election team. Paramedics were called, but it was too late – they say he had been dead for several hours. We have no idea why he would have done something like this. I saw him last night to talk about the excellent progress we were making with the campaign. I saw nothing to make me think that this could be possible. The governor was a loud, enthusiastic, colourful man. This is completely out of character.' He looked away for a moment, swallowing, and then passed a hand over his face. 'More than just being my boss, Joseph Jack Robinson was my friend. He's the reason I'm in politics. He's the godfather to my son. He was a good man. The best.' His voice quavered, almost broke. 'What happened this morning is a disaster for this country and a tragedy for everyone who knew him. Thank you. Good day.'

He turned back and made his way into the hotel.

'It might be a personal tragedy,' Julius opined, 'but a *national* one? Nah. Not for me. Boy had some pretty strident views on things, you know what I'm saying? He wouldn't have got my vote.'

Milton's phone rang.

It was Eva.

'Afternoon,' Milton said. 'Are you watching this?'

There was no reply.

Milton checked the phone's display; it was definitely her. 'Eva?'

'Mr Smith,' a male voice said. 'You've caused us a whole heap of trouble, you know that? And now you're gonna have to pay.'

'Who is this?'

'My name's not important.'

It was a Southern accent. A low and lazy drawl. A smoky rasp.

'Where's Eva?'

'She's with us.'

'If you hurt her—'

'You ain't in no position to make threats, Mr Smith.'

'What do you want?'

'To talk.'

'About?'

'You know what about. We need to be sure you won't mention' – there was a pause – 'recent events.'

'The governor.'

'That's right.'

'And if I persuade you that I won't say anything, you'll let her go?'

'Perhaps.'

'Right. I wasn't born yesterday.'

There was a rasping laugh. 'Perhaps and perhaps not, but if you don't play ball with us now, well then, it's a definite no for her, ain't it? How much does she know?'

'She doesn't know anything.'

'Gonna have to speak to her to make sure about that.'

Milton's voice was cold and hard. 'Listen to me – she doesn't know anything.'

'Then maybe we just need you.'

'Where are you?'

'Nah, partner, it ain't gonna happen like that. We know where you are. We'll come to you. You stay right there, all right? Finish your meal. We'll be along presently.'

42

Milton checked the joint out after he had finished speaking to the man on the phone and could guess which of the other four patrons had followed him inside: a scrawny weasel of a man with three days' worth of stubble and a face that had been badly scarred by acne. Milton stared at him, and the man eventually found the guts to make a sly nod, emboldened, no doubt, by the prospect of imminent reinforcements and his opinion that they had the advantage. That knowledge wasn't enough to stiffen his resolve completely, and as Milton stared at him, his confidence folded and he looked away. Milton wondered if there was some way he could use the man to even the odds, but he knew that there would not be. What could he have done? They had Eva, and that, he knew, eliminated almost all of his options.

They arrived in an old Cadillac Eldorado ten minutes after the call. Milton finished his burger, wiped his mouth, laid ten dollars on the counter and went to the car. He got into the back without complaint. There was no point in making things difficult for them.

That would come later.

There were four of them in the car, each of them wearing a biker's leather jacket and each, helpfully, following the biker habit of having a nickname badge sewn onto the left shoulder lapel. The man in the passenger seat was Smokey. It looked like he was in charge. He was tall and slender, all knees and elbows, and Milton saw a tattoo of a swastika on the back of his neck. The driver was bigger, wearing a denim jacket with cut-off sleeves that revealed heavy muscle. His badge identified him as Dog. The men flanking him both had long hair, like the others, and they smelled of stale sweat, pot and booze. There wasn't much space in the back, and they were pressed up against him. The one on his right was flabby, Milton's elbow pressing into the side of his doughy gut, with a full red beard and shoulder-length red hair. His badge identified him as Orangutan. The one on his left was different, solid slabs of muscle, hard and unyielding. If it came down to it, he would be the one to put down first. His nickname was Tiny.

They had a radio on; it was a news channel, and the show was dominated by talk of the governor's death. They discussed it with animation, and Milton quickly got the impression that they considered it a tragedy.

The four of them seemed pretty secure in themselves and their ability to keep Milton in line. He noticed that they didn't blindfold him or do anything to prevent him from seeing where he was being taken. Not a good sign. They didn't plan on him making a return trip, and so, they reckoned, it made no difference what he found out. They were right about one thing: Milton wasn't planning on going back to wherever it was they were going. There would be no need after he was through. He would be leaving, though, and he would be taking Eva with him. And if they thought he would be as pliant as this once they had him wherever they were taking him?

Well, if they thought that, then more fool them.

They drove out to Potrero Hill, the gritty industrial belt on the eastern boundary facing the bay and, on the other side of the water, Oakland. There were warehouses, some old, others cheaply and quickly assembled prefabs. They navigated the streets to the water's edge, prickling with jetties and piers, and then drew up to a gate in a tall mesh wire fence. The compound contained a warehouse, and Milton saw stacks of beer barrels and trucks with the logo of a local brewery that he thought he recognised.

There were four big motorcycles parked under cover next to the warehouse.

Dog hooted the horn, and the gates parted for them.

They took him into the warehouse through a side door. He paid everything careful attention: ways in and out of the building, the number of windows, the internal layout. The place smelt powerfully of hops and old beer, sweat and marijuana. He watched the four men, assessing and reassessing them, confirming again which were the most dangerous and which he could leave until last when it came time to take them out.

They followed a corridor to a door, opened it and pushed him inside.

It was empty, just a few bits and pieces. It looked like it was used as a basic kitchen and dining area. A trestle table with one broken leg. Rubbish strewn across the table. Three wooden chairs. Several trays with beer bottles stacked up against the wall. A dirty microwave oven on the floor next to a handful of ready meals. A metal bin overflowing with empty food packaging. Breeze-block walls painted white. A single naked light bulb overhead. A pin-up calendar from three years ago. No windows. No natural light. No other way in or out.

Eva was standing at the end of the room, as far away from the door as she could get. There was another woman with her.

The skinny guy stepped forwards and shoved Milton in the back so that he stumbled further into the room.

Eva stepped forwards.

'Are you all right?' Milton asked her.

'Yes,' she said.

He kept looking at her. 'They haven't hurt you?'

'No,' she said. She gestured to the other girl. 'This is Karly.'

'Hello, Karly,' Milton said. 'Are you okay?'

She nodded. There was no colour in her face. She was terrified.

'Don't worry,' Milton told her. 'We'll be leaving soon.'

'That right?' Smokey said from behind him, his words edged by a braying laugh.

Milton turned back to him.

'All right then, partner. We got a few questions for you.'

'You should let us leave.'

'You'll go when I say you can go.'

'It'll end badly for you otherwise.'

Smokey snorted. 'You're something, boy. You got some balls – but it's time for you to pay attention.'

'Don't worry. I am.'

'My questions, you gonna answer 'em, one way or another. No doubt you're gonna get slapped around some, don't really matter if you co-operate or not. Only issue is whether we do it the hard way or the *fucking* hard way. Your choice.'

Milton glanced over. The other three men were all inside the room. Smokey was just out of reach, but the big guy, Tiny, was close. The stack of beer bottles was waist high. The cellophane wrapper on the top tray had been torn away, some of the bottles had been removed, and the necks of those that remained were exposed.

'Who are you working for?' Milton asked.

'See, you say you're paying attention, but you ain't. I'm asking, you're answering.'

'Is it Crawford?'

Smokey spat at his feet. 'You gonna have to learn. Tiny – give him a little something to think about.'

Tiny – the big man – balled his right hand into a fist and balanced his weight to fire out a punch. Milton saw and moved faster, reaching out and wrapping his fingers around a bottle, feeling it nestle in his palm, pulling it out of the tray and swinging it, striking the guy on the side of the head, just above his ear. He staggered a little, more from shock than from anything else, and Milton struck the bottle against the wall and smashed it apart, beer splashing up his arm. He closed in and jabbed the jagged end of the bottle into the man's shoulder,

343

then stabbed it into his cheek, twisting it, chewing up the flesh. He dropped the bloodied shards, grabbed Tiny by the shoulders and pulled him in close, driving his knee into his groin, then dropped him down onto the floor.

Three seconds, start to finish.

'The fucking hard way, I guess,' Milton said. He wasn't even breathing hard.

Smokey pulled a pistol from his waistband and brought it up. 'Get back. Over there. Against the wall.'

Milton knew he wouldn't be able to take them all out, but that wasn't what he had in mind. He just wanted a moment alone with Eva. He knew they wouldn't kill him, not yet. They needed some answers before they could think about that, and he wasn't minded to give them any. He did as he was told and stepped back. The man waved the pistol, and he kept going until he was at the rear of the room, next to Eva and Karly.

'Get him out of here,' Smokey said to Orangutan and Dog, pointing at the stricken Tiny. They helped him up, blood running freely from the grisly rent in his cheek, and half-dragged him out into the corridor beyond.

'Last chance,' Milton said.

'For what?' Smokey yelled at him.

'To let us out.'

'Or?'

'I'll make what just happened to him look like a love bite.'

His bravado seemed to confuse, and then amuse, the man. 'Are you out of your fucking mind? Look at you – look where you are. You're *fucked*, brother. You can have a couple of hours to think about that until a friend of ours gets here.'

'Mr Crawford?'

'That's right. Mr Crawford. He wants to speak to you. But then that'll be the end of it after that. You're done. *Finished.*'

43

Milton tried the door. It was locked. He paused for a moment, thinking. He could hear the deep, muffled boom of the foghorns from outside.

Eva came to him. 'Jesus, John,' she said. 'Look at you.' She pointed to a spot on his shirt. 'Is that yours?'

He looked down. A patch of blood. 'No. I'm fine. It's his.'

She turned to the front of the room and the splatter of blood across the bare concrete floor. Her face whitened as she took it in and what it meant. He could read her mind: the horror at what he was capable of doing, the ease and efficiency with which he had maimed the man. How did someone like him, so quiet and closed off, explode with such a terrifying eruption of violence? How did he even have it in him? Milton recognised the look that she was giving him. He had seen it before. He knew that it would presage a change in the way that she felt about him. She was going to have to see more of it, too, before the day was over. Worse things. It couldn't possibly be the same afterwards. Tenderness and intimacy would be the first casualties of what he was going to have to do to get them out.

'Don't worry,' he said. 'It's fine. I'm going to get us out.'

'Don't worry? John—?'

'Are you sure you're all right? They didn't hurt you?'

'No. They just threw me in here. They asked me a few questions about you, but that was it.'

'What kind of questions?'

'Who you are, what you do, how long I've known you.'

He took her by the shoulders. 'I'm very sorry,' he said, looking into her eyes. She flinched a little. 'You should never have been involved. I don't know how they found out about you. They must've been following me.'

'I don't understand why, though? Why would they follow you? What have you done?'

'Nothing.'

'What you did to that man – Jesus, John, you fucked him up – are you some sort of criminal?'

'No.'

'Then what?'

'It's to do with the girls they've found.'

'Which girls? The ones on the beach?'

'I know who did it.'

'Who?'

'Governor Robinson,' the other girl, Karly, answered. 'Right?'

'Do you know him?' Milton asked.

'I worked for him.'

'And you had a relationship with him?'

She nodded.

Milton asked her to explain what had happened and she did: how Robinson had discarded her, how she had gone to Crawford for help, and how the bikers had abducted her and brought her here.

'You know he's dead?'

'No,' Karly said, her mouth falling open.

'This morning. They found him in his hotel room. They're saying suicide, but I don't think it was that. Robinson was also seeing the three girls they've found up on Headlands Lookout. I'm guessing the same thing happened with them as happened to you, Karly.'

'He killed them?'

'I doubt he knew anything about it. Crawford found out about them, maybe they threatened to expose Robinson, and he covered everything up. I spoke to Robinson yesterday afternoon and told him I knew about him and Madison. I said that if he didn't go to the police and tell them that he was seeing her, then I'd do it for him. The names of the girls came out this morning. If I had to guess, I'd say he found out. It wouldn't have been difficult to work out what had happened to them after that. He went to Crawford and confronted him, and Crawford killed him.'

Eva listened, and as he explained more, her disbelief was replaced with incredulity. 'So who are these men?'

'They're working with Crawford.'

Eva's brow clenched angrily. 'None of this has anything to do with me.'

'I know it doesn't. They took you to get my attention. They've got it now, but they're going to wish they hadn't.'

'John – look around. We're stuck.'

'No, we're not. These boys aren't the smartest. There are plenty of things we can use in here.'

She picked up a utensil from the table. 'A plastic knife isn't going to be much use against a gun, and I doubt they'll let you come at them with a bottle again.'

He picked up a roll of duct tape from the table. 'I can do better than a plastic knife.'

* * *

He didn't know how long they had. Two hours, Smokey had said, but it might have been more or it might have been less, and he wasn't sure how much time had already passed. He had to make his move now. Milton went to the stack of beer, tore away the rest of the cellophane wrapper on the top tray and took out three bottles. He took the duct tape and wrapped each bottle, running the tape around it tightly until they were completely sealed. He needed to make sure the caps didn't pop off. A little resin would have been perfect, but that was asking for too much. This should work well enough. It was the best he could do.

He opened the microwave and stood the bottles neatly inside.

'What are you doing?' Eva asked him.

'Creating a diversion.' He closed the microwave door. 'I've seen four men. One of them won't be a problem, so that makes three. Have you seen any more?'

'No,' Eva said.

'Karly?'

'Four, I think.'

'Did you see any guns?'

'He had a gun.'

'I mean big guns – a shotgun, anything like that?'

Eva shook her head. 'I didn't see anything.'

'I think I saw one,' Karly said.

'Are you sure?'

'Pretty sure. Yes. I'm sure.'

A shotgun, and they would be wary now. It wasn't going to be easy.

'Both of you – get to the back of the room. In the corner. And when the time comes, look away.'

'What are you doing?'

'Trust me, okay? I'm getting us out.'

'"When the time comes"? What does that mean?'

'You'll know.'

Milton set the microwave's timer to fifteen minutes and hit the start button.

He hammered on the door.

Footsteps approached.

'What?'

'All right,' he called out.

'What you want?' It was the red-haired biker, Orangutan.

'I'll talk. Whatever you want.'

Footsteps going away.

There was a pause. Milton thought he could hear voices. They were muffled by the door.

Minutes passed.

The foghorns boomed out.

He watched the seconds tick down on the counter.

14.12.

13.33.

12.45.

Footsteps coming back again.

'Stand back,' Smokey called. 'Right up against the far wall. I'm coming in with a shotgun. Don't try to do anything stupid, or I'll empty both barrels into your face.'

Milton looked down at the microwave timer.

9.18.

9.16.

9.14.

It would be close. If they noticed it too quickly, it wouldn't work, and he didn't have a Plan B. If the man did have a shotgun, he would be hopelessly outmatched. Too late to worry about that. He stepped all the way back, putting himself between the microwave and the two women.

The door unlocked.

It opened.

Smokey did have a shotgun, a Remington. The room was narrow and not all that long. A spread couldn't really miss him from that range, and the man was careful now, wary, edging into the room, his eyes fixed on Milton.

Once bitten, twice shy. He knew Milton was dangerous. He would be careful now. No more mistakes.

That was what Milton wanted.

It was the reason for the demonstration earlier.

He wanted all of his attention on him.

'Change of heart?'

'What choice do I have?'

'That's right, buddy. You ain't got none.'

'What do you want to know?'

'The governor – you tell anyone what you know about him and the girls?'

'The dead ones?'

'Them, that one behind you, any others.'

'No,' he said.

'No police?'

'No police.'

'What about her?' he said, chin-nodding towards Eva. 'You tell her?'

'No,' he said. 'She doesn't know anything.'

'You tell anyone else?'

'I told you – no one knows but me.'

'All right, then. That's good. How'd you find out?'

'I had a chat with Jarad Efron.'

'"A chat"? What does that mean?'

'I dangled him off a balcony. He realised it'd be better to talk to me.'

'Think you're a tough guy?'

'I'm nothing special.'

'I ain't scared of you.'

'You shouldn't be. You've got a shotgun.'

'Damn straight I do.'

'So why would you be scared?'

Milton glanced down at the microwave.

7.17.

7.16.

7.15.

'You want to tell me what happened to the girls?' he asked.

'Obvious, ain't it?'

'They wanted money.'

'That's right.' He flicked the barrel of the shotgun in Karly's direction. '*She* wanted money.'

'And then you killed them?'

'They brought it on themselves.'

'Who told you to do it? Robinson?'

'Hell no. Robinson didn't know nothing about none of this shit. We took care of it on his behalf.'

'Crawford, then?'

'That's right. Crawford and us, we just been cleaning up the governor's mess is what we been doing. He had his problems, y'all can see that plain as day, but that there was one great man. Would've been damn good for this fucked-up country. What's happened to him is a tragedy. *Your* fault, the way I see it. What you've done – digging your nose into business that don't concern you, making trouble – well, old partner, that's something you're gonna have to account for, and the account-ing's gonna be scrupulous.'

'What about Madison Clarke?'

'Who?'

'Another escort. The governor was seeing her.'

'This the girl you took up to the party in Pine Shore?'

'That's right. You all came out that night, didn't you?'

'That's right.'

'You find her?'

'You know what? We didn't. We don't know where she is.'

Milton glanced down at the microwave.

6.24.

6.23.

6.22.

Come on, come on, come on.

'We don't need to do this, right?' he said, trying to buy them just a little more time. 'I'm not going to say anything. You know where I live.'

Smokey laughed. 'Nah, that ain't gonna cut it. We don't never leave loose ends, and that's what y'all are.'

5.33.

5.32.

5.31.

Smokey noticed Milton looking down at the microwave.

'Fuck you doing with that?' he said.

'I was hungry. I thought—'

'Fuck *that*.'

He stepped towards it.

'Please,' Milton said.

The man reached out for the stop button.

He saw the beer bottles inside, turning around on the platter: incongruous.

Too late.

The liquid inside the bottles was evaporating into steam; several atmospheres of pressure were being generated; the duct tape was holding the caps in place; the pressure was running up against the capacity of the bottles. Just at that precise moment, there was no more space for it to go. It was fortunate; it couldn't have been better timing. The bottles exploded with the same force as a quarter-stick of dynamite. The microwave was obliterated from the inside out. The glass in the door was flung across the room in a shower of razored slivers, the frame of the door cartwheeled away, and the metal body was broken apart, rivets and screws popping out. Smokey was looking right at it, close, as it exploded; a parabola of debris enveloped his head, the barrage of tiny fragments slicing into his eyes and the skin of his face, his scalp, piercing his clothes and flesh.

Milton was further away, yet the blast from the explosion staggered him backwards, and instants later, the red-hot shower peppered his skin. His bare arms were crossed with a thin bloody lattice as he dropped his arm from his face and moved forwards.

He looked back quickly. 'You all right?'

Neither Eva nor Karly answered, but he didn't see any obvious damage.

He turned back. Smokey was on the floor, covered in blood. A large triangular shard from the microwave's metal case was halfway visible in his trachea. He was gurgling, and air whistled in and out of the tear in his throat. One leg twitched spastically. Milton didn't need to examine him to know that he only had a minute or two to live.

The Remington was abandoned at his side.

Milton took it and brought it up. He heard hurried footsteps and ragged breathing and saw a momentary reflection in the long, blank window that started in the corridor opposite the door. He aimed blind around the door and pulled one trigger, blowing buckshot into one of the other men from less than three feet away. Milton turned quickly into the corridor, the shotgun up and ready, and stepped over the second man's body. He was dead. Half his face was gone.

Three down.

One left.

He moved low and fast, the shotgun held out straight. The corridor led into a main room with sofas, a jukebox, empty bottles and dope paraphernalia.

The fourth man popped out of cover behind the sofa and fired.

Milton dropped flat, rolled three times to the right, opening the angle and negating the cover, and pulled the trigger. Half of the buckshot shredded the sofa while the other half perforated the man from head to toe. He dropped his pistol and hit the floor with a weighty thud.

Milton got up. Save the cuts and grazes from the explosion, he was unmarked.

He went back to the kitchen.

Smokey was dead on the floor.

Eva and Karly hadn't moved.

'It's over,' he told them.

Eva bit her lip. 'Are you all right?'

'I'm good. You?'

'Yes.'

'Both of you?'

'I'm fine,' Karly said.

He turned to Eva. 'You both need to get out of here. We're in Potrero Hill. I'll open the gates for you, and you need to get out. Find somewhere safe, somewhere with lots of people, and call the police. Do you understand?'

'What about you?'

'There's someone I have to see.'

44

Arlen Crawford waited impatiently for the hotel lift to bear him down to the parking garage. He had his suitcase in his right hand and his overcoat folded in the crook of his left arm. The car had stopped at every floor on the way down from the tenth, but it was empty now, just Crawford and the numb terror that events had clattered hopelessly out of control. He took his phone from his pocket and tried to call Jack Kerrigan again. There had been no reply the first and second time that he had tried, but this time, the call was answered.

'Smokey,' he said. 'What the fuck's going on?'

'Smokey's dead, Mr Crawford. His friends are dead, too.'

'Who is this?'

'You know who this is.'

The elevator reached the basement, and the doors opened.

'Mr Smith?'

'That's right.'

'What do you want, Smith? Money?'

'No.'

'Then what?'

'Justice would be a good place to start.'

'It wasn't me. Jack killed the girls.'

'Come on, Mr Crawford. Don't insult my intelligence. I know what happened.'

He aimed the fob across the parking lot and thumbed the button. The car doors unlocked and the lights flashed.

'I didn't have anything to do with it. There's no proof.'

'Maybe not. But that would only be a problem if I was going to go to the police. I'm not going to go to the police, Mr Crawford.'

'What are you going to do?'

No answer.

'What are you going to do?'

Silence.

Crawford reached the car and opened the driver's door. He tossed the phone across the car onto the passenger seat. He went around and put the suitcase in the trunk. He got inside the car, took a moment to gather his breath, stepped on the clutch and pressed the ignition.

He felt a small, cold point of metal pressing against the back of his head.

He looked up into the rear-view mirror.

It was dark in the basement, with just the glow of the sconced lights on the wall. The modest brightness fell across one half of the face of the man who was holding the gun. The other half was obscured by shadow. He recognised him: the impassive and serious face, the cruel mouth, the scar running horizontally across his face.

'Drive.'

PART V

45

The meeting on the third anniversary of Milton's sobriety was a Big Book meeting. They were peaceful weekly gatherings, the format more relaxed than usual, and Milton usually enjoyed them. They placed tea lights around the room, and someone had lit a joss stick (that had been the subject of a heated argument; a couple of the regulars had opined that it was a little too intoxicating for a roomful of recovering alkies and druggies). Every week, they each opened a copy of the book of advice that Bill Wilson, the founder of the programme, had written, read five or six pages out loud and then discussed what it meant to them all. After a year, they would have worked their way through it and then they would turn back to the start and begin again. Milton had initially thought the book was an embarrassingly twee self-help screed, and it was certainly true that it was packed full of platitudes, but the more he grew familiar with it, the easier it was to ignore the homilies and clichés and concentrate on the advice on how to live a worthwhile, sober life. Now he often read a paragraph or two before he went to sleep at night. It was good meditation.

The reading took fifteen minutes and then the discussion another thirty. The final fifteen minutes were dedicated to those who felt that they needed to share.

Richie Grimes raised his hand.

'Hey,' he said. 'My name's Richie, and I'm an alcoholic.'

'Hi, Richie,' they said together.

'You know about my problem – I've gone on about it enough. But I'm here today to give thanks.' He paused and looked behind him; he was looking for Milton. 'I don't rightly know what happened, but the man I owed money to has sold his book, and the guys who bought it off him don't look like they're going to come after me for what I owe. I might be setting myself up for a fall, but it's starting to look to me like someone paid that debt off for me.' He shook his head. 'You know, I was talking to a friend here after I did my share last week. I won't say who he was – anonymity, all that – but he told me to trust my higher power. If I didn't know any better, I'd say he was right. My higher power has intervened, like we say it will if we ask for help, because if it wasn't that, then I don't know what the hell it was.'

There was a moment of silence and then loud applause.

'Thank you for sharing,' Smulders said when it had died down. 'Anyone else?'

Milton raised his own hand.

Smulders cocked an eyebrow in surprise. 'John?'

'My name is John, and I'm an alcoholic,' Milton said.

'Hello, John.'

'There's something I need to share, too. If I don't get it off my chest, I know I'll be back on the booze eventually. I thought I could keep it in, but . . . I know that I can't.'

He paused.

Richie turned and looked at him expectantly.

The group waited for him to go on.

Eva reached across, took his hand and gave it a squeeze.

Milton thought of the other people in the room and how they were living the programme, bravely accepting 'honesty in all our affairs', and he knew, then, with absolute conviction, that he would never be able to go as far down the road as they had. If it was a choice between telling a roomful of strangers about the blood that he had on his hands and taking a drink, then he was going to take a drink. Every time. He thought of what he had almost been prepared to say, and he felt the heat gathering in his face at the foolish audacity of it.

'John?' Smulders prompted.

Eva squeezed his hand again.

No, he thought. Some things had to stay unsaid.

'I just wanted to say how valuable I've found this meeting. Most of you know me by now, even if it's just as the guy with the coffee and the biscuits. You probably wondered why I don't say much. You probably think I'm pretty bad at all this, and maybe I am, but I'm doing my best. One day at a time, like we always say. I can do better, I know I can, but I just wanted to say that it's my third year without a drink today, and that's as good a reason for celebrating as I've ever really had before. So' – he cleared his throat, constricted by sudden emotion – 'you know, I just wanted to say thanks. I wouldn't be able to do it on my own.'

There was warm applause, and the case of birthday chips was extracted from the cupboard marked PROPERTY OF A.A. They usually started with the newest members, those celebrating a day or a week or a month, and those were always the ones that were marked with the loudest cheers, the most high-fives and the strongest hugs. There were no others celebrating tonight, and when Smulders called out for those celebrating three years to come forward, Milton stood up and, smiling shyly, went up to the front. Smudlers shook his hand warmly and handed him his chip. It was red, made from cheap plastic and looked like a chocolate coin, the edge raised and stippled, the A.A. symbol embossed on one side and a single 3 on the other. Milton self-consciously raised it up in his fist, and the applause started again. He felt a little dazed as he went back to his seat. Eva took his hand again and tugged him down.

'Well done,' she whispered into his ear.

46

It was time. He had already stayed longer than was safe. He had thought about skipping the meeting altogether, and he had gone so far as getting to the airport and the long-stay car park, but he had been unable to go through with it. He needed the meeting, and more than that, he needed to see his friends there: Smulders, Grimes and the other alcoholics who drank his coffee and ate his biscuits and asked him how he was and how he was doing.

And Eva.

He had needed to see her.

She stayed to help him clear away.

'You hear what happened to the governor's aide?'

'Yeah,' Milton said vaguely. 'They found him in his car up in the Headlands.'

'He'd killed himself, too.'

'Yes.'

'Put a hose on the exhaust and put it in through the window.'

'Guilt?' Milton suggested.

She bit her lip.

'You're sure he had something to do with those men? Those girls?'

'He did.'

Milton looked at her, and for a moment, he allowed himself the thought: could he stay here? Could he stay with her? He entertained the thought longer than was healthy or sensible, until he caught himself and dismissed it. Of course he couldn't. How could he? It was ridiculous, dangerous thinking. He had made so much noise over the last few days. The spooks back home would be able to find him without too much bother now. Photographs, references in police reports, all manner of digital crumbs that, if followed, would lead them straight to him. The arrival of the Group would be the first that he knew of it. They would be more careful this time. A sedative injected into his neck from behind; a hood over his head before being muscled into a waiting car; a shot in the head from a sniper a city block away. He'd be dead or out of the country before he could do anything about it.

Thinking about staying was selfish, too. He knew what Control would order. Anyone who had spent time with him would be a threat.

A loose end.

The guys at the meeting?

Maybe.

Trip?

Probably.

Eva?

Definitely.

'What are you doing now?'

It startled him. 'What?'

She smiled at him. 'Now – you wanna get dinner?'

He wanted it badly, but he shook his head. 'I can't. I've got— I promised a friend I'd catch up with him.'

If she was disappointed, she hid it well. 'All right, then. How about tomorrow?'

'Can I give you a call?'

'Sure,' she said.

She came over to him, rested her hand on his shoulder and tiptoed so that she was tall enough to kiss him on the cheek. Her lips were warm, and she smelled of cinnamon. Milton felt a lump in his throat as she lowered herself down to her height.

'It was good to hear you speak. I know you're carrying a burden, John. You should share it. No one will judge you, and it'll be easier to carry.'

He smiled at her. His throat felt thick, and he didn't trust himself to speak.

'See you around,' she said, rubbing her hand up and down his right arm. 'Don't be a stranger, all right?'

*   *   *

Milton drove back to the El Capitan for the last time. He recognised Trip Macklemore as he slotted the Explorer into the kerb outside the entrance to the building. He scanned his surroundings quickly, a little fretfully, but there was no sign of anything out of the ordinary. The Group were good, though.

If an agent was using the boy and didn't want to be seen, he would be invisible. Milton felt an itching sensation in the dead centre of his chest. He looked down, almost expecting to see the red crosshatch of a laser sight, but there was nothing there. He turned the key to switch off the engine and stepped outside.

'Hello, Trip.'

'Mr Smith.'

'Are you all right?'

'I'm fine.'

'What can I do for you?'

'There's someone you need to talk to.'

Milton noticed that there was someone else waiting at the entrance to the building.

She smiled nervously at him.

Milton couldn't hide his surprise. '*Madison?*'

'Hello, John.'

'Where have you been?'

'Is this your place?' she said, rubbing her arms to ward off the chill. 'Can we maybe go in? Get a coffee? I'll tell you.'

47

She explained. To begin with, she edged around some of the details for fear of upsetting Trip, but when he realised what she was doing, he told her – a little unconvincingly – that he was fine with it and that she should lay it all out, so that's what she did.

It had started in April when Jarad Efron booked her through Fallen Angelz for the first time. She had no idea who he was other than that he was rich and generous and fun to be around. They had had a good time together, and he booked her again a week or two afterwards, then several times after that. The eighth or ninth booking was different. Rather than the plush hotel room to which they usually retreated, this was a private dinner party. Some sort of fundraiser. He had bought her a thousand-dollar dress and paraded her as his girlfriend. It was a charade, and it must have been easy to see through it, but there were other escorts at the party, a harem of young girls with rich older men. Madison recognised some of them, but it didn't seem like any of it was a big deal.

One of the other guests came over to speak to Efron. She guessed within minutes that the conversation was an excuse;

he was more interested in finding out about her. She hadn't recognised him at first; he was just another middle-aged john with plenty of cash, charming and charismatic with it. He didn't explain who he was, and when she asked what he did for a living, all he said was that he worked for the state government. They had exchanged numbers, and he had called the next morning to set up a meeting the same night. She reserved a room at the Marriott; they had room service and went to bed together.

He booked her two more times until, one day, she was idly watching the TV in a bar where she was waiting for Trip and she had seen him on the news. The bartender had made some quip about how they were watching the next president of the United States. She googled him on her phone and nearly fell off her stool. He booked her again the day after her discovery, and she had told him, when they were lying on the bed together afterwards, that she knew who he was. He asked if that bothered her, and she said that it didn't. He asked if she could keep a secret, and she had said that she could. He had said that he was pleased because he thought that she could be special – 'different from all the others' – and he wanted to see her more often. Mentioning that there were 'others' didn't make her feel all that special, but she told herself that he was with her, and that she *was* special; she would make him see that, and then, maybe, eventually, it would just be the two of them.

Robinson had been good to his word, and they saw each other at least once a week for a month or so. She had persuaded herself that he really did see her as more than just another working girl and that, maybe, something might come of it. She dreamt that he would take her away from hooking and give her a better life: money, a car, a nice place to live. He had made promises like that, and she had bought all of them. She read about him online and watched him on the news. The fact that a man like him, with so much to lose, had started a relationship with her and trusted her to keep it secret? Man, that was totally *crazy*. The proximity to power was intoxicating, too, and she admitted that she had let it get to her head. He told her that his wife was a bitch, and he would be leaving her as soon as the election was over. She started to believe his spin that, if she was patient, they could be together. At no point did she question how any of that could ever be possible for a working girl. She loved him.

'And then he dropped me,' she said. 'No warning. Just like that. He called me and said he couldn't see me again. I asked why, and he said it was one of those things – we'd had a good run, he said, we'd both had fun, but all good things have to come to an end. No hard feelings, goodbye, and that was it. Just like that.'

She moped for a week, wondering whether there was any way she could put things back the way they had been before. She blamed herself: she had pushed him too fast, talking about the future and the things they could do together once they were a couple. That, she saw then, had been childishly naïve. She had scared him off. She called the number he had given her, but the line had been disconnected. She saw that he was speaking at a rally in Palo Alto and had hitched down there in the vain hope that she might be able to speak to him, but that, too, had been a failure. She had found a space near the front, but he had been absorbed in his speech, and even as he beamed his brilliant smile into the crowd, his eyes passing right across her, she knew that he hadn't even noticed that she was there.

Two days later, Efron called.

'He was having a party,' she explained. 'A fundraising thing for the campaign. He was inviting people that he knew, CEOs and shit, these guys from the Valley, and Robinson was going to be there, too. He asked if I could come. I couldn't understand it at first – I mean, why would he want me to be there after what had happened between me and J.J., but then I realised, there was no way he could've known how involved we'd been and what had happened since. All he knew was that Robinson had taken a shine to me, so he thought he'd get me to be there too because he thought that'd make him happy.' She laughed bitterly. 'That's a laugh, right? I mean, he couldn't possibly have been much more wrong about that.'

'What happened?'

'You drove me to the house. It was fine at first. Robinson wasn't there. Jarad was sweet, looking after me – the place was jammed with rich guys, totally flush, and there was as much booze as you could drink.'

Madison said that Joseph Jack Robinson and Arlen Crawford arrived at a little after midnight. Milton remembered the town car that had pulled into the driveway and the two guys who had stepped out; he hadn't recognised them – it had been dark and foggy – but it must have been them.

Crawford had been aghast to see her. He sent Robinson into another room and came over to deal with her. He had been kind, she explained, taking her to one side and having a quiet drink with her. He explained that the governor couldn't see her that night, that there were people at the party who couldn't be trusted and that it would be damaging to the campaign if anything leaked out, but as she protested, he told her that the governor was missing her and that he would call her the next day. She had been overwhelmed with relief, and as Crawford refilled her glass, and keen to ingratiate herself more fully with him, she had accepted his offer to do a pill with him. He said it was ecstasy, and although she rarely did it these days, she had swallowed it, washing it down with a slug of Cristal. She realised afterwards that he had not taken his pill and then, after that, that it wasn't ecstasy but something that was making her feel woozy and out of it.

'I asked him what it was that I'd taken, and he said not to worry, it was just MDMA, and then when I told him I was feeling worse, he said it was just a bad trip and that he'd get me a car and take me home. He was on his cell, making a call, and he had this weird expression of concern and irritation on his face. Mostly irritation, like I was this big inconvenience for him, this big problem he was going to have to deal with. I knew then that Jack never wanted to see me again and that Crawford was getting rid of me. I told him that. He snapped at me, said I was a fucking embarrassment and a mistake and a liability and why couldn't I have stayed away? I shouted back at him. I went totally nuts, so he lost his cool too, and when I tried to get away, he grabbed me and told me I had to stay until they could drive me back, and that's when I screamed.'

'Do you remember me being there?' Milton asked.

She shrugged. 'Sort of.'

'Why didn't you let me help you?'

'Because I was out of my head and terrified. I didn't believe Crawford, not then, not for an instant, and I knew I was in trouble. Whatever it was he'd given me was seriously messing me up. I didn't even know where I was. I just felt like I was underwater, and I kept trying to swim up, I was really trying, but it felt like I was going to fall asleep. I remember an argument, men shouting at each other, and then I knew I had to get out of there, right that instant, before it got worse and I couldn't move, and so I took off.' She paused, frowning as she tried to remember what had happened next. 'I know I went to a house over the road. There are bits after that that are a complete blank. The pill, whatever it was, totally wiped me out. I woke up in the woods behind the houses. Five, six in the morning. Freezing cold. There was no way I was going back there, so I just kept going through the trees until I hit a road, and then I followed that until I got onto the 131. I hitched a ride back to San Francisco.'

'After that?'

'I've got a girlfriend in L.A., so I got on the first Greyhound the next morning – this is like at seven – and went straight there. I didn't want to stick around. I didn't think it was safe. I just kept my head down. Stayed in the apartment most of the time.'

'Why didn't you call?'

'I heard about what had happened to them . . . those other girls.'

'No one knew that they were connected to Robinson.'

'Yeah,' she said. 'But it freaked me out. It just felt a little close to home. And then when they said who they were, like last week? I was about ready to get out of the state.'

'Did you know them?'

'Megan – I met her once. This one time, at the start, before I was seeing Jack properly, there were two of us. Me and her. She was a sweet girl. Pretty. She was kind of on the outs then, but I liked her. I remember her face, and then, when they put pictures up on the news and said she was one of the girls they'd found, and then I thought what had nearly happened to me, I realised what was going on. I mean, it was obvious, right? Robinson likes to have his fun, and then, when it's all said and done and over, if they think the girl is gonna cause trouble, they get rid of her.'

'You could've called the police,' Trip said.

'Seriously? He is – *was* – the governor of Florida. How do you think that's going to sound – I call and say I've been with him, and they ask how, and I say it was because I was a hooker, and then I say I think he wants to kill me? Come on, Trip. Get real, baby. They'd just laugh.'

'You could've called me,' he said sadly.

'Yeah,' she said, looking away for a moment. 'I know.'

'You have to go to the police now, Madison,' Milton said. 'It's pretty much wrapped up, but you have to tell them.'

'I know I do. Trip's going to take me tomorrow.'

They finished their drinks quietly. Milton had packed his few possessions into a large bag. The apartment looked bare and lonely, and for a moment, the atmosphere was heavy and depressing.

'I'm gonna go and wait outside,' Madison said eventually. They all rose, and she came across the room, slid her arms around his neck and pulled him down a little so that she could kiss him on the cheek. 'Probably wasn't what you were expecting when you picked me up, right?'

'Not exactly.'

'Thank you, John.'

She disengaged from him and made her way across the room. Milton watched as she opened the door and passed into the hallway, out of sight.

He looked over at Trip. He was staring vaguely at the open doorway.

'You all right?'

He sighed. 'I guess,' he said quietly. 'Things aren't what they always seem to be, are they, Mr Smith?'

'No,' Milton said. 'Not always.'

Trip gestured at his bulging travel bag. 'You going away?'

'I'm leaving town.'

'For real?'

Milton shrugged. 'I like to keep moving around.'

'Where?'

'Don't know yet. Wherever seems most interesting. East, I think.'

'Like a tourist?'

'Something like that.'

'What about your jobs?'

'They're just jobs. I can get another.'

'Isn't that a bit weird?'

'Isn't what?'

'Just moving on.'

'Maybe it is, but it suits me.'

'I mean – I thought you were settled?'

'I've been here too long. I've got itchy feet. It's time to go.'

He walked across to the bag and heaved it over his shoulder. Trip followed the unsaid cue and led the way to the door. Milton took a final look around – thinking of the evenings he had spent reading on the sofa, smoking cigarettes out of the open window, staring out into the swirling pools of fog, and above all, the single night he had spent with Eva – and then he pulled the door closed, shutting off that brief interlude in his life. It was time. He had taken too many chances already, and if he had avoided detection, it had been the most outrageous luck. There was no sense in tempting fate.

Quit while you're ahead.

He locked the door.

* * *

They walked down the stairs together.

'What are you going to do now?' he asked the boy as they crossed into the harsh artificial brightness of the lobby. 'With Madison, I mean?'

'I don't know. We're right back to the start, I guess – that's the best we can hope for. And I'm not stupid, Mr Smith. Maybe we're through. I can kinda get Robinson, how it might be flattering to have someone like that chasing after you. Efron, too, all that money and influence. But there's the other guy – the driver. I thought he was kinda dumb if I'm honest. I don't get that so much. All of it – I don't know what I mean to her anymore. So, yeah – I don't know. I've got a lot of thinking to do.'

'You do.'

'What would you do? If you were me?'

Milton laughed at that. 'You're asking *me* for relationship advice? Look at me, Trip. I've got pretty much everything I own in a bag. Do I look like I'm the kind of man with anything useful to say?'

They stopped on the street. The fog had settled down again, cold and damp.

Milton took out the keys to the Explorer. 'Here,' he said, tossing them across the pavement at the boy. He caught them deftly but then looked up in confusion. 'It's not much to look at, but it runs okay, most of the time.'

'What?'

'Go on.'

'You're giving it to me?'

'I don't have any need for it.'

He paused self-consciously. 'I don't have any money.'

'That's all right. I don't want anything for it.'

'Are you sure?' he said awkwardly.

'It's fine.'

'God, I mean, thanks. Do you want – I mean – can I drop you anyplace?'

'No,' he said. 'I'll get the bus.'

'Thanks, man. Not just for this – for everything. For helping me. I don't know what I would've done if you hadn't been here.'

'Don't worry about it,' Milton said. 'I'm glad I could help.'

The corners of the books in his bag were digging into his shoulder; he heaved it around a little until it was comfortable and then stuck out his hand. Trip shook it firmly, and Milton thought he could see a new resolution in the boy's face.

'Look after yourself,' Milton told him.

'I will.'

'You'll do just fine.'

He gave his hand one final squeeze, turned his back on him and walked away. As the boy watched, he merged into the fog like a haggard ghost, melting into the long, bleak street with its shopfronts and palm trees shrouded in fog and whiteness. He didn't look back. The foghorn boomed as a single shaft of wintry moonlight pierced the mist for a moment.

Milton had disappeared.

EPILOGUE

The two newcomers came into the bar with trouble on their minds. They were both big men, with broad shoulders and thick arms. The bar was full of riggers from the oil fields, and these two fitted right in. Milton had ordered a plate of barbeque chicken wings and fries and a Coke and was watching the Cowboys' game on the large flat-screen TV that was hanging from the wall. The food was average, but the game was close, and Milton had been enjoying it. The bar was busy. There were a dozen men drinking and watching the game. Three young girls were drinking next to the pool table. He watched the two men as they made their way across the room. They ordered beers with whisky chasers, knocked back the latter and set about the beers. They were already drunk, and it looked like they were fixing to work on that a little more.

Milton had been in Victoria, Texas, for twelve hours. He had dropped his rented Dodge back at the Hertz office and was just wondering what to do next. He still had four thousand dollars in his go-bag, enough for him to just drift idly along the coast with no need to get a job just yet. He thought that maybe he'd get a Greyhound ticket and head east from Texas into Louisiana and then across to Florida, and then, maybe, he would turn north up towards New York and find a job. That was his rough plan, but he was taking it as it came. No sense in setting anything in stone. He had taken a room in a cheap hotel across the street from the bar, and rather than spend another night alone with just his paperbacks for company, he had decided to get out, get something to eat and watch the game.

Milton took a bite out of one of the chicken wings.

'Good?' said the man sitting on the stool to his right.

Milton looked at him: mid-twenties, slender, acne scars scattered across his nose and cheeks.

'Very good.'

'All in the sauce. Hot, right?'

'I'll say.'

'That's old Bill's original recipe. Used to call it "Suicide" 'til folks thought he ought to tone it down a bit. Calls it "Supercharger" now.'

'So I see,' Milton said, pointing to the menu on the blackboard above his head. 'It packs a punch.'

'Say – where you from?'

'Here and there.'

'Nah, man – that accent, what is it? English, right?'

'That's right,' Milton said. He had no real interest in talking, and eventually, after he made a series of non-committal responses to the man's comments on the Cowboys' chances this year, he got the message and quietened down.

The two newcomers were loud. Milton examined them a little more carefully. One of them must have been six-five and eighteen stone, built like one of the offensive linemen on the TV. He had a fat, pendulous face, a severe crew cut and small nuggety eyes deeply set within flabby sockets; he had the cruel look of a school bully, a small boy transported into the body of a fully grown man. His friend was smaller but still heavyset and thick with muscle. His head was shaved bald, and he had dead, expressionless eyes. The other men in the bar ignored them. It was a rough place, the kind of place where the threat of a brawl was never far from the surface, but the way the others kept their distance from these two suggested that they were known and, probably, that they had reputations.

The bald man saw Milton looking and stared at him.

Milton turned back to the screen.

'All right!' the man at the bar exclaimed as the full back plunged over the goal line for a Cowboys' touchdown.

The two men sauntered over to the table where the girls were sitting. They started to talk to them; it was obvious that they were not welcome. The big man sat down, preventing one of the girls from leaving. Milton sipped on his Coke and watched as the girl pressed herself against the wall, trying to put distance between him and her. He reached across and slipped an arm around her shoulders; she tried to shrug it away, but he was persistent. The bald man went around to the other side of the table and grabbed the arm of the nearest girl. He hauled her up, encircled her waist with his arm and pulled her up against his body. She cursed him loudly and struggled, but he was much too strong.

Milton folded his napkin, carefully wiped his mouth with it and then stood.

He walked to the table.

'Leave them alone,' he said.

'Say what?'

'They're not interested.'

'Says who?'

'I do. There's no need for trouble, is there?'

'I don't know – you tell me.'

'I don't think so.'

'Maybe I *do* think so.'

Milton watched as he sank the rest of his beer. He knew what would come next, so he altered his balance a little, spreading his weight evenly between his feet so that he could move quickly in either direction.

The bald man got up. 'You ought to mind your own business.'

'Last chance, friend,' Milton said.

'I ain't your friend.'

The bald man cracked the glass against the edge of the table and rushed him, jabbing the sharp edges towards his face. Milton took a half-pace to the left and let the man hurry past, missing him completely with his drunken swipe. He reached out with his right hand and snagged the man's right wrist, pivoting on his right foot and using his momentum to swing him around and down, crashing his head into the bar. He bounced backwards and ended up, unmoving and face down, on the floor.

The big man reached out for a pool cue from the table. He swung it, but Milton stepped inside the arc of the swing, took the abbreviated impact against his shoulder and then jabbed his fingers into the man's larynx. He dropped the cue; Milton took a double handful of the man's shirt, yanked him down a little, butted him in the nose and then dumped him back on his behind.

The bald man was out cold, and the big man had blood all over his face from his broken nose.

'You had enough?' Milton said.

'All right, mister! Get your hands up!'

Milton turned.

'Come on,' he groaned. 'Seriously?'

The man he had been talking to earlier had pulled a pistol and was aiming it at him.

'Put your hands up now!'

'What – you're police?'

'That's right. Get them up!'

'All right. Take it easy.'

'On your head.'

'You want me to put them up or on my head?' He sighed. 'Fine – here.' He turned away and put his arms behind his back. 'Go on. Here we go. Cuff me. Just relax. I'm not going to resist.'

The young cop approached him warily, moved his hands behind his back – and fixed handcuffs around his wrists.

'What's your name?'

'John Smith.'

'All right then, buddy. You have the right to remain silent. Anything you say can and will be used against you in a court of law. You have the right to an attorney.'

'Come on.'

The big man wiped the blood from his face and started to laugh.

'If you cannot afford an attorney, one will be provided for you. Do you understand the rights I have just read to you?'

'Of course.'

'With these rights in mind, do you wish to speak to me?'

'Not particularly.'

'John Smith – you're under arrest.'

Turn the page for a preview of

GHOSTS

the next book in the John Milton series

PART I

LONDON – 8 YEARS AGO

1

The van was parked at the side of the road. It was a white Renault and it had been prepared to look just like one of the maintenance vehicles that Virgin Media used. It was parked at the junction of Upper Ground and Rennie Street. The spot had been chosen carefully; it allowed an excellent view of the entrance to the Oxo Tower brasserie on London's South Bank.

The interior of the van had been prepared carefully, too. A console had been installed along the right-hand side of the vehicle, with monitors displaying the feed from the low-light colour camera that was fitted to the roof. There was a 360-degree periscope that could be raised and lowered as appropriate, various recording devices, a dual-band radio antenna and a microwave receiver.

It was a little cramped in the back for the two men inside. The intelligence officer using the equipment had quickly become oblivious to any discomfort. He reached across to the console and selected a different video feed; they had installed a piggyback into the embassy's security system two weeks ago and now he had access to all those separate feeds, as well as to an array of exterior cameras they had also hijacked. The monitor flickered and then displayed the footage from the security camera that monitored the building. He could see the big Mercedes S280 that the chauffeur had parked there, but, apart from that, there was nothing.

The second man was sitting just to the side of the technician, watching the action over his shoulder. This man was anxious, and he knew that it was radiating from him.

'Change views,' he said tensely. 'Back inside.'

The technician did as he was told and discarded the view for another one from inside the restaurant. The targets were still in the main room, finishing their desserts. The first target was facing away from the camera but she was still recognisable. The second target was toying with an unlit cigarette, turning it between his fingers. The second man looked at the footage. It looked as if the meal was finally coming to an end. The two targets would be leaving soon.

'Group,' the second man said into the headset microphone. 'This is Control. Comms check.'

'Copy that Control, this is One. Strength ten.'

'Eight, also strength ten.'

'Twelve, copy that.'

'Ten, strength ten.'

'Eleven, same here. Strength ten.'

'Five. Ditto for me.'

'Eleven, what can you see?'

The agent code-named Eleven was standing at the bar, enjoying a drink as he waited for a table. His name was Duffy and he had latterly been in the Special Boat Service. Control could see him in the footage from the camera and watched as he angled himself away from the couple and put his hand up to his mouth.

'They're finishing,' he said, his voice clipped and quiet as he spoke into the discreet microphone slipped beneath the strap of his watch. 'The waiter just asked if they wanted coffees and they didn't. Won't be long.'

Satisfied, Control sat back and watched. Very few people knew his given name. He was dressed well, as was his habit, in a pale blue shirt and tastefully spotted braces. He held his glasses in his right hand, absently tapping one of the arms against his lips. He had been in day-to-day command of Group Fifteen for several months but this was the first operation that he had overseen from the field. He was a desk man by nature. He preferred to pull the strings, the dark hand in the shadows. The puppet master. But this operation was personal and he wanted to be closer to the action. He would have preferred to smell the gun smoke, if that had been possible. He would have preferred to pull the trigger.

Watching would be an acceptable substitute.

It was an expensive and exclusive restaurant. The wall facing the river was one huge expanse of glass, with doors leading out onto a terrace. The views were outstanding and Control knew, from several meals there himself, that the food was just as good.

The bright sunlight refracted against the watch that the first target wore on her wrist and the diamond earrings that must have cost her a small fortune. Control watched and felt his temper slowly curdle. He had been introduced to her by a mutual Iranian friend. The name she had given him was

Alexandra Kyznetsov. He knew now that that was not her name. Her real name was Anastasia Ivanovna Semenko and, instead of being a businesswoman with interests in the chemical industry, she was an agent in the pay of the Russian Federal Security Service. She was in her early forties but she had invested heavily in cosmetic surgery and, as a result, she could have passed for a woman fifteen years younger. Control had found her attractive and he had enjoyed her flirtatious manner on the occasions that they had met.

Now, though, that just made her betrayal *worse*.

Control stared at the screen and contemplated the frantic action of the last three days. That was how long he had had to plan the operation. Three days. It was hopelessly insufficient, especially for something as delicate as this, but the role that Semenko played cast her as something of a globetrotter and it was difficult to find a reliable itinerary for her; she tended to change it on a whim. She had only just returned from business in Saudi Arabia. Control had only green-lit the operation when it was confirmed that she was stopping in London before returning to Moscow. The team had then been assembled and briefed. Control had considered the precise detail of the plan and, by and large, he was satisfied with it. It was as good as he would be able to manage in the limited time that he had available.

The second target laughed at something that Semenko said. Control switched his attention to him. He had introduced himself as Andrei Dragunov, but, again, that was a lie. His real name was Pascha Shcherbatov. He, too, was

Russian. He was in his early middle-age and he was a long-time KGB agent, an intelligence man to the quick; since the fall of the Wall, he had amassed considerable influence in the SVR, the successor to his notorious previous employer, and was now considered to be something of an operator. A worthy opponent, certainly.

Semenko clasped the hand of the maître d', her face beaming. They both got up, leaving money on the table, and made for the archway that opened into the lobby.

'Dollar and Snow are on the move,' Control reported. 'Stand ready.'

Shcherbatov's phone rang and he stopped, putting it to his ear. Semenko paused, waiting for him. Control stared at the pirated feed, willing himself to read Shcherbatov's lips, but it was hopeless: the angle was wrong and the quality of the image was too poor. He watched, frowning hard. Shcherbatov smiled broadly, replaced the phone and spoke with Semenko. Control hoped that their plans had not changed. That would throw things into confusion.

'Control to One and Twelve,' Control said into the mike. 'They are on the move.'

'One, Control. Copy that.'

Control watched as Semenko and Shcherbatov headed towards the exit. The pair stepped beneath the camera and out of shot. 'Keep on them,' Control said, and the technician tapped out a command and switched views to a new camera. This one was in the lift and, as Control watched, the doors opened and the two of them stepped inside. Shcherbatov pressed the button for the ground floor. The camera juddered as the lift began to descend.

'Targets are in the lift,' Control reported. 'One and Twelve, stand ready.'

'One, Control. Copy that.'

The technician swung around on his chair and brought up another feed on the second monitor. It offered a wide-angle view of the street outside the restaurant. Control could see Semenko's chauffeur. He was a large man, powerfully built, with a balding head. They knew he had a background in the Spetsnaz and would certainly be armed. He wore a pair of frameless glasses and was dressed in a dark suit and open-necked shirt. Control watched as he stepped out of the shadows, tossing a cigarette to the floor and stomping it out.

The lift came to a stop and the door opened.

Semenko emerged into the wide shot first, walking with a confident bounce across the space to the Mercedes. Shcherbatov followed, his phone pressed to his ear again. The chauffeur opened the rear door for his passengers and, as they slipped inside, he opened the front door and got in himself.

He started the engine. Control could see the fumes rising from the exhaust.

The Mercedes reversed and turned and then pulled away, moving quickly.

'Targets are in play,' Control reported.

2

Beatrix Rose was sitting astride a Kawasaki motorcycle on Rennie Street. The visor of her helmet was up and the cool air was fresh against her face. The usual buzz of adrenaline had kicked in as the operation moved into its final phase. She was a professional with years of experience behind her; too professional to let excitement render her less useful than she would need to be.

She listened to the comms chatter in the receiver that was pressed into her ear, the detailed commentary as the Mercedes passed from the back of the restaurant and onto Upper Ground. She had memorised this part of London, at first with the aid of a map and then, over the course of the morning, three hours of careful reconnaissance that had fixed the local geography in her mind. She was confident that she was as prepared as she could be.

'*They're turning east towards the Bridge,*' intoned Control.

There was another motorcycle next to her. The agent sitting astride it was nervous, despite the time he had spent in the army and then the SAS. He had a glittering résumé, with one mission behind the lines during the second Iraq War a particular standout, but it was one thing to go into battle during a war, when the rules of engagement were clear, and quite another to conduct a clandestine extrajudicial operation like this, with no backup or recognition, and the likelihood of incarceration, or worse, if things went wrong. The man had his visor open, like she did, but where she was clear-eyed and focused, he looked ashen.

'Milton,' she called across to him.

He didn't respond.

'*Milton.*'

He turned to face her. 'You all right?'

'Fine,' he called back.

'You look like you're going to be sick.'

'I'm fine.'

'Remember your training. You've done more difficult things than this.'

He nodded.

Beatrix Rose was Number One, the most senior agent in the Group. The man on the second bike was John Milton. He was Number Twelve. The Group was a small and highly select team. Twelve members. Milton was its most junior member and his presence in it was at least partly because of her influence.

Number Four, a cantankerous Irishman who had served with the Special Boat Service before being transferred to the group, had been killed in a firefight with al-Qaeda sympathisers in the Yemen six months earlier. Control had identified ten potential replacements to fill his spot on the team and had deputed the job of selecting the most promising soldier to her. She had interviewed all of them and then personally oversaw the selection weekend when their number had gradually been whittled down, one at a time, until Milton had been the last man standing.

Beatrix had known before the weekend started that it was going to end up that way. His commanding officers described him as a brilliant soldier who was brave and selfless. They also spoke of a steely determination and a relentless focus on the goal at hand. He did not allow anything to stand in his way. He had demonstrated all of that. He was the most promising recruit that she had ever worked with and, in all the time that she had been Number One, she had tutored two men and two women who had replaced fallen team members. There had been more than three hundred possible recruits for those four spots and Milton was better than all of them.

'Here they come,' she called out.

The Mercedes turned the corner and headed in their direction. Beatrix flipped her visor down and gave the engine a twist of revs. Milton did the same, gunning the engine and then, as the Mercedes moved past them, closing his visor and pulling out into the empty road.

'One, Control,' Beatrix said.

'Go ahead, One.'

'We're in pursuit.'

3

'Control, One. Roger that.'

Control had placed his agents carefully: One and Twelve east of the restaurant on Rennie Street; Five and Eight in a second van, currently idling in Southwark Street; Ten on a third bike, waiting on Stamford Street in the event that they went west instead of east; Eleven inside the restaurant. He was confident that they had all eventualities covered.

The driver of the surveillance van started the engine and they pulled out into the traffic and headed north. The Mercedes was out of sight, but One was providing a commentary on its movements and it was a simple thing to follow.

Control twisted the wedding ring on his left hand. Despite his satisfaction with their preparation, he was still nervous. This had to be perfect. The operation was totally off the book; usually, the files with the details of their targets were passed down to him by either MI5 or MI6, but that wasn't the case this time. Neither agency had sanctioned this operation and he would have even less cover than he usually did if anything went wrong. It wasn't just that this was unofficial business – all of the work they did was unofficial – it was personal.

None of his agents knew that. He had deceived them. 'Control, One. Report.'

'Target is waiting at the junction at Blackfriars Bridge.'

Control knew their itinerary for the rest of the day. Semenko and Shcherbatov were going to a meeting. As far as they knew, the meeting was with him.

It was an appointment that Control had no intention of keeping.

4

The Mercedes picked up speed as it turned onto Blackfriars Bridge. It found a small gap in the traffic. Beatrix opened the throttle in response, keeping the Mercedes a few car lengths ahead of them. Their intelligence suggested that the woman she knew as Dollar had an appointment with a contact on Victoria Embankment; it looked as if the intelligence would prove to be accurate.

Beatrix stayed between fifty and a hundred yards behind the car; Milton was another twenty yards behind her. She kept up a running commentary as they gradually worked their way south-east, towards the river. 'North end of the bridge, turning off . . . onto the Embankment, heading west . . . passing Blackfriars Pier . . . coming up to Waterloo Bridge, following the river to the south.'

The traffic started to queue as they reached Victoria Embankment Gardens. Beatrix bled away almost all the speed, ducking in behind a bus that was idling opposite Cleopatra's Needle. She could see the Mercedes through the windows of the bus and, beyond it, the Houses of Parliament.

'One, Control. Waiting at the lights at Embankment Pier.'

'Acknowledged,' said Control. *'They'll continue south.'*

'Copy that.' The lights changed, the traffic started to move, the last pedestrians broke into self-conscious trots as they hurried out of the way. 'He's accelerating towards Hungerford Bridge.'

She gunned the engine and sped forwards, not about to get stuck should the lights turn against her.

Control's voice crackled again. *'Control, Group. This is as good a spot as any. Five?'*

'In position,' reported Number Five. *'Eight, One and Twelve. Get ready. Here we come.'*

Beatrix watched: a white van, not dissimilar to the one in which Control was watching, had been running parallel to them on Whitehall. Now though, it jerked out into the traffic from Richmond Terrace and blocked the road in front of the Mercedes. Number Eight – Oliver Spenser – was at the wheel. Number Five – Lydia Chisolm – was alongside him. Both agents were armed with SA-80 machine guns but the plan did not anticipate that they would need to use them.

Beatrix braked to thirty and then twenty. 'One, Control. They're stopping.'

'Control, One and Twelve. You have authorisation. Take them out.'

Beatrix rolled the bike carefully between the waiting cars: a red Peugeot, a dirty grey Volvo, an open double-decker bus that had been fitted out for guided tours. The Mercedes was ahead of the bus, blocked in between it and the delivery van in front. Beatrix reached the car, coming to a halt and bracing the heavy weight of the bike with her right leg. Milton rolled up behind her. Neither of them spoke; they didn't need to, they were operating purely on instinct by this stage, implementing the plan. Beatrix quickly scoped the immediate location: the inside lane was temporarily clear to the left of the Mercedes, the pavement beyond that was empty and then it was the wide open stretch of the Thames. No need to concern themselves with catching civilians in the crossfire.

Beatrix released her grip on the handlebars and unzipped her leather jacket. She was wearing a strap around her shoulder and a Heckler & Koch UMP was attached to it. She raised the machine pistol, steadied it with her left hand around the foregrip, aimed at the Mercedes and squeezed the trigger.

The window shattered, shards spilling out onto the road like handfuls of diamonds.

Milton was supposed to be doing the same but he had stopped.

Beatrix noticed but didn't have time to direct him. She was completely professional. Even as the machine pistol jerked and spat in her hand, her aim was such that every round passed into the cabin of the car. The gun chewed through all thirty rounds in the detachable magazine, spraying lead through the window.

The driver somehow managed to get the Mercedes into gear and it jerked forwards. He must have been hit because he couldn't control the car, slaloming it against the delivery van, bouncing across the road, slicing through the inside lane and then fishtailing. It slid through one hundred and eighty degrees and then wedged itself between a tree and a street lamp. The horn sounded, a long and uninterrupted note. The car had only travelled twenty feet but Beatrix couldn't see into it any longer.

'Milton!'

She was fresh out of ammunition and he was the nearest.

'Milton! Move!'

He was still on the bike, frozen.

The passenger side door opened and Snow fell out. The car's wild manoeuvre meant that the body of the car was now between Beatrix and him; he ducked down beneath the wing, out of sight.

'Milton! Snow is running.'

'I've got it,' Milton said, but she could hear the uncertainty in his voice.

He was corpsing; Beatrix had not anticipated that.

She ejected the dry magazine and slapped in another, watching through the corner of her eye as he got off the Kawasaki and drew his own UMP.

Beatrix put the kickstand down. There was a terrific clamour all about: the Mercedes horn was still sounding, tourists on the bus – with a clear view of what had just happened – were screaming in fright as they clambered to the back of the deck, and, in the distance, there came the ululation of a siren.

Too soon, surely? Perhaps, but it was a timely reminder; the plan only allowed them a few seconds before they needed to effect their escapes.

She approached the car, her gun extended and unwavering.

It was carnage. The driver was slumped forwards, blood splashed against the jagged shards of windscreen that were still held within the frame. The full weight of his chest was pressed up against the wheel, sounding the horn. Dollar was leaning against the side of the car, a track of entry wounds stitching up from her shoulder into her neck and then into the side of her head. Her hair was matted with blood and brain.

Beatrix strode up to the car and fired two short bursts: one for the driver and one for Dollar. She kept moving forward, the machine pistol smoking as she held it ahead of her, zoning out the noise behind her but acutely aware of the timer counting down in her head. The man and the woman were unmoving. She looked through the driver's-side window and saw a briefcase on the passenger seat. They were not tasked with recovering intelligence but it was hardwired into her from a hundred similar missions and so she quickly ran around to the passenger door, opened it and collected it.

'Control, One,' came the barked voice in her earpiece. 'Report.'

'The driver and Dollar are down.'

'What about Snow?'

'He's running.'

There was panic in his reply: 'What?'

'I repeat, Snow is on foot. Twelve is pursuing.'

5

Milton left the bike behind him and sprinted. Snow was already fifty feet ahead, adjacent to the Battle of Britain memorial. The great wheel of the London Eye was on the other side of the river and, ahead, a line of touring coaches had been slotted into the bays next to the pavement.

The man dodged through the line of stalled traffic; nothing was able to move with the shot-up Mercedes blocking the road ahead. He turned his head, stumbling a little as he did, saw Milton in pursuit and sprinted harder. He was older than Milton, but he had obviously kept himself in good shape; he maintained a steady pace, driven on by fear. Milton's motorcycle leathers were not made for running and the helmet he was wearing – he dared not remove it for fear of identifying himself – limited his field of vision.

He took out his Sig and fired a shot. It was wild, high and wide and shattered the windscreen of one of the big parked coaches. It inspired Snow to find another burst of pace, cutting between two of the parked buses. Milton lost sight of him. He ran between a truck and the car in front of it, passed between the two buses behind the ones that his quarry had used and saw him again. A second shot was prevented by a red telephone box and then a tall ash tree.

Milton heard the up-and-down wail of a police siren. It sounded as if it was on the Embankment, behind him, closing the distance.

Milton stopped, dropped to one knee and brought up the Sig. He breathed in and out, trying to steady his aim, and, for a moment, he had a clear shot. He used his left hand to swipe up his visor, breathed again, deep and easy, and started to squeeze the trigger.

Snow ploughed into the middle of a group of tourists.

Shit.

Milton dropped his arm; there was no shot. He closed the visor and ran onwards, just as he saw the man again: he had clambered onto the wall that separated the pavement from the river and, with a final defiant look back in his direction, he leapt into space and plunged into the water. Milton zig-zagged through the panicking tourists until he was at the wall and looked down into the greeny-black waters. There was nothing for a moment and then, already thirty feet distant, he saw Snow bob to the surface. The currents were notoriously strong at this part of the river. The rip tides were powerful enough to swallow even the strongest swimmer, but Snow was not fighting and the water swept him away, quickly out of range.

The siren was louder now, and, as Milton turned to face it, he saw that the patrol car was less than a hundred feet away, working its way around the stalled queue.

Milton paused, caught between running and standing still. He froze. He didn't know what to do.

'*Milton,*' came Number One's voice in his ear.

He turned to his left.

Beatrix was on the pavement, between the river and the row of buses, gunning her Kawasaki hard. Milton pushed the Sig back into its holster and zipped up his jacket. Beatrix braked, the rear wheel bouncing up a few inches, then slamming back down again. Milton got onto the back; Beatrix had a slight figure and he looped his left arm around her waist and fixed his right hand to grip the rear of the pillion seat. Milton was six foot tall and heavy with muscle, but the bike had a 998cc four-cylinder engine and his extra weight was as nothing.

It jerked forward hungrily as Beatrix revved it and released her grip on the brakes.

6

Beatrix looked out of the window of Control's office. It was the evening, two hours after the operation. It was a habit to debrief as soon as possible after the work had been done and, usually, those were not difficult meetings. Normally, the operations passed off exactly as they were planned. They were not botched like this one had been botched.

Control was busying himself with the tray that his assistant, Captain Tanner, had brought in; it held a teapot, two cups, a jug of milk and a bowl of sugar cubes. He poured out two cups. Beatrix could see that he was angry. His face was drawn and pale, the muscles in his cheeks twitching. He had said very little to her, but she knew him well enough to know that the recriminations were coming. The crockery chimed as he rattled the spoon against it, stirring in his sugar. He brought the cups across the room, depositing one on her side of his desk and taking the other one around to sip at it as he stood at the window.

'So?' he began.

'Sir?'

'What happened?'

Beatrix had known, of course, that the question was coming. The mission had been an unmitigated failure. The watchword of the Group was discretion, and the shooting had been the first item on all of yesterday's news broadcasts and websites were leading with a variation of the same picture: Milton, in black leathers and a helmet with a mirrored visor, his arm extended as he aimed at the fleeing Snow, his abandoned motorcycle in the background. The headline on *the Times* website was typical: MURDER ON THE STREETS OF LONDON.

'It was just bad luck,' she said.

'Luck? We plan so that luck isn't a factor, Number One. Luck has *nothing* to do with it.'

'The driver managed to get the car away from us. That was just bad luck.'

'It was Twelve's responsibility to neutralise the driver. Are you saying it was his fault?'

She had given thought to what she should say. The honest thing to do would be to throw Milton under the bus. This had been his first examination and he had flunked it. He had frozen at the critical moment. They had the targets cold, helpless, and it had been his corpsing that had given Snow the opportunity to make a run for it. And even then, she knew Milton was a good enough shot to have taken him down.

She could have said all of that and it would have been true. She could have burned him but it wouldn't have been the right thing to do.

She had some empathy. She remembered her own introduction to the Group. The operation when she had lost her
own cherry had been a fuck-up, too; not quite like this, but
then she had been in Iraq and not on the streets of London,
far from prying eyes and the possibility of your mistakes being
amplified by a media that couldn't get enough of something so
audacious and dramatic. Her own wobble had been between
her, the female agent who had been Number Six in those days
and her victim, an Iraqi official who was passing information
to the insurgency; she had paused at the moment of truth and
that meant that the man she had just stabbed in the gut had
been able to punch her in the face, freeing himself for long
enough to hobble into the busy street outside. Number Six
had pursued him outside and fired two shots into his head
and then, keeping bystanders away with the threat of the gun,
she had hijacked a car and driven them both away. Beatrix
remembered how Control had asked her how it had gone. Six
had covered for her, telling him that the operation had passed
off without incident and that it had all been straightforward.
Beatrix would have been cashiered without hesitation if Six
had told Control the truth. So she understood what had happened to Milton. It did not diminish her opinion of him. It
did not make her question her decision to recommend him.

'It wasn't his fault,' she told Control, looking him straight
in the eye. 'He did his job, just as we planned it.'

'So you say. But he went in pursuit of Snow?'

'Yes.'

'And?'

'He never had a clear shot, not one he could take without a significant risk that he would hit a bystander. The rules of engagement were clear. This had to be at no risk.'

'I know what the bloody rules of engagement were, Number One,' he said sharply. 'I wrote them.'

'If you want to blame anyone, blame me.'

Control flustered and, for a moment, Beatrix was convinced that he was going to blame her. That would have been all right. She had been a member of the Group for six years and that was already pushing at the top end of an agent's average life expectancy. It wasn't an assignment that you kept if you had something to lose. Beatrix had a daughter and a husband and a family life that she enjoyed more than she had ever expected. She had done her time and she had done it well, but all things had to come to an end eventually. She wouldn't have resisted if he blamed her and busted her out of the Group. There would be something else for her, something safer, something where getting shot at was not something she would come to expect.

But he didn't blame her.

'It's a bloody mess,' he said instead, sighing with impatience. 'A bloody, *bloody* mess. The police have been told it's an underworld thing. They'll buy that, if only because the prospect of their own government sanctioning a hit is too bloody ludicrous to credit.'

'The only thing we left was Milton's bike, and that's clean. There's no way back to us from that.'

'You're sure?'

'Absolutely sure.'

Control took his saucer and cup to his desk and sat down. He exhaled deeply. 'What a mess,' he said again. He was frustrated, and that was to be expected, but the immediate threat of the explosion of his temper had passed. 'Where is Milton now?'

'Training,' she told him.

That was true. He hadn't left the quarters where the Group's logistics were based since the operation. He was firing a target pistol over and over until the targets were torn to shreds, then loading another target and pushing it further out and doing it all again.

'Are you still sure about him?'

'He'll be fine,' she said. 'When have I ever been wrong about a recruit?'

'I know,' Control said, leaning back. 'Never.'

He exhaled again and sipped at his tea. Beatrix looked beyond him, beyond the plush interior of his office where so many death warrants were signed, and out into the darkness. London was going about its business, just as usual. Beatrix's eyes narrowed their focus until she noticed the image in the glass: the back of Control's head and, facing him, her own reflection. She stood at a crossroads, with a choice of how to proceed: she could say nothing, and go back to her family, or she could do what she had decided she had to do and begin a conversation that could very easily become difficult.

'There was one more thing,' she said.

'What?'

'I pulled some evidence out of the car.'

Control sat forward. 'That wasn't in the plan.'

'I know. Force of habit, I suppose. It was there, I took it.'

'And?'

'And you should probably take a look.'

She had travelled to the office on her own motorbike and had stowed the case in a rucksack. She opened the drawstring, took it out and laid it on Control's desk. It had been locked and she had unscrewed the hinges to get it open; it was held together by one of her husband's belts at the moment. She unhooked it and removed the top half of the case. There was a clear plastic bag with six flash drives and, beneath that, a manilla envelope. Inside the envelope was a thick sheaf of photographs. They were printed on glossy five-by-eight paper and had been taken by someone from a high vantage point, using a powerful telephoto lens. It was a series, with two people in shot. The first person was a man. He was wearing a heavy overcoat and a woollen hat had been pulled down over his ears. The picture had been taken in a park during the winter; the trees in the foreground were bare and a pile of slush, perhaps from a melted snowman, was visible fifty feet away. The man was bent down, standing over a park bench. There was a woman on the bench.

Despite the distance and the angle that the picture had been taken, it was still obvious that the standing man was Control.

'What is this?' he asked brusquely.

'It was in the case . . .'

'Yes,' he snapped. 'You said. I have no idea why.'

'That's you, sir, isn't it?'

'If you say so.'

The atmosphere had become uncomfortable, but Beatrix couldn't draw back.

'The woman on the bench . . .'

Control made a show of examining the photograph more closely.

'It's Dollar.'

He said nothing.

'I don't understand, sir . . .'

'Your job is not to understand, Number One. Your job is to follow the orders that I give you.'

He paused; Beatrix thought he was hesitating, searching for the words to say what he wanted to say, but he didn't say anything else. He just stared at her instead.

'Sir?'

He indicated the flash drives with a dismissive downward brush of his hand. 'Have you looked at these?'

'No, sir,' she said, although that was a lie.

'Very good.' He shuffled in his chair, straightening his shoulders. 'I want you to keep a close eye on Milton. It might be that we were wrong about him – and we can't afford passengers. If we were wrong, we'll need to reassign him. Understood?' She nodded that she did. 'That will be all for now. You're dismissed, Number One.'

She stood, still uncomfortable and confused, and then turned for the door.

She was halfway across the room before Control cleared his throat.

'Look, Number One ... Beatrix. Please, sit down again.' She turned back and did so. He had come around the desk and now he was standing by the mantelpiece. 'You're right. I did meet her. A couple of times. Looks like she decided she'd like some pictures to mark the occasion. I can't tell you why we met and I can't tell you what we spoke about, save to say that it was connected to the operation. The details are classified. All you need to know, Beatrix, is that you were given a file with her name on it. And you know what that means.'

'I do, sir. Termination.'

'That's right. Is there anything else you want to ask me?'

She looked at him: a little portly, a little soft, his frame belying his years of service in MI6, including, she knew, years behind the Iron Curtain during the Cold War and a distinguished campaign in the Falklands. He was looking at her with an expression that looked like concern but, beneath that, she saw a foundation of suspicion and caution. Beatrix was a professional assassin, Number One amidst a collection of twelve of the most dangerous men and women in the employ of Her Majesty. She was responsible for the deaths of over eighty people all around the world. Bad people who had done bad things. She was not afraid of very much. But Control was not the sort of man you would ever want to cross. She looked at him again, regarding her with shrewlike curiosity, and she was frightened.

The thought began to form that she had just made a very, very bad mistake.

MARK DAWSON is the bestselling author of the
Beatrix Rose, Isabella Rose and John Milton series
and has sold over four million books. He lives in
Wiltshire with his family and can be reached
at www.markjdawson.com

www.facebook.com/markdawsonauthor
www.twitter.com/pbackwriter
www.instagram.com.markjdawson

A Message from Mark

Building a relationship with my readers is the very best thing about writing. Join my VIP Reader Club for information on new books and deals, plus a free ebook telling the story of Milton's battle with the Mafia and an assassin called Tarantula.

Just visit www.markjdawson.com/Milton.